THE ESSENCE OF DECAY

Steven Bliss

FOR MY WIFE.

The one who brings me hope.

The one who has patience while I chase my dreams.

And the one who supports any and all decisions I make.

For love is the key to hope.

TABLE OF CONTENTS

PROLOGUE

"It seems even God has realized that this world is no longer worth saving." She clenched as a scream in the background echoed through the thick twilight air. "Another young lady taken, I wonder if she will be happier dead?" She sighed while looking down upon a single green sprout of grass, reaching up between the broken concrete. Staring upon its hopeful sprout, she released a soft whimper, as if someone would listen to her cries. "How have we gotten to this place? How did we let this happen?"

The cold breeze licked at her chapped and bleeding lips as the sun's light slowly dissipated through the thick haze, declining behind the crumbling skyscrapers that surrounded her. "I remember sixteen years ago, when I was only twelve, having nothing to worry about. Spending my days running around with my friends as my dad yelled at the TV, saying, 'This country, heck this world, is all going down. At this rate, we will be fighting just to keep a job for a few more days. Most have already lost their homes.'"

She returned her gaze to that hopeful piece of grass. Its vibrant green stem shimmering within the dim light and, without a second thought, scraped her foot across it. "Why should there be beauty in this world when all hope has been taken from us? No one can be happy in this chaotic place of ruin!" She glanced down at the green sprout, now smeared across the cracked concrete, then gazed up at the darkening sky as her frustration conceded to the sadness within. "If only my father would have known. If only I could go back there, back to the days when I had no worries."

Back then, back when everyone complained, but no one acted. Everyone thought that someone else would solve the problems, voicing their dislikes on social media. Everyone wanted things fixed, but they sat idle, as the few people that acted grasped the disparity with their bare fists, without resistance, and for a profit. She noticed chunks of concrete on the ground as she looked around. With a long groan, she once again whispered to herself, "Where did we go wrong?"

Another cold gust of wind caressed her thin hair within its frigid hands. The same hands that played a dangerous game with the brittle skyscrapers around her. Their I-beams screaming and creaking as the fissures within them grew a little larger with each gust.

She clenched her eyes shut as the pain of the past echoed into her mind. These streets, these very same streets, she remembered walking down them with her dad. Back then, back when she was just a kid. Back when they were still bright. When that despair, now seemed to be a shimmering pathway within this dark world.

Back when the city still shined, when her dad's voice still hung onto a fragment of hope as he promisingly stated, "This city resembles the significance of our country; of human achievement and on how far we've come. Soon, we will break free of this. We will rise again. We always have; we just need to get through these rough times."

Those rough times never ended.

Screams of terror were so frequent now that it no longer affected her. Rape, murder, and slavery all seemed like a daily occurrence. She knew it would only be a matter of time before it was her turn. She looked behind her, at an old crumbled building with ancient flame ridden walls, with more broken glass on the ground than hanging onto each window frame. Tears started to stream from her eyes as she moaned, "Father, why did you vanish from us when we needed you most? Why did you leave mom and me right before the world erupted in riots before this terror embraced us all?"

She pulled out a picture from her barely recognizable sock. It's worn elastic, desperately attempting to hold onto its only prize. Her tired eyes rested upon that picture. Upon the three of them, her father positioned with one arm around her and his other arm around her mother. She looked back at the broken and flame ridden building, wondering if that building was destroyed the same night that her mother was killed. She still didn't understand why her mom never hated him for leaving that night; why her mom had said he had to do what he believed in. How had she always supported his decision to leave them at a time so crucial?

Struggling to place the picture back into her worn and tattered sock as her weakness only increased with the passing of each day. She barely had the energy to move anymore, yet, that was probably their goal.

The night had arrived, the sun had gone. Not that the sun offered warmth, but the night was worse. The darkness seemed to engulf everything. Shadows were the new tyranny, and not even one's soul could hide from such desperation. She looked up where the moon should have been if it were not for the swirling fog that had allied itself with the darkness, choking out its light.

Escape seemed impossible. She whispered as she glanced down at a puddle by her feet, filled with more dead bugs than water. "How can I escape if light can't even break free?" She watched as the few bugs that were alive strived to climb on top of the corpses of their once alive companions, knowing that they too would soon drown in their comrades' blood. She wondered how she had stayed alive this long, existing from day to day, and realized she didn't care how much longer she had left to live. Her eyes began to become cumbersome as thoughts of the past numbed her mind and eased the passing of time.

She jumped. Her mind racing as a slow scraping sound in the distance echoed, only to dissipate seconds later. She strained to see into the darkness of the alley. Light was a commodity that few could afford; she doubted that anyone could afford it in this wasteland of prosperity.

Forcing herself to relax, she whispered in an attempt to calm her racing heart. "I know better than to let myself fall asleep at night."

Those who survived on the weakness of others came out at night. Sadly, everyone seemed weak now, but she knew that the night was when the worst predators came out to hunt—for the boogieman was no longer a child's story, and it was definitely a man.

"I am but only an animal, hiding within the night, trying to survive."

Another soft scrape echoed from within the darkness. Her mind racing once again while her feeble voice drifted into the air as she weighed her options, struggling within herself. "Is someone there?"

"Someone was definitely there. Coincidences don't exist."

"Should I run?"

"If I run, then they will know I'm here. I can barely stand, let alone run."

The scraping continued.

She knew that if he continued down this alley, he'd soon find her either way. She pushed herself up against the cement wall behind her, taking her first step away as quietly as she could manage.

The scraping sound dissipated, being replaced by the sound of shoes beating against the pavement.

"Crap," she mumbled under her breath. She knew he must have heard her, and if he was running toward her, it wasn't to help. She broke out running, pushing herself, knowing her weak body could only flee so long before it too would succumb to the predator. A hand grasped the back of her shirt as she fell onto the pavement.

Looking at the ground before her, a small red trickle began to spread out a few inches from her face. She no longer felt pain. When life was pain, it was hard to notice something that was part of everyday life; its presence as easy to accept as the next breath of air rushing into her lungs.

A voice drifted through her ears, growling from within the darkness, for where it came from was part of the shadows.

"You think you can get away from me?" He turned her around. "Oh, you're a pretty one; you're going to fetch a prime price once you're cleaned up."

She didn't bother to struggle. She knew it was useless.

"But why shouldn't I have fun with you first? They usually don't like tainted goods, but heck, a guy's got to enjoy himself every once in a while."

She stared at him without emotion, without any sense of fear, with an effect, simply put, that said, screw you.

He growled once again as his putrid breath fell upon her, "Don't look at me that way, you wench; you should be grateful!" He raised his hand, striking her across her face.

She returned his gaze, defiantly looking into his eyes.

"My Sir, would you please remove your hands from the lady?"

She looked behind her growling predator and noticed another man. His attire resembled the current fashion trend of society, which was dirty, decaying, and tattered clothes. She peered closer at that particular man, beneath the dirt that hid his wool suit with splotches of paint speckled across his vest. She peered past his greasy brown hair that was slicked back, deeper, past his skinny and starved looking figure. She looked into his eyes, and although the dark engulfed everything around him, his eyes showed through. Gold erupted around the blackness of his pupils. A deep blue embraced that gold as if the sun was escaping the darkness and creating a serene blue horizon. Hope seemed to leak from those eyes, from the eyes of the young man with a strong stance—the one who peculiarly grasped a cane within his hands.

The growling man on top of her hesitated, tactically analyzing his options, and then stood up to proclaim his prize. "Go away! You have no business here. She's mine now!" he snarled with rotting teeth.

"My Sir, although you are right in the matter that I have no business here, my request remains the same. Please, withdraw your presence from the lady."

The predator sneered at the young man again, "Who the heck do you think you are anyway? I said she's mine. Now leave, while you have a chance to draw breath for another day!"

The young blue-eyed man calmly replied while giving a slight bow. "I am Damian Gardge, and I insist you withdraw, for drawing breath for another day is better than ceasing to exist now."

The predator leaped forward, pulling out a knife, rushing Damian. Damian dropped his cane as the blade attempted to plunge forward into his flesh. Taking a quick step back, he grabbed the knifed hand, pulling the assailant forward and towards his side while twisting his wrist, breaking it within one swift movement. The man staggered forward as Damian grabbed his neck with his unoccupied hand and turned his planted foot behind the predator's back leg, slamming the assailant onto the cement.

The man looked up into Damian's eyes, with the look of a predator that had just been defeated by its prey.

Standing above him, he calmly confessed, "Now, Sir, I warned you that you'd cease to exist if you did not withdraw. Your arrogant perseverance has ended. You will now fade as those before you have, as you led them into the darkness."

Taking the predator's broken wrist, with his knife still in his hand, Damian placed one foot on his neck while drawling up the assailant's own knifed hand to his collar.

The man on the ground struggled as fear consumed his face.

"Now, now, that will only cause you more pain." He advised as a snap echoed down the alley, breaking the silence of the night as the predators' elbow was split into two.

Damian placed the knife against the assailants' neck once more, and with that motion, the man started to sob. Those same sobs began their transformation into gurgles mere seconds later as he asphyxiated on his own blood, staining the pavement red as his life faded from his eyes.

Then he raised his own to the lady in front of him, releasing a soft yet commanding question. "What is your name?"

She looked up at Damian, unable to speak, as both confusion and wonder-filled her.

"I am Damian Gardge, and I mean no harm. So, may I ask of you, what is your name?" He said while offering his hand. Her fingers clutched his as he helped her to her feet. "You know, it is improper not to introduce yourself when presented."

"Sorry," she said while attempting to stand straight, wiping the blood from her nose and lower lip. "I am Coretheen Nerites. Thank you, Damian." Then bent over, reaching for his cane lying upon the ground as a small stream of blood trickled towards it, originating from the corpse before her.

Damian lunged forward, grasping at his cane with great speed, ripping it out of her hands.

She looked down at her trembling hand in shock, then peered up at Damian. "Sa-sa-sorry, I, I was."

"It's ok, Coretheen," he interrupted her, "I was rude, but we all have something precious to us, and this is the one thing I cannot let go of for long." She looked down at the cane and saw a strange symbol etched in white along the glossy black shaft. Three curved lines crossed each other, making up an oddly curved triangle, surrounded with vines as their thorns reached in, breaking inside the symbol.

"Ahh, so you noticed my symbol." He smiled. "It's called an Elpis, named after a spirit of hope and expectation. It's a symbol of who I am and what I will soon start. Sadly, it's just a dream I follow, so I must learn while I grow in strength and determination. If you wish, you may follow me. I can offer you some safety, a shelter, and maybe some food." Releasing a soft chuckle, "If we have any food, that is. But if we do, you're welcome to share it. Man, you're a quiet one."

She looked up at Damian, noticing how his demeanor became more relaxed, as if he was a different person entirely, and shrugged. "Where else do I have to go?"

She followed those hopeful eyes.

CHAPTER ONE

E ston Tavernier woke up every morning, walked to his window, then peered down upon the freshly paved streets of New Chicago. Even though the sun had yet to rise, the city glistened with light. The new-found architectural design resembled a modern approach to the Romanesque and Gothic forms; instead of long granite columns, there were giant glass and stainless-steel towers that shimmered and reflected their surroundings, making a rare emerald dull in comparison.

These cities were rare, few, and only those who held political positions were granted allowance through the entrances of the gates—for they had to watch over the masses as God's hands, guiding them throughout life. They had to appear proper, as leaders who watched from

1

afar. They couldn't dwell in filth, for the new weekly poll would come out, and their peers judged them. And peers were, of course, a person whose status was the same as themselves. Those who were positioned outside of these cities had little control or influence, but it was their choice. They knew that for their own survival, they had to sign away their problems and let those who were more, more caring guide them.

He walked over to his mirror and turned on the light. He noticed stubbles of hair protruding from his face. He needed to keep a smooth face. He found himself shaving at least twice a day. For if he was not clean-shaven, he could lose up to five points in the next poll. He slicked back his short blonde hair with water while looking at his smooth face and his protruding cheekbones. A clean-cut was important, for even a week without a trim could result in a loss of three points in the polls. He brushed his teeth and noticed that his white luster seemed to be fading. He had to remember to go see his dentist soon because his campaign manager told him that his friendly smile and attitude brought him more votes than his agenda. He reached into his closet and pulled out his suit. A suit given to him by the hard work of those taxpayers he tried to protect and without thought put it on, knowing that it cost more than most would make in a year. He knew it was his duty to further his agenda, for he needed to make a name for himself, or else he too would be thrown aside. He was warned not to make too much of a splash. The goal was to cause a ripple, to be noticed, not to knock those off who were already sitting on the log.

He grabbed his overcoat and looked upon himself. He hesitated, noticing that his shirt cuffs were buttoned. He unbuttoned them, for he too wanted to appear to be a hard-working citizen of the order—ready to roll up his sleeves and get the hard work done. It was told to him that it would raise his poll by up to seven points.

He pulled out his agenda. Thinking as he looked at himself what his campaign advisor told him, "Eston, you have to lose a few pounds. No, no, no, you're of average weight for this city, but you wouldn't want to appear greedy. You want to appear as if you care and only take what you need. We need those extra five points in the next poll! We need you to win. Just think of the nice benefits you will receive. You deserve it, Eston. You worked so hard. The taxpayers owe you for you are serving them, aren't you?"

Looking into the mirror once more, he smiled, pompously saying, "Hi, I am Eston Tavernier, and I approve this message."

A knock was heard on the door. "Yes?" Eston inquired, as his young assistant entered the room.

"Sir, the progressive Alliance of Coordinated Governments meeting is in one hour."

Eston sighed, "Go get my car ready." Then he grabbed his computer and walked out of his sky rise apartment.

Upon arriving at the car, he noticed his campaign manager sitting in the back. In one of his hands, he grasped an egg sandwich, devouring the food while talking.

"Now you know Eston; we must follow whatever the Alliance's goals are, for it's for the party. We are not individuals rushing towards separate goals."

Eston wasn't looking at his face as specs of food shot across the car, littering the fresh upholstery. His mind in a trance, watching as every word he spoke seemed to span across his rolls of fat, reverberating with every vibration from the man's vocal cords.

The fat man scolded, "Eston, are you paying attention?"

"Yes, Lorne."

"Like I was saying, we are not individuals rushing towards separate goals. We need to act as one. Even if you disagree, your turn will come in time. Just follow and listen to the party, as it is for the further advancement of the Coalition, and the Coalition is all that matters. Oh, Eston, would you like one?"

He felt the back of his throat curl with disgust, thinking to himself, "Yea, you thought of the perfect way for me or anyone to lose weight. Watching you eat." Although replied with a, "No, thank you, Lorne, I had a hefty dinner last night."

Arriving at the Alliance of Coordinated Governments, they pulled up in the circular drive that was miles long. The center building itself resembled the old Roman Colosseum, though well over one thousand feet tall, with an even loftier obelisk protruding from its center. The building was made of thick glass with polished steel as the support. Its shimmer was the greatest in the Alliance. He remembered reading how the glass had sets of prisms and specks of rare earth metal so fine that when the lights behind the wall shined, it put the fabled aurora lights to shame. The color scheme transformed not only as you changed your position but as the time of day changed too.

The entrance resembled the Pantheon, or the temple of the Gods, with thousands of stairs just to reach the doorways. They walked into the magnificent building, his eyes settling upon the letters "Perpetuus Foedus" thickly carved into the stone.

"Eston, this way to the main hall," Lorne hurried, urging him as he struggled to lift the fat off of his chest in an attempt to take another deep breath. "The meeting is about to begin."

The suits settled into their habitat as a man who he knew as Ashling walked to the stage. He didn't know his true name. Not many did, for he would just explain, "This name describes me better, for I too was just a sprout, and I have risen." Ashling, the house majority leader, stepped up to the podium. He cleared his throat and began the opening. "Can we have a motion to start the session?"

The whip stated, "Motion granted."

The house majority declared, "Can we have a second motion."

Another representative shouted, "Second motion granted."

"We are brought here today to inform you of the recommended movements to further the Alliance of Coordinated Governments. Let us all stand to state the pledge. Raise your hands to your hearts, for we feel with our hearts. Our hearts lead our way; they lead our compassion."

He looked at his hand and smirked to himself, accidentally whispering out loud. "I thought we used our brains to lead our bodies."

"Shhh," Lorne sternly glared at Eston, "stop your mumbling. We need to make an impression today."

Eston looked around at the few hundred people that controlled the fate of the world, all with proud eyes holding their hands on their hearts. Then followed suit, raising his hand to his heart. He took a deep breath and slowly exhaled. He realized he had to get past what he once thought; he was here to help further the Alliance. If the leaders of the world followed their hearts, then he, too, would obey those greater images before him.

Without even thinking, hundreds spoke the pledge, for it was imprinted on them, as easy to state as their names.

I pledge allegiance, to the Alliance of
Coordinated Governments.
To promote the General party, to put
their needs above myself, an individual.

To give the Alliance my body, mind, and
heart, for as long as I stand.
To strive to further the Coalition under rule.
Our nations, indivisible, with health and
prosperity for all.

The speaker began, "You may be seated. Now our agenda is set out before us as the recommended movement to further the Alliance of Coordinated Governments. In recent history, the slums have started to resemble a third world nation, struck by war and plague. The businesses that were handed over to us seem to be lacking a profit again. So, in turn, we have increased the leverage tax on anything bought or exchanged. This tax will be applied on top of the current sales tax, raising the tax from forty to fifty-two percent. Of course, the Alliance of Coordinated Governments realizes that those who serve the Coalition need their resources—in order to serve the people—and the exclusion act remains in effect for all who serve, making you exempt from this increase."

"With good news, I'm delighted to inform you the forefronts of the Alliance's military have made some headway in Ukraine. We have expanded our territory, and during the process, a significant part of land and wealth was claimed for redistribution for the Coalition. So, we are proud to announce that we will now be serving sixty percent of the world, to better health and prosperity for all!"

The crowd started to clap as Ashling continued, "This, in turn, will allow a five percent increase in the cost of living allotments for those who serve the masses. Now let us get back to the heart of the issue. We are disheartened to state that seventy-five percent of our housing remains unclaimed or unwilling to pay rent to the Alliance. We now have to start taxing all those who don't serve the Coalition. For in these tough and trying times, all have to do their part and make sacrifices. No allowances can be allotted, not even to the poor. Food supplies will continue to be distributed for those who work at any business, except those businesses that continue to run a deficit. The helping hand of the Alliance will have to withdraw or nationalize their process. For if they are unwilling to put the Alliance above themselves, then we will have no choice but to concentrate our efforts on those who are more, well … more motivated to serve the masses."

"In other news, I do regret to inform you that the police of the Alliance will soon abandon Seattle. It breaks our hearts that another great city of the past has fallen. Their resources will be better provided for those cities that are still growing. So it will be placed on the unrecoverable list. We understand that a large majority of our once-great cities are now lost. We must not dwell on the past but turn to the future and protect our new and few great cities left. Our heart goes out to those left in the city as we fence off the population. Remember my comrades, that even a wolf sometimes bites off his paw if it becomes useless so that it can save the body."

"On a lighter note, I am pleased to inform you that Amendment twenty-four has passed with a unanimous vote. I am glad to know that all of you see the importance of what I recommended. That any idea created or presented will now belong to the Alliance, allowing us to use these fresh new insights to serve the greater good, which will truly benefit the masses that we serve. Let them not forget that those thoughts were nourished by the sustenance the Alliance gave them in the first place."

Eston was staring at his shoe as his consciousness came back with the simple words he was longing to hear. "Thank you all for your consideration in these important matters as we continue to serve the population below us. Now, unless anyone has further inquiries, may I have a motion to end the Alliance of Coordinated Governments session?"

The whip once again responded, "Motion granted."

Ashling boomed, "Would anyone like to second that motion."

Another representative stated, "Second motion granted."

Ashling nodded to the crowd before him, "The motion is granted; we are adjourned."

Lorne quickly turned to Eston, "Watch how he moves effortlessly through the crowd. His presence is felt, and he knows he has the power to do as he wishes."

He studied Ashling, noticing his graying hair and his aging face. His mature body remained strong, and behind his brown eyes, a gleam seemed to leak through that Eston just couldn't place. It appeared those eyes were hiding the knowledge that no one else knew, a secret just waiting to escape.

"Now Eston, quickly, I'll go introduce you to him, only talk when spoken to." Lorne directed. "Let me do most of the talking for you." Then he approached Ashling while raising the pitch of his voice, "Hey Ash, I see you're running the world without even crossing a speed bump. How are your beautiful family and that gorgeous house coming along?"

Ashling slowly turned around, "Ahh, Mr. Lorne, I see you're doing quite well for yourself still. The family is keeping busy, as usual, and the house is coming along quite nicely. Who is this young new face?"

Lorne was beaming proudly, "This is Eston Tavernier, recently duly elected and appointed to represent the eighteenth district, presiding over the northwest region of America. He is going to do great things for the Alliance."

"It is a pleasure to meet you, Mr. Tavernier," slightly bowing his head as he spoke, "always pleased to see new men interested in furthering our goals."

"No, it is my pleasure to see you, Mr. Ashling," Eston smiled and squared his shoulders, "especially after reading so much about your avenues and your recent advances for the Coalition."

"Well stated, Mr. Tavernier!" Ashling complimented, "The party is my only goal, and you will do well here, as long as you follow the path we set before you; for the good of the masses, of course."

"Well, Ash, I heard that studies show that Amendment twenty-four will bring great prosperity to the party." Lorne offered.

Eston's mind drifted as his ears began picking up on other representatives talking about their agendas. He listened as one was urging, "We need more control over the citizens. They seem like a wild horde of animals, and animals need controlling, don't they?"

Another demanded, "We need to regulate trade between Alliance nations and set a higher levy on those who are not part of the Alliance."

He looked at the ground as a few hundred people each pushed for their own regulations. Speaking to himself, "It's no wonder why every year I have to read a new manual on the latest rules."

Lorne placed his hand on Eston's shoulder as his attention shot back to the conversation in front of him. "I expect to see you doing great things, Eston," Ashling nodded, "and it was a pleasure to meet you. Eston, never forget, you really do have the best manager possible. Lorne, I need to speak with you regarding more private matters, if you're available?"

"Of course, Sir, of course, whatever you need. Eston, make yourself comfortable, my dear lad; I'll talk with you later tonight."

"Walk with me, Lorne." He watched Lorne toddle away with Ashling, his bile once again rising out of his stomach. How could one call that walking? It was waddling at the very best.

CHAPTER TWO

Grasping her hand within his, Damian led Coretheen into the crumbling subway system below. They slowly descended the rotting stairway—swaying under their weight with every step they took—until he pushed open a thin metal door with rust falling off its brittle frame.

Squinting down the damp tunnel, stretching out before her, a thick musk pulled at her nostrils until her gaze settled upon the walls surrounding her. She peered upon the banners that were draped down the moist and molding stone. Within such darkness, beauty still could show through. For imprinted upon each banner was an eagle holding onto an olive branch, tightly grasping it within its sharp talons, as flames behind the eagle reached forward and consumed each end of the branch.

"Yes," Damian said, "we are getting close. These are the symbols of the Dicade. Here, right down here, this way." He led her as the lantern's flames flickered across the walls, revealing the wooden stairs pieced together out of old tables and chairs that squeaked under their pressure.

"Let me look at you, Coretheen." His eyes settled upon her as he wiped the dried blood from her mouth. Then brushed her ragged black hair from out of her dark glowing hazel eyes. "Well, you are a beautiful girl. Skinny, but ehh, who's not these days." As he laughed to himself, "Ahh, there you go; finally, a hint of a smile released upon that face of yours. Now Miss, be prepared. There will be quite a gathering tonight. We don't have much down here, Miss, but what we do have is plenty of rallies. Pointless, I think. But hey, if it improves morale, I guess I can't complain. It does give quite a spectacle for those newcomers, though."

Coretheen heard a single loud voice shouting from below, growing louder as he continued. "We better keep moving, Miss, for I am expected. It's proper to be punctual, especially to these blasted social ramblings. I just had to make one wrong turn in this pesky city. It is so hard to get around when everything looks the same. A broken, collapsed building to the right, and oh wait, what's that up there to the left? Of course, another broken, collapsed, and decaying building. Then I start to run late. But, then again, I can't complain. I wouldn't have run into such a pretty gal. Ahh, I hate talk. We should just act. I guess I am just too impatient. That's why I must be stuck in the background, whispering in other's ears. Maybe one day, my whispers will reach across this land, but for now, patience is the best course of action."

Coretheen's eyes opened wide while she nervously scanned the dark tunnels before her as the loud voice echoed off the sheer walls surrounding her.

"Coretheen, stay close now. It's going to get crowded quick. Don't be afraid, for I will not leave your side. Stay close, my Lady. Don't be afraid."

She clutched his hand tightly as they entered the hall, brushing past the masses of people until arriving at an elevated slab of concrete. She gazed upon the large hall illuminated by the dancing flames. Upon the pillars rising to the ceiling, carved out of stone and covered in brass, with banners bearing the symbol of the eagle positioned on each one.

Reaching the concrete platform, Damien climbed on top and extended his hand towards hers once again. "Come, Coretheen," he said while lifting her up. Then proceeded to take a seat behind the speaker, who was wearing a vest that was one size too small.

She looked at the man in front of her—with badges draped across his shoulders—and on his back, the

Dicade symbol was proudly displayed. Her eyes were nervously drifting towards the one who saved her, towards Damian Gardge.

"Come, sit here, Miss. I'll explain after." Assuring her with his steady and kind smile.

The speaker's voice echoed down the halls as he spoke fluently, seizing everyone's attention. The room was filled with hundreds of men and women, all quieter than the sound of a lucky soul mashing food around their pallet. "To our wise general, under the command of the Dicade, here is our Lieutenant General, Damian!"

Coretheen's eyes gleamed over as the crowd's attention was fixed on the one who saved her, the one called Damian.

"This rotten city," Damian bellowed, "this soiled country, this decrepit world, where the so-called Government grasps everything, claiming their actions are for the many. They destroyed our companies, forcing us through their lead bullets and protected by their bulletproof vests, tainting our morals through the disguise of innocence. Guiding our hands-on paper as we signed away our rights, being told it was for our own good, for the better of the whole. They stated we did not know what we needed, that we had to act before it was too late and that it was our own greed that leached the country dry. That even our thoughts and our innovations were loaned to us through them. That without them, we would be nothing and could have never become anything. So as they gave to us, they persuaded us that we had to return what was given. We followed blindly, thinking that moving in any direction was better than sitting still. We ignored logic. We ignored ourselves, and we lashed out at anyone who claimed logic, who claimed an idea. So, we signed over our souls to them, for we were unable to bear the strain or torment of everyday life. We handed over the hands that fed us, forcing them into submission and giving them over to those who claimed it was needed."

"We did this because we were jealous of those who worked before us, who had more than us. Though what we did not realize or fathom, that those who we were listening too, had greater wealth than those we were handing over, those that gave us food, and those who worked hard for what they had achieved. Just as most of you worked for your living, the masses lived off of the crumbs leftover; that were handed out by the Government. It progressed. Soon the middle class fell, for why should they have more? Even if they worked hard for what they acquired too. They farmed, produced, sweat, and strived to have a family, bettering themselves, striving for better than the crumbs that were leftover. Though, they too did not have the loudest voice, for they had no time to head to the streets to raise theirs. Those living off the crumbs, provided by the Government, raised their voices in protest and yelled 'without you standing on our back, you too, wouldn't be where you are now!'"

"Then, those in charge on paper, the Alliance before you—whose fortune was amassed from the many; whose wealth was acquired by that of a signature; whose only strength was that of a pen and a threat; whose work was minimal, other than to harm the whole—gained strength. Their worth grew by leaching the wealth from those who worked before them as the masses rotted below them. Who soon would realize that tyranny of darkness is where they would thrive. Who took upon the task to eclipse the sun and bring darkness to their own people. For what good is freedom of choice when it could go against those in power? The rest, you know. They persuaded those on crumbs to lash out, to tear down any achievement built by those who claimed self-achievement."

"So, the buildings came crashing down onto the bodies below them. New cities were built upon those skeletons, but only those elected could enter the buildings. Only those who the Alliance deemed select and of national importance to the vitality of the country could even approach those sanctuaries. Corpses were pushed aside as one would push away an insect as an inconvenience to their existence. Therefore, we continue to live on our knees as they give us our scraps of food, only so we can work and maintain their existence. I ask you, what happens if we stand on our own two feet? We are first pushed down to our knees. If we attempt to stand again, we are pushed to the ground, and our shoes are taken. If we manage to stand again and start to thrive, we are killed, pushed away as a threat to the corrupt status quo. So, we obey as we always have."

"Though, I ask you this question, what if we stand together? What if we stand together and we don't scatter like insects, as they expect us to? The answer is, we may once again rise based on the foundation of what this empire was built upon. Freedom to do as one wished; freedom to thrive; freedom to make one's own choice; freedom to profit and live one's life. For that is the greatest gift a nation can give to its people."

Damien paused, glancing over his shoulder at Coretheen. Calmness was in his eyes, and this calmness was absorbed by every single person in the crowd. He returned his gaze upon the masses. His voice rising with every word he spoke. "But, each time they took from us, they gave us something in return. They gave us the time to plan, to collaborate, to retaliate against their Alliance of so-called Coordinated Governments." The crowd below started to stand slowly, one by one, "We, who used to be on our knees. We, who no longer scatter. We, who now stand. We, demand our freedom! For if one is not free to think for themselves, then they are as useless as the cattle that follow blindly into a slaughterhouse. Soon to become sustenance for those who set its fate in stone."

Coretheen watched with awe, shocked by the group below. She looked around and noticed something she hadn't seen for a long time: hope, motivation, and determination. The crowd did not cheer; the mass did not scream or yell. Their eyes said it all—that they believed. That this was their choice and that this is what they wanted. More than what they wanted, what they needed.

Damian growled, "We will not let them carve our names in stone and throw it upon the mass graves. Our names will remain ours; they shall not relinquish what was given to us at birth, for our thoughts are ours. With those thoughts, we proclaim life and that life will be used as each and every individual chooses. We will proclaim our own mistakes and suffer our consequences. We will bear only the burdens we choose and wish to carry out."

"Would they sit by while a robber stole their possessions at night? No, they would arrest the villain and deem him unfit for life! Yet, they claim their acts are different. They claim that it is for the better that everyone should listen to their hearts as they rip it out of our bodies. So I ask, do we accept their act? Do we allow them to steal our thoughts? Do we allow them to steal our few last goods? Do we allow the villain into our heads and grant them the right to do as they please? So, I ask, what is the difference between a villain who stalks at night and those of the Alliance?"

"The Alliance no longer needs to hide in the veil of darkness. The Alliance does not need to fear consequences because they control what is deemed evil and immoral. So, I ask again, what shall we do? The choice is yours, but we cannot sit idly by. The time has come for us to reclaim what was unrightfully taken. The time has come for us to reclaim our freedom!"

Damian slowly walked back to Coretheen as the crowd clapped and slowly departed back to whatever hole they crawled out of. He noticed her eyes glazed in wonder, focusing upon the few guards that remained, one in front of each pillar within the vast hall until he took her hand. The mysterious man before her, who mistakenly walked past her at precisely the right time, and as he grasped her side, her eyes settled upon another man.

Damian abruptly turned and stood erect. "Sir, my apologies. I didn't realize that you would compliment me with your presence."

A smile appeared upon the new man's face. "Now, now, Damian. I have known you for quite some time, and I wouldn't have put you in charge of this city if I didn't think we could be on at least a first name basis."

Damian put his hand to the back of his head, then looked down at the ground anxiously. "Well, Sir, I couldn't possibly call you by your first name, Mr. Kamon." Pulling Coretheen to his side as a grin erupted across his lips, "Sir, pardon my manners. This is Coretheen, ahh…"

She looked up at Kamon's face, noticing his graying hair and wrinkles that seemed to signify his years of wisdom, along with his robust and assertive stance. "Sir, I am Coretheen Nerites, and I am pleased to meet you."

"Man, Damian." Kamon started laughing, "Still can't remember the simple things, can you?"

"Hey, now. Come on, Sir, I just met this pretty gal tonight." Damian bristled.

"Yea, sure you did, kid. I go and make you Lieutenant General, and you're running around picking up gals?"

"No, no, no, no, Sir, that's not it at all. Come on, Sir; I was on my way here…"

Kamon interrupted, "In which you barely made it in time to make your own speech."

"Come on, Sir, it's not how it appears. This young miss seemed to be in some trouble."

Kamon pulled Coretheen close to him and stared into her eyes, "You do seem to have a certain look to your eyes, almost a defiance, and longing. So gal, what do you think of tonight's convergence?"

Coretheen opened her mouth to speak but was interrupted by Damian, "Well, Sir, let's be proper and let me introduce you. Miss Coretheen, this is the leader of the Dicade, not many know him by face, and only his commanders know him by name." Damian smiled and kind of giggled, "It's not like our organization believes in hanging giant pictures of their leaders in some sort of self-inflicted lust to be loved."

"Nice to…"

"Come on, Damian." Kamon interrupted her, not seeming to notice that she was even speaking. "You know we are not about self-image."

She opened her mouth once again, attempting to talk, without any success. Her eyes began to narrow as her lips started to tighten.

"Sir, with due respect," Damian declared, "the only reason you don't gloat your image around is for lack of funds to promote the printers or to obtain the ink, don't ya think, Miss Coretheen?"

"Well…"

Kamon lunged forward, "Now Damian, we all know that I would designate funds if it were important but,"

"Yes, yes, Sir. We highly realize that the only reason you don't lust over your own image is the fact that you wish to remain an individual—instead of a delicately placed memorial over your martyred body. In defense of the old capitalism constitutionalists, which would soon be defiled by many rodents."

"Now, do you see what I have to put up with? Do ya, Miss?" Kamon looked at Coretheen. "I don't know how you ended up with this guy, but if I were you, I would choose to flee from him. If ya want, Miss, I can offer you a nice little position in another city, so you are not burdened with his lack of thought."

Coretheen, attempting to speak once again, "Well…"

"Mr. Kamon," Damian burst in, "as you well know, I bring in the most well-fitted recruits and the most skilled self-thinking candidates. I also acquire the most funding." Coretheen started to clench her hands into fists next to her body as Damian continued, "I think you're just afraid of me donating my time to someone other than you. Sir, with respect, I think your jealously is flattering. Though let's be honest, Sir, we both know you're just jealous of me being with such a pretty lady."

"Hey, I am not judging if you drag a woman off the street to help her. Though, let me be honest with you, Damian, forcing someone is another situation." Kamon teased, "You should know better than to pry or sneak into her head, convincing her that she needs to be with you."

"Sir, I can and am able to find a lady if I was willing. Though, I decided to dedicate myself to more important matters, unlike your excessive waste of time traveling to check up on the situation instead of coordinating a movement. I just don't have..."

Coretheen, full of rage, roared, "First of all, I, in no manner, stated I was with Damian like that!" Turning to Damian, she proclaimed with a fiery stare, "Second of all, who the heck said I was a waste of time? I thought you were all about being polite. Yet, here you are only hours after I met you, and you seem to ignore the fact that I am even here. I am hungry, thirsty, and beyond all annoyed with the both of you!"

Turning to Kamon, she continued her rampage, "And for you, I have no idea who you are, nor do I care. It does not give you the right to interrupt me after trying to converse with me. After hearing a speech like that, I thought the general and the coordination leader would be..."

"I actually resemble, in a similar sense, the President of old," Kamon defended himself, "though, the head military general really has all the power in times like this. I guess you could say I am second in command. With my responsibilities on tasks of organization, yet still the face of this resistance, only having to collaborate with one."

Coretheen snapped back, "Like I stated, I don't care who you are. Stop interrupting me! As I was saying, I came here thinking you had manners. I listened to your speech Damian, and I admired that someone, somewhere, wanted to act instead of hope... Someone who could draw strength out of weakness. Now, I don't know what to think. I don't know how the heck anyone can get a single word in with you two by each other. Kamon, I am surprised someone hasn't killed you out of your sheer disrespect because you never seem to shut up!"

"Woah, Damian, you sure know how to find a lady!" Kamon started to laugh as Coretheen glared at him. "After a lecture like that, you just got to laugh." He put up his hands in a gesture of defeat. "Though you got to admit, young Lady, what you stated wasn't exactly respectful or proper either. I do apologize for our lack of reverence. We do kind of get carried away sometimes, Miss."

Damian smiled, "See, Sir, like I was saying, I find all the self-minded individuals for ya."

"Yea, you sure do."

Coretheen glared once again, "You were just walking by me; it was luck, and who said I was joining you?"

"Well, Miss Coretheen, I never claimed you were joining us. I just said I find all the self-minded individuals. Actually, I don't even remember offering you a spot in my city."

"If I do remember, the so-called President himself offered me a position in another region. As I remember from history books, the President seemed to have authority in placing subordinates wherever he wishes."

"Well, you got me there," Damian started to laugh as he began leading her behind the raised concrete platform, "but technically, generals control most war matters. I'll retract my statement, and as long as you're willing, I'd assume that you would be a worthy addition to this organization. Though first, let us find you some food and get your strength back. I don't want you saying yes before you're well informed of what our resistance goals are."

She watched as he pulled out a seat for her to sit at in front of a small and splintering wooden table. Her anger faded as her eyes focused on his earnest smile until a warm cup of coffee and stale bread rested in front of her.

"Sorry, Miss, that's really all we got, though we do got lots of coffee, so drink up."

Kamon started to whisper, leading Damian to the back of the room, "Damian, there is a reason I came here today. Some of the businesses that were supporting us will soon be shut down or nationalized by the Alliance. As you know, they were secretly donating every penny to us, so the Alliance of Coordinated Governments could not re-distribute their profit. My most serious concern is that we have received notice from my informant in the Alliance that the twelfth military manufacturing division is sched-uled for decommissioning in three months. We will lose one of our biggest arms and explosives manufacturers. We have agreed to accommodate all their workers, per their request, and to help the Dicade movement. The manager of that building is a dear friend of mine, Damian. He as-sisted us in getting most of our income from other busi-nesses, who still managed to maintain their mind while being forced to watch their creation go to the Coalition. They were willing to work for free under harsh condi-tions, till the time came to rise and strike back."

"Well, there goes our hope of getting all the equip-ment we needed." Damian sighed, "It would have been at least another five years before we would have had enough to mobilize. With our current rate, we may have even needed longer to accommodate and train all our forces. This is disappointing. What does the director of defense, Mr. Pikon, think of this?

"Why do you think I am here? He requested me to come to get your insight personally. We need your expertise in this situation to properly form a plan. He apologizes that he could not come down here himself. So we must discuss this in-depth and make a strategy Damian, we can't let our people down, and we have to endure this as we always have. The only positive thing is that he found us an informant in the Alliance so that we won't be out of the loop." Damian's eyes rose to Coretheen as she continued to eat.

Her gaze met his as she watched the two men talk and then glanced down at the bread in front of her. Food used to be a commodity that everyone had. Supplies were vast, and shelves were filled with more food than one could eat in a lifetime. Now she was grateful just to have a drink and some stale bread to eat, accompanied by a few flies filling themselves upon the crumbs that remained. She thought to herself, "And I thought I had it bad back in college."

Those were supposed to be the hardest times in her life, and now they seemed to be some of the best. She remembered the excitement that built up inside of her when she got accepted to Stanford. How proudly her dad had beamed at her, knowing that she would soon take over his global business of logistics. The business that, a few years later, was ripped from the family name and grasped by the newly formed Alliance—who proclaimed it was necessary for the betterment of humankind—to serve those more in need. Their vast amount of transportation vessels were taken first to help with the war efforts, of course. The Government claimed any resources that were needed, putting millions out of work for a "good cause." The Government justified it by saying that competition drew money away from the government's personal services and that they needed the current network of her father's business to distribute goods to the population in need, which held the riots at bay for a time. The Government even paid her father well, at first.

She watched a fly land on her bread, rubbing its legs together as if it was praying before its last meal. She shooed it away and took another bite. Just as the Government had shooed her father away from his company, declaring that it was a part of the nation's infrastructure and it was essential to keep the population healthy. His wasn't the first business they took over and not even close to the last. Not long afterward, their bank accounts were secretly confiscated to pay the workers. They were allowed to keep a considerable amount of funds, though it didn't matter after inflation hit.

Even worse, the Alliance set a motion to tax current wealth at twenty percent a year instead of taxing income. Within ten years, all of their money was gone. There was nothing to invest in, nothing seemed safe, and there were no sacred cows. For what is holy to one person can be devoured through a gluttonous mouth of another. She soon returned from college, just one-year short of earning her degree. It was no longer safe to be away from her family; the riots began to become much more severe. Thousands were being killed, and the military had to be called in. She had guessed that they probably were transported using some of their own vessels and planes. The murder and mayhem spread and multiplied like the maggots that would spawn on her bread if left untouched. So the Government did what anyone would have done to maggots, they crushed them.

Coretheen's attention returned to the room around her as the dust began to pepper her hair from the ceiling above. She watched as Damian and Kamon both froze, just as a dog does when a stranger approaches the door, knowing something was coming before those around him senses adjusted to the situation.

A scream was heard in the distance as a thunderous explosion erupted down the hall. Coretheen clapped her hands to her ears while Damian and Kamon walked calmly towards the door as cracks in the ceiling began to spread. A loud crash was heard from the main hall as another deafening explosion ripped through the underground tunnels. She nervously looked towards Damian.

He smiled at the woman in front of him, whose trembling hands tightly grasped her head, then gently whispered. "Don't worry, my girl; I made a promise to offer you shelter from the world. I keep my promises; you will be safe."

The cracks in the ceiling began to grow as if branches from a trees trunk slowly stretching out across the sky. Pieces of rebar pierced out of the ceiling as if they were a spider's web desperately trying to hold onto the cement from above. She watched as the look returned to Damian's eyes, the look she had first seen when he had saved her from that venomous man. A glimpse of ferocious determination, as his presence in the room, became more prominent than the room itself. He seemed to change, and with that, she knew—she was not going to become someone else's prey tonight—that she would be safe.

Those eyes, his fierce eyes, gave her more hope than she'd felt in a long time; a blue fire grew in those eyes, and she knew that not even death could extinguish their fire. The Elpis symbol on his cane began to emit a faint light as a man lunged into the room. Taking his cane, Damian grabbed the back of the man's leg with its curve, pulling it up over his head, flipping the assailant forward onto the ground. Another man was already through the door, thrusting a knife at Damian; before the blade could puncture his flesh, he grabbed his arm and twisted the assailant, causing him to stumble forward. With that, Kamon wrapped his arms around the attacker's neck and, with one swift movement, broke it against his knee. Damian calmly walked to the man on the floor, put his foot to the assailant's shoulder, and broke it, as Kamon grabbed the knife off of the ground and tightly held it against the man's throat.

A small whimper echoed down the collapsed hall as the dust began to settle.

CHAPTER THREE

E ston stared at the ceiling of his apartment, thinking of how he had just met the most powerful man in the country. No, Ashling wasn't only the most powerful man in the country, but the entire world. Ever since they rescinded the power of the president, other than for ceremonial purposes, the house majority could remain in control as long as he lived. He remembered how far he had come and how a much skinnier Mr. Lorne approached him when he was running one of the working unions in a small manufacturing plant under the Alliance. Lorne had taught him how to talk, dress, and how to make those around him do as he pleased, without directly telling them to do so. Soon he was offered a council spot in his district, followed by him becoming the district representative—replacing his predecessor during an emergency session—knowing that in the next election, it was almost a guarantee for him to be reelected.

He remembered Lorne's words, "Now, if you do well as district rep, I'll make sure you'll get regional manager, putting you in direct contact with the board and Mr. Ashling. Just keep doing the favors I ask, and you'll be there within two terms end." Eston closed his eyes, letting the cool night air relax him a little more with every breath he took. He listened to the sounds of the night until his ears concentrated on footsteps in the hallway, slowly becoming louder with each stride. He thought to himself. It's odd as one sense is dulled; others seem to become heightened, a fact that he learned too well while living on the streets.

The footsteps stopped as his door opened. Eston jumped up, rushing to see who had come unannounced. His shirt was unbuttoned, showing his formed chest as a calm and well-postured man dressed in black appeared before him.

"Mr. Lorne has sent for you." The man's stale voice indicated that this was not a request but a command.

His eyes rested upon a pin on the man's shirt before him. It bore the symbol of an iron tree with its branches grasping the shadows in an attempt to cover the sun.

The man noticing his confused expression, explained, "Representative Tavernier, we could not go through the usual channels tonight. So, disregard this inconvenience, for you will accept the request of Mr. Lorne."

Eston smiled and shrugged, "No, that's not it at all. Of course, I will accept the invitation of Mr. Lorne. I was just shocked to have an unannounced guest, without first allowing my assistant to be notified so that I could present myself properly." Buttoning his shirt up, he began to walk towards his suit jacket and started to prepare his hair as the man reached for his hand.

"Sir, that will not be necessary, for where you are going, structure and formality will not be the norm. We leave, as you are, now." His last words lingered in the air as Eston followed the strange man before him until he was gestured to sit in the back of a shimmering black car.

The car was put into gear. And as it pulled away, the driver flicked a switch, and his view of the world vanished into the darkness.

CHAPTER FOUR

Coretheen's mind snapped back to reality. What just happened? She lifted her hands off her head as the rubble fell from the ceiling. Then she sat on her knees, peering towards the sounds of two voices as the dust began to settle. Straining her eyes, she began to make out Damian's figure, standing above a man on the ground as Kamon pressed a knife against the man's neck. Thinking back, she could barely track their movements, their attacks so swift, without any hesitation. Her mind began to clear as the situation settled in, and her anxiety faded. No longer was she nervous as their voices stretched out across the room.

"Now, now, Mr. Transgressor," Damian calmly spoke, "I have to admit, a valiant effort on your part, though it seems failure is in your nature, isn't it?"

The assailant smirked, a sense of arrogance filling his voice. "You just don't understand; you have no chance. If not from me, then from those who sent me, the Alliances' power is far-reaching and is only growing every day."

Kamon pressed the knife deeper into his throat as a trickle of blood started to form a small pool underneath him. "Mr. Transgressor, do not play games of implying my ignorance, especially in the presence of the pretty lady. Let's make this easier on the both of us and tell me about your sacred Alliance. While you're at it, could you throw in how you found this location in the first place, for this gesture would be vastly appreciated?"

The assailant started to laugh, then paused to spit out the blood accumulating in his mouth. "You just don't get it, man, are all of you so dumb? You can't stand up to their might. Every single one of you is just a bunch of fuc..."

A snap was heard as Damian broke his other arm and corrected, "Now, my Transgressor, there is no need for that, especially in front of the young lady. Just think, I still have two more limbs that I can play with. Doesn't that sound fun, mmmmm? Where were we? Ohh, yes, that's right, you were just about to tell me how you found this place. Weren't you, my kind Sir?" A soft whimper echoed out from the man on the floor as Damian adjusted his grip. "Yes, that's better, isn't it?"

"They have been tracking your so-called president's movements for weeks." He paused every few words to stop himself from screaming out in pain. "We tracked him here and were told to infiltrate your compound, eliminate the general of this city, and capture the president."

"Look, Kamon; it appears that we are both quite popular these days. It seems I am more disliked than you, though. Well, my new-found friend, kindly tell me who sent you to us, and spare yourself another limb, hmmm? I warn you, the response of the Alliance will not suffice either."

Another large mouth full of blood was spat upon the ground. "How do you think we knew how to track you? Heck, I am just military spec ops, and even I can see you have a leak. How do you even manage to run your Goddam..." Another crack echoed through the hall, followed by a loud, piercing scream.

"Sir, please refrain from causing yourself this agony. I will not allow you to continue to speak as you have been, and I am running out of limbs to break. I guess you still have your left knee, though. So, I ask kindly once again, so the perseverance of your pain can cease, who sent you?"

The man shook on the ground as pain ripped through almost all of his joints, and the puddle of blood only grew larger under his neck. "I don't know, we just get the orders to carry out the mission, but I will tell you what I do know. I can't wait till that glimmer in your eyes fade as your followers suffer and are fuc..." A gargle was heard, followed by muffled coughs, while the assailant choked on his own blood as Kamon's knife plunged deep within his throat, releasing his pain.

"Mr. Transgressor, I do apologize, but it seems that your eyes will fade much before mine."

Coretheen looked up towards Damian, noticing that the strong, fierce gleam was retreating from his eyes, as he began chastising the dead man on the ground. "Geesh, it wasn't necessary to redecorate our halls, though. I guess it resembles the rest of the city now, just a pile of rubble."

Wiping the blood off the blade, Kamon then put it into his pocket while whispering to himself, "Never a reason to waste a good knife now, is there?" Then sighed while looking at Damian. "My friend, I am sorry for the short notice, but I must contact the informant and figure out how this happened. We are losing ground, not only in our armament of the resistance but now they are somehow privy to our inside operations. I must depart to investigate. I will be in contact with you as soon as I can, you know when and where to meet me. To you, Miss Coretheen, it was a pleasure to meet you, and I hope I will have the pleasure to do it again." He looked toward Damian as they both gave each other a slight nod, understanding one another without exchanging a single word. Kamon turned into the dark, crumbling tunnels as the shadows engulfed any presence he once had.

"My dear girl, sorry for that inconvenience, though it could not be helped." Picking his cane up off of the floor, he walked to Coretheen and stretched out his hand to her. "It is time for us to move, my Lady, for time is something we never have the luxury to waste. Take my hand, and I will lead you and all the people to the freedom that they deserve. For together, we can put the light back into this dark world."

CHAPTER FIVE

Eston heard a click, and after being confined in darkness for hours, the windows once again became clear. He peered down the dark tunnel that stretched past where the headlights of the vehicle illuminated. To his left, there was a door—with a large shadow that stretched past its frame—as he heard a bellowing laugh.

"Lad, you ought to see your face. You look like you are on your way to an execution."

Glaring, Eston stated, "What do you expect when I am pulled out in the middle of the night by you, Mr. Lorne?" Whispering to himself, "I should have known that something larger than a door itself could have only been you." Then smiled at Lorne while walking toward him, "A man of your stature, I shouldn't have expected any finer of an entrance. Though I will admit, I am curious why you summoned me in this manner, let alone at this time?"

Ashling walked out behind Lorne and spoke with a soft yet commanding voice. "My dear Eston, this inconvenience was recommended by Mr. Lorne here." Gesturing with his hand towards Lorne. "We needed fresh blood, one who is committed to our cause, who will work on behalf of the Alliance. One who will have new insights on certain matters and can learn and grow to our needs."

"Why the secrecy, within the dead of the night?"

Ashling said, grinning, "For Eston, a structure as large as the Alliance cannot grow without guidance. At certain times, this guidance needs to be led, not in the light of the day, but in the darkness of the night. For in the darkness is where one stalks their prey, where one takes hold and expands their boundaries. It is where one snuffs out the light of the resistance. That is why I called you here tonight. You have been summoned to take part in the shadow unit of the Alliance, led by me. Our tasks are many, from political advancement to maintaining order; we are the secret that is kept in the night. We are the shadow that hides in the darkness, pulling the strings of the Alliance itself. Only the few and privileged learn about us. That is why you have been chosen. But before any information is released to you, you must accept this privilege. And pledge to us your mind and your heart—for the sake of the Alliance, of course."

Eston hesitated, knowing that those who denied likely became part of the shadows themselves, never seeing the light again.

"Well, my dear Eston, the Alliance awaits your response, in full, now!" His last word echoed down the tunnels.

Knowing this would be the quickest way to advance within the Coalition, Eston took a deep breath and affirmed, "Let me be but clay to be molded to what the Alliance seems fit. From a weapon, or to a tool, from whatever to whomever the Alliance deems necessary of me. Till they are ready to cast a permanent mold out of me, for the future that is planned for me, by the Alliance, for the good of the Alliance, I will be whatever you command."

"Once again, Mr. Tavernier, well-spoken. Then from here forth, you are accepted into this unit that hides in the dark and bends the light to their own wishes." Ashling handed him a metal coin with the same symbol he saw on the one who collected him. "This is our symbol." He explained, "You will keep this coin hidden from others, and if it is seen by others, you will become a relic of the past, soon to be forgotten. Only show this coin to those who wear the pin, like the one you saw on your escort who brought you here. These people that display the pin are only used when necessary; they will come in through the shadows, and this coin will be your redemption and your savior in these times. My Eston, only a few, have these coins. This symbol is that of the true force of the Alliance, the force of the shadows."

"Congratulations on behalf of the Alliance. I commend you on becoming a shadow of the night, a true guardian of our great nations. Let us convene inside." Ashling walked back through the door behind him as Eston exhaled with relief.

"Lad, you almost had me there. I thought you were going to break." Lorne slapped Eston on the back, laughing, "I would have lost one of my prime students. I knew you wouldn't let me down. You're never one that lacks the right words at the right time. That's my boy!" Once again, smacking Eston on the back while leading him into the room. "I promised you great advancement when I found you, my lad, past those all around you. I promised that you'd climb the greatest mountains. This is your time to prove yourself. To reach the inner circle, I know you won't disappoint. You never do."

He looked at the octagon-shaped room. Each side plated with a TV, with images on them from around the world. Between each set of TV screens hung a banner on the wall, signifying the Alliance. In the center of the room was an iron tree; he pulled out his coin and looked at it.

"Yes, Eston, it is indeed the same tree. This tree consumes the shadows of the world and the screens that surround you display our endeavors across the earth." Eston stared at the iron roots, piercing out of the marble floor, grasping at the screens around the room. Ashling continued, "Its roots are the cause of the world's problems, and yet, it is also the cure. It is the vaccine that prevents absolute chaos in this world, holding fast and never letting go, entangling the problems and choking them out—making its substance a part of its own."

In the middle of the room, he peered at the octagon table surrounding the iron tree. He observed how the table and the floor were made from a single magnificent piece of marble, with its sides and corners laced with gold.

"These are the seats of eight," Ashling gestured to the shimmering crystal chairs, "they signify the eight leaders of the Guardians of the Shadows. One day you may gaze your eyes upon the eight, but only when you are one of them, as I am. We are the only ones who can allow new guardians to join our ranks, and those who are accepted only ever see those who have brought them in. Each of us has a room identical to this one, secret to all other members of the eight, other than to me. A sanctuary of sorts, to bring their followers to for the viewing and for other personal matters." Ashling looked toward Lorne, questioning, "Lorne, shall we proceed?"

"Let the viewing commence of our newest addition, Eston Tavernier," Lorne roared, "for he is here to prove himself in becoming a true Guardian of the Shadows." The screens on each side of the wall went black and, within a moment, showed only shadows of silhouettes.

"This is Eston Tavernier, representative of district eighteen, here for the viewing. Newly accepted to our unit, I nominate him in accordance with our laws, to be advanced past a new cadet and placed into the trial of shadows." Ashling commanded.

The silhouettes spoke in unison. "We, the eight, in accordance with our laws, accept your candidate to begin the trials."

"We must advance your stature and put you into the trials, so we can utilize what we need from you." Lorne notified Eston, "We must first be sure you're a true follower of the Alliance. To prove this, you must blindly follow without knowing our wishes or what we wish of you for the future. You must prove yourself in the coming weeks as a true follower of the eight."

"Don't worry, my boy," Lorne whispered into Eston's ear, "Ashling is backing you. This is pretty much just following protocol. No one ever goes against his wishes, and he wishes to have you, and he always gets what he wishes for."

Ashling walked to the center of the room, turning slowly as he spoke. "Eston Tavernier, I nominate you for your first trial, the trial of acceptance. After completion, you will become an elite member of the Guardians of the Shadows. Though you may be accepted, your allegiance will have to be demonstrated continuously to maintain this title that has been bestowed upon you. In accordance with our laws, we the eight, bequeath the necessary information upon you to accomplish your tasks, in strict confidence, till the day your service is no longer needed. Or, until death claims you and the shadows take you in secrecy, within the dead of night, such as we found you on this very evening."

The shadows on the screen spoke in unison, "We the eight, bequeath the necessary information upon you to accomplish your tasks, in strict confidence, till the day your service is no longer needed. Or, until death claims you and the shadows take you in secrecy—in accordance with our laws—in the dead of night, such as we, the guardians, found you."

Ashling gazed upon Eston, "My new guardian, it is time to see the true power of the Alliance; speak now so the shadows can embrace you."

While squaring his shoulders, Eston slowly turned as the shadows of the world looked upon him. He dare not shake in fear, for if he did, he knew he would be discarded. He dare not show pride, for pride was a sign of independence, and he would be cast aside, just as one casts away a stray animal on a frigid winter night. He only showed the emotion of acceptance. For this elite force of the Alliance wished to mold its foes and its allies to their will. Bowing his head, he declared, "This piece of clay before you will be as you wish when you wish of it. Let words not separate us, nor blades, for blades cannot cut into the shadows. As shadows engulf whatever is thrown into them, as I have been consumed by your might, in secrecy, for the rest of my service under the Alliance. I vow that as long as the Alliance allows me to live, that I will bend to their will."

A mutual smirk slowly spread across Lorne's and Ashling's faces. In particular, Ashling's cold, dark, and brown eyes seemed to scream with excitement as he claimed another soul. "My Eston, I couldn't have put it better myself."

Lorne nodded, smiling as pride filled his eyes, as a parent would smile at a child after receiving their first trophy.

Ashling continued, "As of recent, My Eston, we made some advancements in taking down the resistance. We have been tracking the president of the resistance since its beginning. We now have a face to the movement, against us, on our own soil. This is not the only thing that we have achieved. We have also located a great Lieutenant General, one whose face still eludes us. A General whose wisdom is only second to that of the Alliance, to that of me; his tactical ability is superb, and he is able to move with great speed. He is one of the last pieces of the puzzle that we need before we can break that puzzle into hundreds of pieces. Their compound has been destroyed, being as fragile as a twig inside a hurricane, torn and shattered without mercy. As our plans progress, we now have insight into their movements. Their usefulness will soon end, and when it does, we will make them just a story of the past. The population will whisper their names as if just legends in a book, questioning even their existence."

"So we, the eight, set you on your first task. This task comes with some risk, but it will show where your true allegiance lies. Earlier at the congressional hearing, you heard of the police force withdrawing from Seattle and the population soon to be fenced off, leaving them to the shadows of the night. You, Eston Tavernier, will now oversee this great sacrifice of our land in order to save the whole. Close off the borders, fence off the population, and withdraw our assistance while minimizing casualties on our side. If resistance shows, eliminate the resistance as the shadows consumes the light, for you are now a Guardian of the Shadows. Do not hesitate, do not falter, for we are now putting the might of the Alliance behind your hands."

"With fury and might, in accordance with our laws, purge our weakness and show the Alliance's true strength, My Eston."

The eight silhouettes chanted together, "Purge our weakness and cleanse our land. Purge our weakness and cleanse our land."

"In accordance with our laws, the viewing is over." Ashling's voice drifted over the chanting shadows. "My thanks goes to all of you, the true guardians of the Alliance." The screens crackled, and the shadows were once again replaced with images of the Alliance's dominance across the globe.

CHAPTER SIX

Damian grabbed Coretheen by her hips and swung her body over an area of broken glass as he chuckled, "Sorry, my Lady, heh, seems like I kinda got lost again," while rubbing the back of his head.

"For a general, you have no sense of direction." Coretheen gleefully stated as a hint of a smile tugged at her cheeks. "You can't even seem to find your way out of what you call your city."

"Well, Miss, you see, these tunnels sure look a lot different since they were remodeled with C4."

Coretheen gave Damian a small punch on his shoulder, "And whose fault is that?"

"Geesh," he laughed, "you sure know how to hit a guy when he's down, don't you?" Once again, rubbing the back of his head anxiously while looking down at the ground.

Climbing up a slab of concrete, he reached down for Coretheen's hand as she replied, "You aren't exactly down right now, are you?"

"Well, I guess you're right about that. You are sure a specific one, aren't you?"

"Damian, look!" she exclaimed, "I see light." He stopped as they both peered down the dark tunnel as a faint light trickled in towards them.

While exiting the tunnel, Damian looked down, noticing he was still grasping Coretheen's hand. He stopped walking and smiled as the gentle and warm breeze brushed their faces. And as the light hit them, Damian gripped Coretheen's hand a little tighter within his own.

She looked briefly up at the man next to her, thinking how everything seemed so much more comfortable with him. She bit down on her lip, musing, just for a second, that it almost seemed there could be beauty in the world again.

He returned her stare as the light shimmered down upon her face, and the dust fell away, showing the purest of beauty not masked by the makeup of old. He took his hand and gingerly placed it under her chin. "There is still beauty in this world that we must work hard to grasp. Even a flower starts as a seed, and that seed must take root before it can bloom and release its true allure on this planet. We, too, are but seeds, waiting to take root and spread the beauty in this once great land. Though, we must not wait too long, for we have a duty to the people who wish to see that beauty unleashed upon this earth."

She gazed up at his face as he raised his line of sight to the sun, filling him with strength. Coretheen closed her eyes, just for a moment, and when she opened them, she stared towards Damian, the one who filled her with strength.

"Come, my Lady. We must not delay, for we have many to warn that the compound is no longer a safe haven, as it once used to be." Brushing the dust from her hair, he looked down upon Coretheen as their gazes met.

"Then what are we waiting for?" She smiled, starting to walk ahead of him, "If I were to let you lead the way, you would just get us lost." Coretheen turned around quickly, winking at him while he took another deep breath as a strange peace washed over him.

CHAPTER SEVEN

Eston awoke as his helicopter landed outside of Seattle. He had been given control of the Alliance's great military might; its satellites, vehicles, and manpower were all available to him for his assignment. He was greeted by the Colonel as he stepped out of the helicopter.

The Colonel saluted him and spoke, "Sir, I presume you are Representative Tavernier?"

"That I am." Eston curtly responded.

"I am Colonel Wikerson, and I will be delivering your commands throughout this assignment."

In front of him, Eston looked upon tens of thousands of men in the encampment. Hundreds of vehicles sat on the road on either side of him. He had never gazed upon such a force in a single area before. He thought such forces were only present at the forefront of war. The thought had never occurred to him that the Alliance would keep such an army as this, on their own homefront. "Colonel Wikerson, how many troops do we have available to us?"

"Sir, we currently have a garrison stationed here numbering forty-thousand, though if ordered, I could call assistance from other garrisons, and in that scenario, hundreds of thousands could be stationed here within weeks." He hesitated, "Sir, we were wondering what the timetable would be for the de-escalation of the city?"

"The city will be notified tomorrow evening, while the sun sets, to give us a strategical advantage against the population." Eston continued to peer at the might that would beckon to his voice. "I want a stage set up in the center of the city, with an escape route that allows air support. Then the population will be notified of what is best for the masses and will be thanked for their service and cooperation."

"Colonel Wikerson, I want you to take me to the command room immediately."

"Yes, Sir, immediately, Sir." The colonel pulled out his radio and demanded transport.

Moments later, a young private pulled up in a jeep. They climbed in, and soon the private was calmly and appropriately weaving between encampments on the way to the command room. While driving around tents, the private came within inches of striking another soldier, but neither the driver nor the young men on the field seem to notice how close they came to death. Then again, Eston thought they probably came closer to death every day in battle.

The jeep soon came to a stop as the Colonel signaled toward a large tent. "Sir, this way, please."

As they walked inside, the soldiers at the entrance saluted in unison, their voices booming, "For the glory of the Alliance, we salute our representative."

The makeshift command room was covered with screens as several young men were typing on keyboards methodically. In the middle of the room stood a marble octagon-shaped table with one of the sides missing; Eston walked into the middle of the table and touched the top. The marble finish lit up and turned into an outline of the city. "So this is the once-great Seattle! Well, Colonel, I want you to get the fencing vehicles in place around the city tonight. Just to be safe, I want one every half a mile."

Touching the screen, he pulled up an image of a fleet of boats on the waterfront, "I want boats blocking Bainbridge Island and the old Southworth Fauntleroy. I want charges set on the 520 and the I90 bridges tonight. I want the boats equipped with sentinel deploying mines for the coastline. I will not have this population reaching society."

"Sir, can I speak freely?" The Colonel queried.

"You may Colonel," he pompously smiled, "but remember my words are absolute, for I speak for the Alliance, and they speak for the world."

The Colonel squared his shoulders. "Sir, if this city isn't worth saving, then why not just use a seeking missile and save the population the suffering and agony that is bound to come? It seems more humane, and a better allocation of the Alliance's funds."

Eston snickered at the colonel, "Yes, that does seem more appropriate, though, after great thought and insight, it is not. History can teach us many things. The Alliance knows this. They must preserve the nations and guide the people. Remember Colonel, we are here for the people, and we were put in place by the people for their own protection. Colonel, this happened out of necessity and out of the fact that the people do not know what is best for themselves. So, we were selected to make this choice for them, by them. The Alliance may seem fierce and uncaring, but we care so very much. Besides this fact, we can't just destroy the population who lives here because of the repercussions that would inevitably happen, due to our rashness, if we did. Every massacre in history caused by a nation has led to a revolt, and in the end, it only weakened those in control. Even this very nation's revolution began with a massacre that took place in the Boston of old. Leading the population to unite and, with time, overthrow its captors. The Alliance are not captors, for we give the population a chance to survive on their own and once again become a productive city for the Alliance."

"We have hope that this day will come for the betterment of all who live under the Alliance. In case this doesn't come to fruition, we need to take caution, for a disease can spread quickly if it is not cut off from the rest of the population. So, we too must cut of this disease of laziness, of non-productivity, until the day that they have cured this disease, and we welcome them back to the Alliance; as a parent welcomes back their child after becoming lost in the world—with loving open arms."

"Colonel, the population has to live or die on their own accord, till they become of use. These poor souls aren't against the Alliance. They are not our enemies. Simply put, they are just no longer useful to our society as a whole. That is why we do not give up hope. The Alliance are not savages. They just have to keep in mind the whole is more important than the few. Do you understand this, Colonel Wikerson?"

"Sir, I am honored to have you with us in this time of great importance. The Alliance truly does understand the need of the many, over the few."

He gleamed as he looked upon his work. He truly was about to outdo himself this time. He would now have Ashling's full attention after this demonstration of flawlessness. He directed, "When you lower the stage from the heliocarriers, I want five-thousand troops to be present with me. The rest, I want moving in from both the north and the south sides; that is, after my speech to the masses. This will turn out to be a profitable venture for the Alliance. Take all raw material and goods from the population, for the Alliance has given these civilians what they had, so is it not our right to repossess it? That will be all Colonel."

Eston awoke in the afternoon, having given himself a good night's sleep before the decommission of Seattle. The whole city seemed to lay still in anticipation of what was to come. The city's population should have been notified this morning that the Alliance was hosting an event in the town's center and that it would occur this evening. Most of the population would crawl out of their holes, covered in their own filth, in the hope of receiving a few scraps of food and supplies.

A voice from outside trickled in, "Sir, as you requested, I've got your suit and your tie for the speech."

"Come in and lay it out on my bed. Be sure not to wrinkle it."

The private quickly entered and laid the suit and tie on the silk linen sheets, saluted, and departed as quickly as he came in.

Smirking, Eston looked at his suit. He wanted the population to feel welcomed by his presence, so he requested a blue tie with a lightly faded undershirt. "I wouldn't want the population to feel intimidated by me tonight. I need their cooperation, or at least until the time is right." He remembered how Lorne had taught him never to wear a red tie, for red was a color of aggression, the color of blood. It naturally made people feel defensive. Blue was a color of welcoming, the color of a clear, peaceful sky during the summertime, relaxing one's mind and soul. Still smiling, he looked into the mirror and noticed the clock in the corner. With every second that ticked by, his excitement seemed to grow accordingly. Just a few more hours, and his agenda would start.

"I request the Colonel's presence." Eston called out, "Someone go find him for me. I wish to leave and see the stage being set." He picked up his briefcase and opened it for a second time, making sure his speech was still in place. The Alliance required the residents to be placated before decommissioning a city. The population deserved to be acknowledged and thanked for their undying allegiance and cooperation, a sort of sweet goodbye.

Colonel Wikerson walked into the room, "Sir, your helicopter has been prepared. It will set out whenever you're ready."

"Colonel, I have been ready for this since well before I first landed here. Let us go see this once great city of old."

CHAPTER EIGHT

Coretheen walked silently out of the massive storm drain into the depths of the city. There was no need for words, for Damian and the sun's warmth provided her with all the strength that she needed. She was no longer alone in this cold, dark, and decaying world.

"Looks like someone has procured some new clothes." Damian mused as he observed a dead body lying naked on the ground, wearing a thick gash across his throat.

Bile rose to Coretheen's mouth as the smell of rotting flesh entered her nostrils as if it was a wave breaking upon a shore.

"At least someone is getting a feast today," Damian closed his eyes tightly in an attempt to wipe away the image of the abundance of maggots consuming the dead man's flesh. "Let us depart from this filth, letting the city consume it as part of itself; for my Lady, we are close to our destination."

He turned around and stopped, looking curiously at Coretheen as she gazed upon a large granite building a few hundred feet away. She smiled, fondly remembering how it used to be one of the most prestigious state libraries in the entire country. Without looking back, she walked into the building, making her way to the center as her feet crunched on the glass that had fallen from the broken skylight above. She looked around, gazing at the granite pillars that circled the room, stretching to the heavens themselves. Tilting her head back, she bathed in the sun as a warm, gentle breeze entered from the broken skylight above. Coretheen peered at the thousands of books that had fallen off the shelves, only to be sitting on the floor, gathering dust. "Such a waste, all of the knowledge left here to decay, never to be read, never being able to give its wisdom away again."

"Coretheen, it will not always be wasted, although it may not be as organized and renowned as it once was. This building still serves a great purpose." He calmly walked to the middle of the room and pronounced, "Dicade, the strength of the many, above the few!" His voice was resounding around the columns.

One by one, men began appearing from behind the granite pillars as Coretheen stood motionless, bewildered, and frozen. The serene scene before her stretched out as men continued to appear, and all she could manage to do was to stare at them.

"These are my runners, they spread my word, they pass supplies, and they are the core of our resistance. Much like the days of old, where a runner would run down the battlefield to deliver a message in the face of great odds, informing his nation of an incoming threat." As the runners gathered, Damian looked toward each one of them and spoke. "This is a sad time, for we have been compromised, though I assure you that a plan will soon be set in motion to rectify this grave wrongdoing." Taking a deep breath, he closed his eyes, "Does not a fortress walls have to break before it comes crashing down upon the enemy? Soon, we shall crash through their vast cities and reclaim what was given to us at birth."

He gazed towards a runner and commanded, "Jacob, come here. You will need to break into our food reserves. We must maintain the morale of our troops."

Coretheen looked upon the one he called Jacob. He was thin and appeared to be nothing but a child. He, too, wore a torn suit covered in dust, but he spoke with strength, and his posture was strong.

"Sir, as you request, though we have heard rumors that your demise was already a fact."

"Yes, it seemed that was their plan," Damian put his hand on the young man's shoulder, "but it has not come to be. The compound of old is no longer safe.

It is compromised, and we must seek those who have destroyed it. We are afraid that we have an informant in our midst. So we must scatter now, for just a single moon, till we can reformulate a plan. I will give further instructions at that time where our new meetings will take place. For when one swats at a mosquito, he too scatters before attacking again; to suck the substance from its victim. We will not scatter for long, safeguard this city, for we have hope that we can soon control it. We will hold those who hide in the night accountable for their actions. No one will be able to prey on the weak as this poor lady has seen."

"We will move forward and take control of this city, protecting its people, just as we will soon protect the cities across this nation. The cities that they claim unfit and unworthy of protecting. The cities they fence off to devour themselves in dying agony. We will use these cities to lash out against the ones who say they are protecting the masses. So, depart now, let it be known to disseminate 'til the new moon when we will reconvene with a fury that has been long held within us all."

The men disappeared behind the cracked pillars as the sun seemed to shine a little brighter.

"My Lady, I must now know of your intentions. I do not mean to be rude, but so much is at stake. As a gentleman, I cannot fathom a need to leave you here, unattended, and your company is pleasant in this dying city. I wish nothing more than to be blessed with your company, but nonetheless, I must not only consider myself in these times—for I do bear a vast responsibility."

"I feel safe next to you, Damian," Coretheen said, taking a slow and deep breath as her words lingered in the air. "I may not know you. I may not fully know what you stand for, but I can tell one thing, you're an honest man. You are a lantern within the darkness of this city. Every person that touches your light Damian starts to emit their own light," she looked above her at the crumbling skyscrapers towering over the skylight, "into this darkness, this darkness that attempts to consume all hope. I won't say that I will follow you until the end, but I will say that I will be by your side until I learn your world. I want nothing more than to leave this city behind me and look to the future. To build a new city and to have something worth living for feels like the only sane thing in this entire world. So, I ask you, Damian, to show me your world. Spread your light into my eyes and destroy the darkness that surrounds these people. Let me help guide your way through this darkness. Do not trust me, but let me gain your trust."

Turning to Coretheen, Damian smiled while gently grabbing her arm with one hand and her head with his other, pulling her close to him. "And let me gain your trust. Let me show you what this dark world has to offer. We must leave this city, for now, only to return stronger than before. We have to reach past this city and meet Kamon, for he will have information for us. The spot where I am taking you to is saved for the direst of situations. It is one of the few places left in this dying world where beauty still remains." He tilted her head up, looking deeply into her eyes. "Beauty is hard to find, and trust is even harder. Though even in the darkest and most decaying places in this world, a rare gem can still be unearthed. And it seems to me that I have just found the rarest of gems, in the darkest of places."

Coretheen looked back at the edge of the town as the sun began to set. The screams once again returned as the darkness took hold of the city. Yet, the city seemed to stand strong as the setting sun shimmered off the broken glass of the buildings; even the clouds seemed to resist the urge to consume the sun, for the first time since she could remember.

As Damian left the town, he grasped her hand within his, thinking to himself that the task now seemed so much easier and so much shorter than before; he momentarily glanced at Coretheen and smiled, for they now had one another.

CHAPTER NINE

Gazing upon the city from above, Eston felt his heart pulsating through every single crevice of his body, as excitement built with each passing second. He examined as four heliocarriers slowly approached downtown Seattle, carrying the metal stage over the crumbling skyscrapers, thinking to himself that in only a few more minutes, he would be standing on top of that very stage. He pulled out his tablet and zoomed in on the city using a satellite link. Thousands of army personnel were coordinating the population away from the landing area. The Alliance soldiers were using lasers to mark where the future platform boundaries would be. The heliocarriers soon started their descent as the army personnel withdrew from the area, pushing civilians away from the landing zone. Within a few minutes, the stage hovered only mere meters from the ground as they coordinated its final resting place.

"Sir, the stage is secure," Colonel Wikerson declared, "we are going to start our descent."

Eston peered out the window as they landed onto the metal stage; he stepped out of the helicopter, noticing the sheer size of the platform beneath him. It spanned hundreds of feet in length, width, and towered fifty feet above the population below. Imprinted on the shimmering metal floor was the flag of the Alliance, with the congressional buildings waving in the background. He watched as the large screens rose from the floor's frame, slowly becoming taller than the remnants of the skyscrapers around him. The Alliance army stood in formation, stationed on all sides of the stage, twenty men deep.

Walking next to the raised podium, Colonel Wikerson spoke into the transmitter on his wrist. "The Alliance of these great nations requests your attention, in these trying times that our nation faces. They present to you, your representative, to speak to you on behalf of the Alliance. Without further ado, I present to you, your newly appointed district representative, Eston Tavernier!"

Eston climbed up the stairs to the podium and peered onto the streets of the decaying city, noticing thousands of civilians as far as he could see—lining the roads in all directions. Even the decaying buildings had civilians at each window, observing the great Alliance coming to their decrepit town. As he began to speak, the clouds darkened, and the sun began to set. Lights from the stage flickered on, illuminating the crowd ahead of him.

"The Alliance requests your help. They acknowledge your existence and your loyalty to these great nations. But," hesitating for a moment, he gave a conniving smile, "but, let us begin this commencement by acknowledging your perpetual devotion to us, by stating our loyal, and undying pledge, to the Alliance. So, I ask all of you to raise your hands to your hearts, for we feel with our hearts what is best for all." Eston raised his hand to his heart, and the civilians followed suit as he began.

"I pledge allegiance, to the Alliance of
Coordinated Governments.
To promote the General party, to put
their needs above myself, an individual.
To give the Alliance my body, mind, and
heart, for as long as I stand.
To strive to further the Coalition under rule.
Our nations, indivisible, with health and
prosperity for all."

Eston witnessed how more civilians than he could count blindly pledged their allegiance to the great Alliance.

As they finished, he saw many with tears in their eyes, as hope sprung forth, gleaming at their savior who would free them of their agony. "The Alliance thanks you for your cooperation and knows that your participation is for the best of the nations that we protect. We understand the trials your city has endured, spanning across the numerous years. We, the nations of the Alliance of Coordinated Governments, though must look to the future, as a whole."

Examining the crowd, he watched as their eyes resembled those of children, who blindly trusted in their parents, walking with them wherever they were led. "So, I ask all of you to listen with your hearts and continue to think of the greater good. Think of the billions of people on this earth who need our assistance, who are still producing for the whole. Remember, my civilians of the Coalition, self-sacrifice for the better of the whole is the greatest servitude and honor that any civilian could ever hope to grasp. It is a true honor that I myself will never get to reach."

A slight rumble of thunder echoed in from the distance. Eston took a deep breath while looking up to the sky and watched a single raindrop fall from the heavens as if God himself was crying for the people who resided here. He hesitated, clenching his jaw tight as another drop landed onto a young soldier in front of him—who, without a single thought—wiped the raindrop off the flag strapped to his bulletproof vest. Taking another deep breath, he closed his eyes tight and disregarded the fate of the city before him, for he was the pride of the Alliance, one of the elite. This future was for the best of the Alliance and its citizens. He had to prove that he could carry out what was best for the world and not just for a single soul in such troubling times.

He opened his eyes, raising his voice in serene encouragement. "The Alliance thanks you for your service, for the betterment of the masses under the coalition. They expect your cooperation and understanding in this new transition in your lives. For the good of the country, we will be taking all raw materials such as gold, copper, and food. Any fine goods and or material found will be confiscated by the Alliance for the Alliance. The Alliance would appreciate if its civilians would hand over these goods of their own free accord, for the betterment of the population, as it is needed, and is expected."

Eston watched as the crowd stood still in shock from the command that was just given to them. Not a single citizen moved, and not a single noise was heard, except the sound of raindrops falling onto the hard plates protecting the soldiers below. Whispers started to spread through the crowd, spreading as fast as a wildfire consumes a dry field on a windy day. A child's cry echoed in the distance, and with that cry, the crowd was released from their paralysis, shaking them into motion as the true terror of the situation settled in.

A loud voice yelled up towards him, "You're abandoning us?"

"What are we supposed to do?" Another broke out.

"The Alliance is not abandoning you, my civilians." He attempted to placate. "We wish the best outcome for you, but our resources need to be better allocated to do the greatest good, and sadly, in this case, your city must be sacrificed for the whole. It is a great honor, one you should be proud of, I assure you." He looked upon the crowd below him as a few men with a patch on their shoulders moved through the masses below. The patch they were wearing depicted an eagle holding an olive branch, with flames consuming each end of the branch, unique and hauntingly familiar.

One of the men yelled, "You expect us to just hand over the few things we have left. You expect us to let you leave with everything, as we are left with nothing? Haven't we given you enough? We gave you our money. We gave you our bodies. We even gave you our blood, in the name of the greater good. Now you ask us to give you our lives?"

His mind raced. He knew that symbol from somewhere. Where had he seen it? Within a moment, his memory grasped ahold of the answer. It was the symbol of the resistance, the symbol of the Dicade. He was warned of their movements. Although, to his understanding, they had not spread this far from the heartland of the country. He saw the crowd begin to move like waves in a storm, slowly building with each gust, picking up speed and ferocity by the second. Yelling and shouting erupted across the population below him. Eston hollered over the noise. "The Alliance urges you to comply with its wishes. It is truly for the good of this nation, for the good of all those around you."

The men bearing the symbol of the Dicade raised their voices. "We will not throw away what we have left."

Another yelled, "We are not pawns that you sacrifice to protect the king."

A bottle shattered across the stage as another member bearing the symbol dissented, "We aren't your troops, and we will not do as you command!" Eston paused, seeing the anger in the crowd grow. "We will not let you kill us! You don't own our lives. You don't own us!"

His eyes went wide in horror. This resistance was taught in psychology, and they knew how to move the masses at just the right time. He remembered how Lorne had taught him crowd or "mob psychology" and how "just a few can push a large number of people to do as they wished." He had used this tactic many times himself to change the direction of a large group. To have the crowd cheer for him, to increase morale, and even increase his standings in the population's eyes. These men, the Dicade, were moving the crowd to revolt without even lifting a finger. These people were not just rebels. They were organized and educated. He had to stop them. He had to destroy them. He lifted his hand to his mouth, whispering into the transponder. "Lockdown the city, and somebody stop those men from speaking."

It was too late; the Dicade had already gained control. Eston watched as the soldiers pushed forward, and as they did, the civilians became even more enraged. They took whatever they could find, throwing it at the soldiers in front of them, even pieces of concrete and rebar from the structures of the buildings surrounding them.

The Colonel grabbed Eston and began pulling him towards the helicopter, and as he was being dragged, he saw the men bearing the symbol of the resistance fall back into the buildings. The Colonel pulled back his sleeve and pressed a button on the screen attached to his forearm. Metal plates erupted out of the floor of the stage, rising thirty feet into the air. He could no longer see the crowd, protected from all angles, except from above. He watched as the soldiers on the stage placed their guns through the small openings within the metal plates. His ears rang as a loud scream pierced his very soul. The Colonel pulled him inside the helicopter as flames exploded behind him from a Molotov cocktail.

"I've never seen chaos like that before. I have never heard such a death pitched scream erupt within in my own ears. It was, it was as if the world was falling apart, collapsing upon itself." He quivered as the helicopter ascended.

The Colonel looked down at the ground, whispering gently. "Sir, you were the only one screaming." He paused for a minute as the thick silence filled the air. "Sir, you told me before that in times like these, you have to consider the whole over the needs of the few. This is a necessary evil, and it is why I carry out the orders from those above me. Someone has to do it, and I am glad to serve my purpose for this great land." Eston looked out of the window as the helicopter continued to rise. "Sir, these are the times we require the most direction; these are the times we require your direction."

"Of course," Eston took a deep breath and solemnly stated. "Then I shall not delay, for the many count upon me, and their weight needs to be placed over the few." He returned his gaze back towards the city center, where thousands of civilians below him cried out in anguish. He pulled out his tablet as the helicopter banked back towards the command room, forcing himself to forget what was taking place below. "I want the fence in place within minutes. Have you started the drilling?"

"The process is commencing as we speak." The Colonel affirmed. "I'll pull up the feed."

He gazed as the tanks rose up on their treads, turning their barrels straight into the ground, and firing their shells within the earth, penetrating deeper into the surface with every shot.

Stepping out of the helicopter as it landed, Eston began to run into the command room as Lorne's voice flashed into his head. "Those in charge never run to any situation, for the world slows for them, the world waits for them; they wait for us, my dear boy."

Forcing himself to slow down, he commanded, "I want the fencing up on screens one through three. I want the fleet of destroyers on screen four, five, and the bridges on screen six. I want images of the city's downtown area to cycle on screens seven and eight."

"Sir, the drilling is complete." Wickerson declared.

Speaking with no hesitation, Eston rose, for the shadows could not hesitate. He spoke with confidence, for the shadows did not ask for permission before they engulfed the light. He spoke swiftly and fluently, for the shadows do not delay before they strike. He spoke without emotion, for shadows contained no emotion. "Release the rods." He slowly turned as he saw a man lurking within the shadows, his hand resting on his face. Eston's heart skipped a beat, then dropped, and as the gravity of his guest was realized, he quickly saluted.

"Now, my Eston, that is not needed, nor desired at this time. This is your moment. I have only come to gaze upon your great plan being delivered, for the betterment of the Alliance."

Bowing slightly, Eston affirmed, "Yes, Mr. Ashling, of course. I am honored with your presence."

"Now, let us not delay, continue your campaign, my dear Eston."

The civilians in the town hesitated, struck with both amazement and fear as they looked upon the sky, beholding the might of a thousand red beams encircling their city. The heavens above them darkened, turning the color of blood. The crackling of rocket motors boomed across the landscape as thousands of missiles began to bear down around them while the lasers guided them to their destinations. Explosions erupted in the heavens above them as a thick black film spread around the city, and metal rods pierced through the mist, raining down around them, with each metal rod replacing the missile that concealed it. The ground began to shake as the dirt rose, encircling the perimeter of the city, as each rod penetrated the ground in the precise spot that was being drilled by the tanks only moments before.

The tanks turrets repositioned themselves, aiming at the rods stretching thirty feet out of the ground in front of them. Their thick barrels spinning, emitting a strong light, as the shafts began to glow, and molten metal began dripping down their sides, creating perfectly cut circles within their structures. The heavens opened wide as the rain began to pour down upon the shimmering rods, and with every drop that landed on the shafts, steam rose back into the heavens, as if a symbol of the Alliance's defiance to God himself.

As the rain dragged the dust back to earth, the Alliances army unleashed their might upon the masses. Bullets ripped through the civilian's flesh, and the rain mixed with the blood dripping out of their body cavities, creating a dark red lake in the town's center. Those who were not wounded fled, tripping over their dead comrades, choking on the blood that leaked from their once breathing friends, their once breathing families.

Eston watched as both men and women ran to the border of the town, trying to escape the horror surrounding them. "Don't let them escape; finish the perimeter!" He shouted, and with that command, the tanks moved forward, putting their barrels through the smoldering holes in the rods. Hundreds of tanks fired at once, shooting thick metal wires through each shaft, trapping the city's occupants. He examined the scene as thousands of unlucky civilians were impaled by the wires as the tanks continue to shoot the cables, from rod, to rod.

"Fehahaha," a ghoulish laugh erupted from Ashling, "like Christmas decorations strung out on a tree, for all those who go against the Alliance to see, what beauty to behold, what beauty indeed."

Stuck in a trance, Eston's eyes were drawn upon a single unlucky soul whose leg had been impaled by a wire—watching as he grabbed at his leg, desperately pulling with all of his strength—seeing his flesh being torn with every pull he made. Tears began rolling down his filth covered face, creating streams of clean skin underneath. The man stood up straight, digging his nails deep into his own skin, pulling his flesh out from around the wire as his hands became stained with his own blood. Eston watched as the man opened his mouth, screaming in agonizing pain. A series of cracking roars erupted as another wire penetrated through the man's hip. The tanks rose a few more inches, getting ready to fire again, slowly building a barrier of steel around the city. The man now slumped over, grabbing at his hip while attempting to look up towards his god screaming. Another shot rang out, as a wire impaled him through his chest. Eston watched, horrified, as the poor man started to cough up blood on the screens before him, trying to maintain his composure, with Ashling laughing hysterically from the corner of the room.

"Ah, my Eston, I have not seen a show this worthy of me since the very first decommission. It is a splendid spectacle, a splendid spectacle indeed."

A staggering eruption of crackles echoed from a distance. He raised his head slowly, daring to look at the screen another time. The man now lay motionless, with a fresh wire piercing through his neck. Eston stared into the man's eyes. Even in death, his fear and agony were trapped upon his face. Another fire reverberated across the city as he saw a wire pierce through the man's eye, erupting through the back of his head, as his gray matter was strung out on the wire. Blood dripped not only from the man's head but also from the wires that had impaled him so many times. He looked upon the man's horrified face one last time, knowing it would hold his anguish as rigamortis set in. The tanks continued to unleash their fury, raising a few inches on their treads, then firing, until they reached the maximum height on the shafts, encasing the entire city in steel.

"So my Eston, what's next on the agenda, hmmm? I know that such a young and brilliant mind as yourself will not let this conclude so early."

"There are still many possibilities yet to cover." Eston delicately offered while looking up at the screen, seeing the few civilians who were privileged enough to own vehicles converging towards the bridges. He pressed the screen imprinted on the table and quickly demanded. "Blow the bridges now, before they reach them." He watched as the bridge began to vibrate furiously before breaking and crumbling into the river below.

Looking depressed, Ashling sighed, "Now, now, my Eston, you could have waited a few mere seconds, couldn't you? Wouldn't that have been so much more pleasurable? Come on; I know you're one for theatrics, my child."

His eyes watched Ashling's face mix with emotion, half-filled with bloodlust, the other half filled with anger. That anger and bloodlust seeped out of Ashling's soul and entrenched the entire room. "North Garrison, along with the south, I command both of you to move in on the city." The soldiers began walking towards the town, in lines ten wide, by forty deep. With every step they took closer to the center of the city, the screens became even fiercer. "I want you to locate the Dicade then display them on the screen."

Ashling's face grew grimmer as he questioned. "Eston, what do you mean, the Dicade?"

"During my speech, I noticed that some of the crowd bore their symbol. I am not sure how entwined they are in this city, but I do know they share occupancy with its masses."

"I see my Eston, do not let any escape, not a single one. This decommission has now turned into the annihilation of the Dicade. We, the Alliance, must not let one of these rebels escape, for they are worse than a plague in which quickly infects everything around it." Ashling roared, "For today, we offer this town a cure from that same plague, from their disease, and that cure is obliteration."

CHAPTER TEN

Coretheen gazed upon the vast mountains before her, covered in trees. Having been walking for close to a week, she began rubbing her sore feet.

"My Lady, now is not the time to rest, for we are almost there." Damian urged while leading Coretheen through the foliage until a small opening appeared in the rocks before them. "My dear Lady, by any chance, do you know how to swim?"

"Yes, of course I do," Coretheen said, hesitating, "but there hasn't been clear water in ages."

"This place where I am leading you, you cannot show to anyone else. You may not speak of it. You may not talk of it. It is a rarity in this world. Few can transverse the mountains ahead of us, and even fewer have the ability to fly above them. This path is reserved for the longest and gravest of meetings, and its natural resources are near the days of old. One could live here for years without danger; because of this, precautions have to be taken." He knelt down and peered into the entrance of the small cave. On its walls, vines stretched across the ceiling, seeming to support the weight of the entire mountain above. Damian indicated Coretheen to follow him as he crouched down to squeeze between the crevices. "Those who have the wealth, also have the girth, making this a natural barrier for those who are against our cause, who may have been watching." The light faded behind them as they moved forward into the darkness.

With every step Coretheen took, the damp air became thicker until she heard the sound of water dripping into a pool. She felt a hand grasp hers, pulling her into a standing position, as sparks erupted next to her. Her eyes attempted to focus within the darkness, with sparks bursting forth once more as Damian struck the wall with a piece of flint. The room awoke in flames, revealing the pool of water in the middle of the cave.

Turning, he gestured around him, "The oil naturally flows from these walls, collecting in the carved rock around the chamber. If you need to rest, now is the time to do it. For ahead, we must dive into the depths to reach our safe haven."

"Damian, I am ready to follow you anywhere." She said, standing up strong, allowing no fear to show through her face. "Through anything, for when I am with you, there is no darkness." With one deep breath, they grabbed each other's hands and jumped into the abyss before them, swimming forward through the darkness.

She felt her lungs begin to tighten; as a sense of urgency engulfed her, seconds seemed to turn into minutes. Damian gently smiled and squeezed her hand as he felt her anxiety climbing. Knowing that her mind was playing a deceitful and cruel game, screaming at her, telling her that she only needed to take a single deep breath, which they both knew would lock her fate in stone. She closed her eyes and clutched his hand, and as she opened them again, a light appeared to surround him—the light of warmth, the light of hope, the light of the sun. The sense of urgency and the sense of panic faded into a sense of hope, a sense of endearment, a sense to push forward into the unknown. She grasped his hand tighter as they swam to the light. Now, a minute passed in what seemed like a second, and as they broke through the water's surface, the sun's heat pounded against her body.

Taking a deep breath of air, oxygen began to fill her lungs, as the color returned to her face. Collapsing upon the soft grass, she looked upon the mountains surrounding all sides of her. The trees stood tall, creating a wall of protection around her that made her feel safe. There were no screams here; those screams were replaced by the sound of birds chirping, by the sound of crickets squeaking, and their sounds brought hope. There were no predators here, only salvation from the wicked. Here, air could be breathed with relief. This fresh air filled not only her lungs but also filled her soul. The worry drifted from her, and she now remembered what it felt like to be safe, what it felt like to relax, and what it felt like to not have to worry about what was coming the next day. They laid down together, on that soft grass, as the sun beat its warm breath upon their bodies.

Coretheen awoke the next morning, being greeted by Damian cooking on a newly lit fire, as the smell of food drifted towards her nose. She peered over as he smiled and handed her a piece of meat from a slain deer behind him, confessing. "I just couldn't bring myself to wake you, my Lady. You looked so peaceful. I know it isn't bacon and eggs, but this is as close as you can get nowadays."

She grabbed the meat and delicately placed it into her mouth, feeling the moisture seep from its flesh as its taste overpowered her senses.

"There's a cabin not too far from here that was built a long time ago." Handing her a carved wooden cup filled with what appeared to be tea, "We should make it there in an hour or two if we get moving soon."

Coretheen took a sip of the tea, then put another bite of meat into her mouth. She lay back upon the soft grass closing her eyes, taking in the warmth of the sunlight, and pleaded. "Damian, let us just rest here for a while."

He settled down next to her and closed his eyes with a smile still on his face. "It has been too long since I've last been here."

Damian awoke, feeling soft lips pressing down upon his as a hand brushed across his forehead. A sense of well-being overwhelmed him, the sense of finally feeling at home. He opened his eyes, peering into the glimmering hazel ones that were fixed upon his from above, smiling as she spoke. "I see clouds coming in, Damian. I think we should get moving soon."

He nodded and stood up, helping Coretheen to her feet, then tilted her head up to meet his. Wrapping his arms tightly around her back, he gently kissed her. "Thank you, Coretheen. Knowing that I am not alone, even for a little, is a serene feeling."

"No, Damian," she spoke tenderly, whispering into his ear, "ever since I saw your eyes during that speech, I knew who you were. I knew that I belonged next to your side, and you next to mine."

Damian started to laugh as Coretheen glared at him, "What's so funny?"

"Ohh, just wait till Kamon hears about this. He's never going to let me forget this one. He'll be on me all day."

"Yea, I guess you're right." She started to giggle. "But I was too stubborn and scared at the time to admit it."

She kissed him again as a slight rumble was heard in the distance.

"Let us go. I don't think the weather will hold for much longer." He said as he grabbed her hand.

The thunder released its might upon the mountains, its power booming and echoing off of their sheer edges. The rain started to trickle upon their heads. Letting go of his hand, Coretheen looked at Damian and then began to run.

Becoming mesmerized, Damian stood still, watching as she ran through the rain ahead of him. Watching as her body swayed with every pump of her arms. Watching in awe as her muscles propelled her body through another leap and through another lunge until her voice broke him from his trance.

"You do realize I don't know where I'm going?" Coretheen yelled out, "Or did you forget that too?"

Damian yelled back, "Of course, you're right, my Lady. May you pause for just one second?" He glanced at her body once more as the rain weighed down her clothes, showing off her sleek form. Her damp black hair was holding straight, sticking tightly against her face. Briefly kneeling down, he tightened his grip on his cane, planted his weight onto his back leg, and then plunged forward.

Coretheen now returned the gaze she was not aware she'd received first, her eyes sinking into the man racing towards her. Not a single muscle in his body wasted energy as he moved. His speed was like nothing she had ever seen before. Even a panther pouncing on its prey lacked the velocity, the accuracy, and the swiftness compared to him. Within mere seconds he was upon her, grabbing her hand while rushing forward, dragging her with him.

The rain poured down over them as they sprinted through the woods. Coretheen noticed how even their breaths were in sync. He leaped forward, grabbing her by her waist, swinging her over a fallen tree without even missing a step.

A path made out of broken rocks appeared ahead as their feet pounded through the mud while the thunder continued to roar around them. As she followed the path, she raised her line of sight upon a small cabin sitting on top of the hill, with vibrant green vines covering the entire outside of the home. Water poured onto the thatched roof and swirled down the vines around the cottage, which was carved out of the stone from the hill it stood upon.

They burst through the door, not paying attention to the warm dense air that filled the room. Damian pulled Coretheen's hand close to his, causing her to lose her balance. His stance was strong, steady, and as she fell, he reached his arm around her hip, catching her. Leaning over, he gently stroked her face as they gazed into each other's eyes. She closed her eyes as if accepting what was to come.

Gently pressing his lips onto hers, Coretheen's hands began to move to his head until she was grasping his hair, pulling at his roots, and with that pull, a fury was released from Damian. He picked her up and threw her against the wall—forcing her head back as he kissed her neck—using his weight to pin her up against the cool stone. Reaching her legs around him, Coretheen grabbed at Damian's shirt, pulling it open, exposing his chest, and then lowered her head to meet his soft lips once again.

Their lips felt as if they belonged, as if they were made to be together. Her body began to heat up, despite the wet rain dripping off of her. Damian reached for her neck and began to slide his hand down to her shirt, unbuttoning the first button while slowly kissing an inch lower with every button he undone. She exhaled forcefully and tilted her head back, reaching towards his belt, undoing the first latch.

"Damian!" A voice boomed through the cabin, "I see you lost your sense of awareness. Then again, I guess I can't blame you, seeing you brought the beautiful lady with ya." Kamon's loud laugh reached across the cabin. "I see you're still taking advantage of this young gal; sometimes I told you so, just doesn't quite do it. To you, Coretheen, I guess you aren't as strong-minded as I thought." Another laugh joined in, though, this time it wasn't Damian's, or Coretheen's, as they both stood frozen in the position they had been caught, with lips locked together, up against the wall. "Let me introduce both of you to Mr. Pikon, the true leader of our military might."

Pikon stepped forward, still laughing gently as Damian quickly removed himself from Coretheen and repositioned his shirt by tucking it back into his pants.

Coretheen followed suit and began quickly rebuttoning her shirt as she glanced at the one they called Pikon. His suit was not torn but smooth and firm, his face slender, though his cheekbones protruded with might, and even though he was laughing, his pale face seemed to lack a smile. His black hair was brushed cleanly to the side, keeping it out of his smooth and freshly shaven face. He stood with a strong stance, his feet apart, and his height towered over everyone in the room.

Damian instantly stood erect. "Sir, Mr. Pikon, it is a pleasure and an honor to be in your presence."

"And yours too, Damian. I am here to discuss plans with you and Kamon. He came to retrieve me as I hear the urgency of the matter has grown. With the destruction of your main compound at the forefront of the resistance, it leads me to ponder at the possibility that we have a leak within the Dicade. They observe our movements with such accuracy that the traitor has to come from a high-ranking officer. That being said, it leads us to our present situation; we came here for solitude to discuss our options, away from the piercing eyes of the Alliance. We will begin discussions tomorrow; 'til then,

I recommend you both get some rest and regain your strength, for we have much to do."

Kamon started to laugh as Pikon retreated back into the room he came from, sitting down with a drink of rum in his hand. Kamon looked upon Damian and Coretheen standing next to each other. "Well, my dear Damian, I have to admit, I didn't really expect to find you like this, but when I am right, I am right! Poor girl, she's already fallen into your trap."

"Ohh come on, Sir, it's nothing like that!"

"Sureeee, whatever you say, but we did catch you red-handed. Or should you suggest that this girl was only in need of some excess oxygen? Then she must have been catching hypothermia from her cold clothes, and you were actually innocently assisting her in removing them?" Kamon paused while smirking toward Damian, "Yes, yes, that's what I thought. I will admit, though, that this is the first time I have heard you speechless, making this a fun and eventful day for the both of us, Damian, a fun and eventful day indeed."

Damian smiled while whispering, "Yes, Sir, yes, it is."

Speaking up, he looked at Kamon, "Sir, the runners have been sent. Do we yet have a plan?"

"No, not yet, Damian. Information is being accumulated for the three of us to go over. Considering my expertise in organization, your planning, and insightful ideas, and of course, the military leadership of Mr. Pikon, we will think of something. For now, let us enjoy the rest we all need, so we can begin to think clearly tomorrow."

He gazed upon Coretheen, "In a serious matter, Miss, this man is of vast importance to me. I have known him for a long time. He will treat you kindly, and he will remain by your side. All Mr. Pikon and I ask is for you not to betray his trust. For if he trusts you, and as the first lady we have ever seen him gaze upon, you're a welcomed addition. Just looking into his eyes, I see his spirits have risen, and yours have too Miss, for you have a new gleam in your eye."

"Damian, just remember why we are here, and let this woman help reinvigorate your might and fury towards our cause."

Damian nodded at his President.

"Sir," Coretheen lowered her line of sight, speaking softly, "I do not know what this organization holds for me, though for the limited time I have been by his side, I believe that your main goal is just. From those of the Alliance who hold our minds at bay, who no longer let us speak what we wish. I will not betray the dream that you all seem to hold so close to your hearts."

With that, Kamon smiled and patted Coretheen's head lightly, "Thank you, my kind, strong, free-minded girl. I welcome you into the Dicade. You will now be within all of our reach." He nodded slightly to Damian and walked to join Pikon, pouring himself a drink.

Leading Coretheen to the couch, Damian sat down and smiled at her as the night fully set in. Pikon and Kamon could be heard talking in the background, with a burst of laughter that would follow every once in a while. Damian pulled Coretheen close to him, wrapping his arms around her as she leaned her head against his chest and whispered. "When I was a little girl, my life was great. There was nothing to be afraid of. My dad ran a large business, but soon the wars and riots broke out. I remained strong; I set out to learn in my father's footsteps and went to college. Before I finished school, my dad's company was being absorbed by the government for the effort, of course. The riots became fiercer, and I retreated to be by my family's side. I never let them know my fear until the day my dad joined the resistance ranks. I never understood why he left, until now, as I sit here with you. He couldn't stand seeing the country he used to love fall prey to those around him. I am glad to follow in his footsteps once again; I want to help Damian, I want to play a part, I no longer can sit idly by as the world burns down around me. I want to fight." She raised her head and looked into his eyes with those words.

Damian returned her stare, not with his eyes but with the emotion in his voice. "When the time comes, my Lady, a chance will present itself. You just have to learn to take hold of that chance and grow with it." He said while rubbing the top of his cane with his thumb, picking it up within both of his hands as she laid down on the couch. "Coretheen, do you know why I carry this cane? Why I never leave if far from my reach?"

"You once mentioned to me that the Elpis resembles your hope and expectations that are carved upon it."

"Yes, that is a part of it." Damian spoke as he laid down next to her, "It carries my hope. It reminds me of what I must do, and that hope emits a light that seems to shine not just from me but from the Elpis itself. It gives me strength when I feel I have none left to give. I received it from a man I almost consider my father. He is the one who not only taught me every piece of knowledge I know but the one who taught me to have the strength to remain calm, even in the direst situations. In time, I finally understood that thinking allows one to react quickly and resolve any threat. Yes, he trained me to fight, but even a rabid dog can fight. To be able to draw a conclusion on an enemy before they even move, while intelligently forming a plan to counter their movements, without emotion, but with logic, is even more lethal. Sometimes it isn't just my hope that shines through this cane; it is his too, for this cane was his. This symbol carved upon it is not mine, but the one I consider to be my father from whom I took it. So, for him, I carry it across this land to make his wish come true, which now has also become my own wish. I do this for me and no one else. This land will become free. Coretheen, I do this for me and no one else."

He closed his eyes and laid his head upon Coretheen as he fell asleep upon her chest.

CHAPTER ELEVEN

The Dicade men raced forward through the falling buildings, not knowing how great the Alliance force was. "Scerion, we must send a scout to notify Damian. He has to be told about the slaughter that is occurring before our own eyes. We cannot let this sinful act be unaccounted for, for us to be wiped from this earth as if we had never even existed in the first place. We cannot become part of the silence that rests within the shadows."

"I have been entrusted with this town. I had believed the Alliance would show mercy upon its own people. I thought the mob would hold them back. They did not show mercy; they slayed the innocent along with those who rebelled, not showing even an indication of remorse." Scerion growled while closing his eyes tightly, then took a long deep breath. "We must fight back. We must send out runners, for Damian is the one who entrusted this city to me, the one who spreads our cause. I want four running units sent to the beachside and two units sent north. Your task is to live, to escape, to spread our story of what unfolded here today. Show the nation the relentless destruction the Alliance is capable of. Go now, before we vanish, not even becoming memories entangled within other's minds."

"I have been told the bridges have been blown, that the city is encased in steel and wire. There are only two fronts from which the rest of us can escape. That is one from the main road held high by the Alliance's might, and the other being the outstretched waters of the sea. We will take to the sea."

The Dicade pushed forward as Scerion demanded, "We will break our force in three units. The first unit will distract the enemy from the rooftops by performing guerilla tactics. I will take part in this team; we are team Alpha. Team Beta will take the beach, and team Omega, you will be the small reserve in case of a flanking maneuver. Let us not delay, for every minute that passes allows the Alliance to tighten their grasp upon our city, upon our home!"

Scerion moved forward through the buildings gaining access to the beachfront, noticing only a few dozen men from the Alliance with a single tank. Every once in a while, he would notice a young soldier raise his gun and shoot at a civilian who became courageous enough to run to the shore, taking their life as swiftly as one would kill a mosquito trying to acquire a quick meal. He radioed team Beta, "On the sniper's signal, I want you to take the beach." He motioned team Alpha, "I want my ten best snipers on top of the building next to me." The men looked at him in hesitation as Scerion bellowed, "Go now before this massacre comes to an end, and their blood is on your hands!" The men lunged forward towards the building.

Gunfire erupted as Scerion watched in anguish as his men were killed as they opened themselves to the enemy.

"Team Alpha, draw the enemy out." Scerion thundered as bullets rained out of their encampment.

Scerion heard screeching from above as he hollered, "Take cover!" Artillery shells pounded around them, causing the fragile building to sway with every blast. "Cease fire!" He watched as the artillery rounds slowed then stopped entirely. The dust masking the Alliance's soldiers moving forward towards their building in silence.

He watched, tactically analyzing the enemy as they moved ever closer. Then he raised his hand, waving his troops forward as his men leaped into battle. Gunfire erupted from the Dicade, mowing down the Alliance troops. Scerion's hand came to rest upon his side as the last Alliance soldier fell, littering the ground with his dead body as Scerion screamed, "Go now, my Dicade. Go now and reclaim what was once ours!"

Eston saw a faint explosion on the screen. He moved his hand across it, enlarging the display. He watched a flag being hung on top of a building, freely waving in the wind on the west side of the town. Enhancing the image on the screen, he watched in amazement as the symbol of the Dicade was proudly sown onto that same flag.

He peered closer as hundreds of men bearing the same banner were on top and around the base of the building. "Reroute the north garrison, have them move into the city and march west," Eston commanded.

"For we will crush them as if they were but sand under our feet."

Scerion smiled as he saw his men take the top of the building. "Unleash the volley that will claim our salvation!" The snipers began to fire at the troops on the beach. Scerion continued, "Let your accuracy be as true as our cause is just." With each bullet shot, Scerion could see another Alliance soldier meet his demise, imprinting the soft sand on the beach with their bodies as they fell. "Let the mutts of the Alliance cower back to their masters."

The few remaining Alliance soldiers began running to the tank. With their flight, Scerion roared, "Team Beta, let us show them what fear truly is!"

The full might of the Dicade stormed the beach before the tank's turret could fully rotate, launching dozens of thermite grenades upon it. Within minutes the tank became only a pile of molten metal. Scerion, standing on top of the building, yelled, "Take to the beach, my city, for it is your only escape. The path has been formed; all you have to do is take it yourself."

His words echoed across the city as thousands of civilians in hiding plunged towards the beach, toward their salvation.

Ashling gradually turned, questioning Eston. "So, my Eston, what will you do now? Will you let them escape into the waves? Will you let the insects taunt the Alliance, their masters? What will you do with the might that I have bestowed upon you? What will you do to the mere insects before you?"

"Our forces from the north are not yet in range, and our air superiority is masked by the black mist we ourselves created." Eston softly replied, then took a deep breath and slowly exhaled. "Though, that is not our only option, for a shadow does not need eyes to see into the darkness."

A soft chuckle slowly grew louder, "Well, well, my Eston. This, I hope, will be entertaining, entertaining indeed." Ashling walked over to the table, "Play Requiem, K. 626: Lacrimosa Dies Illa."

Eston listened as the daunting classical music erupted around him. He gazed upon screens four and five, observing the fleet of destroyers he put in the water for just this scenario. Images of the man impaled by the fence flashed back into his mind. Closing his eyes, he whispered to himself, "For the good of the Alliance, release the scarabs."

He remembered Lorne laughing at how they got their nickname, speaking as he was holding onto one of the scarabs, "These little guys are no bigger than my hand but do they ever pack a punch. They resemble a beetle but are launched like a clay pigeon using a sophisticated and modernized skeet thrower. They spin at incredible speeds as the head propels these little explosives. They are of little use anymore, but back in the day, they were great. They need to land in soft soil; because of how quickly they rotate, they burrow under the ground, hiding only a few feet from where they land as someone takes a step over it, bam! The scarab's body will explode, creating a shockwave that rips anything in its path in half. It's a clever little thing. Sadly, it is now a relic, too, as its use ended with the invasions. For there are few places left on this earth that still require beach assaults."

Glancing over at Ashling, Eston noticed a smile spread across his face as he walked towards his seat placed in front of the screens. Ashling raised his arms out to his sides as if composing a symphony before him. He turned his attention back to the screen as the ship's metal decks opened. On each deck, hundreds of launchers filled with scarabs were now ready to be thrown onto the beachfront. He peered over at Ashling, whose eyes lit up in excitement over what was yet to come. Two flashing words appeared on the screen. Eston slowly pressed the one that read confirm.

A loud squealing sound erupted across the sky as Scerion scanned the heavens above him. He attempted to place the sound but couldn't; to him, it resembled the scream of a cicada on a warm summer evening. He watched from the top of his building as thousands of people ran onto the beach below as the squealing became deafening. Covering his ears while squinting towards the sky, he attempted to locate what was making the sound. Small specs appeared on the horizon, slowly growing larger as they flew closer. The entire sky was now filled as if a swarm containing millions of locusts would soon come down upon them.

The scarabs began to make landfall. Eston watched as they began skipping across the water until finding their resting place within the sand. A young woman was running helplessly towards the water. He recognized the agony on her face as a scarab tore through her chest, creating a crevice so deep he could see out the other side. The men bearing the Dicade symbol began to retreat as he watched the civilians continue rushing forward desperately towards the water, as the rest of the scarabs peppered the beach, concealing themselves underneath the earth as quickly as they arrived.

Ashling burst out laughing. "Look at them all flee my Eston. Look at them all run, ha, as if they had a chance in hell to escape our might. My Eston, do they not know? Do they not know that we are hell, reincarnated? If not, they will know it now, my child; they will know it now." Ashling continued to stare at the screen with his arms stretched out as if he was composing an orchestra while the civilians were ripped apart with every thunderous explosion.

Eston watched Ashling's smile grow with every single blast. He watched how he closed his eyes for a moment, taking a deep breath, attempting to take in every second, every death, and every scream of agony as an eerie peace seemed to fill Ashling's soul. Opening his eyes, he watched Ashling sit down in a chair, still composing, with his eyes fixed on the screens in front of him as a man and a woman rushed forward together.

In a cloud of smoke, sand, and blood, he saw the couple flying apart from one another with their hands reaching out towards each other, attempting desperately to hold onto one another for their last few seconds alive. He watched as they both landed only feet from each other, as the man bleeding profusely attempted to crawl to the woman he loved. Another scarab unleashed its hidden might upon them as its shockwave ripped both of their bodies in half, sending body parts skidding across the beach. As each body part landed upon the ground, another scarab would be found underneath the surface, unleashing its fury upon anything near it. Ashling grinned, his eyes piercing the screen before him as the raining blood and body parts were now triggering more explosions than the people still fleeing for their lives.

Swallowing hard, Eston turned his attention back to Ashling, who now sat on his chair, kicking his legs out in front of him in excitement, with the same demeanor that a child would when watching fireworks. "Ohh, look at that one. Another, another, ohhh that was a good one, look at them go, haha I think that one was the best of them all!" as hundreds of civilian's bodies were shredded apart before his very eyes.

He took a long, slow, and deep look into Ashling's eye's, and although his voice was filled with emotion, his eyes remained empty.

⊷⊶

Scerion heard another deafening pitch and gazed at the sky as a second swarm was coming towards them. He looked down, screaming, "The beach is no longer an option. We must focus all of our remaining forces in getting the runners to the north free." He peered down at his men as they continued to flee. The second swarm seemed even more deadly than the first. He watched in agony, being helpless as his own men ran through the chaos of the deadly mines. Thousands were being ripped to shreds as they played Russian Roulette with every step they took, and those who were too scared to move were ripped apart by incoming mines, just as quick as those who were running. For whoever was on the waterfront, there was no salvation. There was no escape. There was only death. He sorrowfully looked at the beach, knowing that the Alliance would not risk taking a step onto it for hundreds of years. The mines would be left there until the city's residents stepped upon them, one by one, until the end of time. No one would be able to safely walk those shorelines for many generations, not until the triggering devices rusted through, releasing their hidden might.

As the remaining Dicade regrouped, Scerion declared, "I want the remaining snipers and marksmen from team Alpha in the towers surrounding the street. We will move slowly. The arrogant Alliance will focus all their power on us, confronting our main force on the street. Use this chance to cause chaos; split their forces, instilling fear inside of them. When the battle begins, take the high ground and unleash your strength upon them—for we will continue to fight, as long as we can still draw a single breath into our lungs."

Eston watched as the second volley of scarabs landed; the whole beach seemed to erupt. For when one scarab landed, it would strike another hidden underneath the sand and dirt, causing a wave of explosions so powerful the ground could be felt shaking from where he stood, tens of miles away from the city. As the vaporized blood and dirt settled, he peered upon what remained of the shoreline; what he saw horrified him. The dirt and the sand were dyed red, dyed red with the blood of this once fine city's inhabitants.

Ashling stood up and bowed towards the screen as the song was coming to an end. His demeanor now reserved in comparison to before the bloodbath. "My Eston, that was a splendid show indeed, though your work is yet to be finished." He looked toward screens seven and eight, those that were looking over the city, seeing what Ashling had pointed out. A few hundred Dicade soldiers remained, marching north in formation, to what he knew would be their death. He wondered if they, too, knew of the fate waiting for them ahead.

Scerion took the lead and marched with the remaining of his men. Speaking to them with determination and vigor, "Men, our goal is no longer survival of the masses. It is the survival of the few. We must push forward into this chaotic world."

"We know not what lies ahead, other than our own death and agony. As we exhale our last breath, we will know that our pain has ended. We will know that with our struggling last steps that our message will be heard. We will know that we pushed a hole into the enemy. We will know that with that hole, the last of our runners will escape, delivering our tale of death and dismay. We will know that our movement, in union with Damian's and the Dicade, will live on through him."

He straightened his back, raising his voice louder, "We do this last act out of the freedom that we have, the freedom that we love. For on this very night, every one of you will truly be free. So my men, my companions, let us march towards our freedom. Let us march towards our salvation."

CHAPTER TWELVE

S craping echoed down the street as feet slipped across the broken concrete. Eight men moved forward through the night, stopping every few moments to allow an Alliance soldier to pass them. They climbed between the fractured walls, pushing themselves through the breaks in the rebar, only to gain a few more feet in complete secrecy. The commander of the runners, sent out by Scerion, raised his hand, signaling his men to stop. He stared ahead, upon three men bearing the symbol of the Alliance, standing between him and an old sewer system. He whispered, "The only way to the edge of town lies before us. It is the single path that has not yet been infested by the epidemic of the Alliance." Soundlessly wedging himself into a crevice of a building, he slowly proceeded to push himself up the sides until reaching the floor above his men.

Leaping forward, he tackled two of the three Alliance soldiers before him. As the third Alliance soldier turned to look at the assailant, three members of the Dicade rushed forward. Grabbed him, covered his mouth, and began choking him—while two more men took out their knives and stabbed the remaining Alliance soldiers on the ground. The commander raised his hand and signaled them to move forward. They silently opened the sewer lid and began lowering themselves down into the old tunnels.

The commander pulled out a candlestick, lit it, and dissected the map as they waited in silence. Then he directed, "I want unit one to move northeast, and my unit will move northwest. We will emerge on the borders of the city only a few hundred meters apart. You will await my signal upon your arrival, and then we will move in unison. Let us hope that there will be an opening for us to breakthrough. Load your guns and use your ammo sparingly, for we have to break free and notify the Dicade."

CHAPTER THIRTEEN

S cerion and his men continued to march towards the
enemy. As they walked every few yards, they would
shoot down an Alliance soldier plundering the city.
He glanced at two men, who appeared to be brothers,
walking down the street towards him. Scerion raised his
hand, signaling his men to stop.

One of the two men spoke, "We saw what you did
on the beach. We have some weapons, and we want to
fight."

"We are here to defend the city with what we have,
and we welcome any additions." Scerion acknowledged,
"It will be an honor to walk with you in this hour of
darkness." One by one, Scerion saw the civilians creep
out of their hiding places. Both men and women now

stood in his force, growing by the minute. Soon, his numbers reached past the thousands as civilians picked up whatever they could find—from weapons taken off of the dead Dicade and Alliance soldiers—to knives and bent pieces of metal from the building's foundations.

Reinvigorated, Scerion raised his voice to those before him. "Men and women of this city, I thank you for your support. As we stare down the barrels of the great Alliance, we renounce our citizenship, and we renounce our enslavement to them. We, the true citizens of this once great country, reclaim what is ours. We will reclaim our freedom."

Eston turned his attention back to the Alliance's army as the rebels approached his forces. A few hundred against a few thousand, it hardly seemed fair.

"Well, my Eston," Ashling yawned, "it seems our fun has almost reached its conclusion. Let's wrap this up and destroy them. So, so I can return to something more, more entertaining. They don't offer us any threat now."

"Understood, as you command." He looked over to the quiet Colonel Wikerson, "Destroy the remaining Dicade."

The Colonel raised his radio to his mouth, "The order has been given, and the rebels are positioned less than a mile from you. Attack, until not even a single one of their hearts remains beating."

The Alliance soldiers stopped their march as Eston watched the Dicade troops approach his forces. He moved the surveillance satellite to the approaching enemy, as his body became stiff. "My Speaker, I urge you, look at the surveillance."

Looking at the screens, Ashling saw thousands of civilians walking behind the few hundred Dicade, his face filled with anger. "Their insolence!" He fiercely growled, "How can they disregard the wishes of the Alliance? How can they disregard my commands? Do they not strive for the best in this world?"

Ashling took a deep breath, and as his tense face relaxed, he sighed. "Though, in the end, I assume, it makes no difference. We will break them nonetheless. Their demise is certain, and that I can assure you my Eston."

"Wait for your freedom until our snipers are in position." Scerion whispered to his men. Glancing behind him, he saw the frightened faces of thousands of men and women, though, in all their eyes, he saw something more powerful than fear. He saw relief, relief from the life they had allowed to consume them. He saw a sense of purpose, a sense of control as they decided their own actions for the first time within their miserable lives.

A flash of light shone down from above, signaling to Scerion, as he shouted. "For liberty and freedom, for all!"

With those words, they sprang forward upon the Alliance. Holding formation in the middle of the street, the Dicade began to fire upon the enemy of the nation, upon the enemy of the world. The civilians remained behind the Dicade, unleashing Molotov cocktails and rocks at the Alliance, as the few with guns fired widely ahead of them. Bullets began to plow into the vests of the Alliances soldiers, forcing them to fall onto the ground from the energy of the projectiles. They struggled to stand as more bullets pummeled into them until their vests weakened, giving way to the forces against them, allowing the bullets to pierce deep within their flesh.

The Alliance soldiers regained their stance and attacked with a vengeance. Scerion peered around him, noticing his men falling to his left and to his right. He pulled out one of his few grenades and threw it upon the enemy. With that explosion, the Dicade snipers let loose upon the army underneath them, breaking the Alliance's forces. Scerion and the Dicade pushed forward, followed by an army of the cities inhabitants that continued to grow by the hundreds with every minute that passed.

≈‡‡≈

Ashling and Eston watched the Alliance's men being pushed down by bullets, only to become engulfed in flames by a Molotov cocktail seconds later. The men who began to run fared no better as the bullets from the Dicades snipers pierced their skulls in an instant. With every soldier's death, they watched the resistance power increase as the men and women began picking up the dead and fleeing soldier's weapons.

Ashling calmly walked up to Eston, grabbing his shirt he lifted him off the ground and pushed him against the wall.

Shock spread across Eston's face as he was taken aback, not only from the sheer surprise of the act but by the strength of Ashling himself.

"Sir," Colonel Wickerson stepped forward towards Ashling, "may I ask you..."

Before he finished his sentence, Ashling removed a knife from his belt and threw it into the Colonel's neck, keeping his eyes fixed on Eston the entire time.

"My Eston, you will fix this. You will destroy them. For if they escape, the guilt and shame will fall upon your head, alone, with an ax... Do you understand this, my dear Eston?" Ashling serenely and sarcastically elucidated as the colonel fell to the ground, his blood pouring out around the knife lodged within his throat.

Taking a deep breath while keeping his composure, he replied. "My speaker, no, not just my speaker, my leader. As you have requested, shall be done, for they have not yet seen the full fury of your power." Ashling lowered him to the floor, turning his head slightly to the side like a confused dog analyzing the situation—not yet sure how to respond.

He straightened his shirt while walking to the command table. "I want the battle to be positioned on screen seven, and on-screen eight, you will track the movements of our patrol guard to the north."

He pressed a button on the command table, "This is Eston Tavernier, your representative, your commander. The Alliance commands the north patrol unit to move southwest, reinforcing our troops. I want the garrison moving from the south to be repositioned as the patrol guard around the perimeters of the entire city, tripling our defenses as soon as possible. Reinforcements from the north are to collect brigade bullets and depart immediately."

"This is the will of the Alliance, and it will be carried out. The Coalition calls for a strict defensive assembly until the rebel forces begin to flee. Do not give chase, or advance, until only the back of their heads are seen. Then and only then may formation be broken to kill those attempting to escape. You will not let even one of the rebels live; we will track them, and you will remove them from existence."

"I repeat, this is the will of the Alliance and will be carried out as commanded. There will be no exceptions to this command, and any deviations will be considered an act of treason. Go forth and commence; that is all."

CHAPTER FOURTEEN

The commander of the runners, Falkor, gazed in amazement as the forces surrounding the perimeter began to take marching formation and move south. The north road was now almost completely open. Only a small fraction of their men were left behind. Falkor continued to watch, giving the Alliance a few more minutes to put distance between the perimeter and them. He lit two candles and waved them quickly, then extinguished them, indicating to the other unit that it was time to move.

Analyzing the few Alliance soldiers that remained, he counted two men within each watchtower—positioned on either side of the road—guarding the only opening in the fence the Alliance had erected. In the center of the road stood four men with two more under each tower, totaling twelve men. Whispering under his breath, he instructed, "Runners, get ready. I don't think we're going to get a better chance than this. I don't know what made them move, but Scerion must have had some tricks in store for them. Who said you couldn't teach an old dog new tricks, heh?"

Sprinting towards a broken, rusted, and ruined car a hundred yards from the towers, Falkor peered at the guards. A quick smirk tugged at his dry and cracked lips as he noticed the look of boredom plastered upon the enemy's faces. He watched the men on the ground pacing back and forth while the men in the structures seemed no better, yawning every few seconds. The other Dicade unit began moving up, crawling into a ditch parallel to him on the other side of the road. He put one finger to his head, signifying that his unit was to lead and that the other would flank.

He nodded to the three men with him. They rose in perfect harmony from behind the car, firing at the troops in the middle of the road as they fell without resistance.

The soldiers in the guard towers snapped into action, hammering the vehicle that Falkor hid behind with bullets. The men at the base of the towers began to move up on the car, trying to flank to the sides, as the turrets kept Falkor's squad pinned down.

Two men from the second Dicade unit struck, taking down the four men moving in on their commander—streaking the cracked pavement with their blood—as the two remaining Dicade began a flanking maneuver on the enemy's fortifications.

Both turrets turned their attention to the two Dicade men, now out in the open, as they attempted to run and take cover. It was too late. Bullets ripped through them as if they were just paper used during target practice. The towers returned their guns on the force positioned behind the car, unleashing another bombardment of bullets.

"Suppressing fire!" Falkor yelled as he witnessed two of his men approaching the bottom of one of the fortifications. The men behind the car unleashed a volley of bullets while his men, flanking, entered their position underneath the first structure.

The men immediately fired, shooting through the wooden floor above them and into the enemy. They began their ascent up the fortification's stairs, as blood began dripping down through the splintered and cracked wood from above.

Falker watched as the structure on the right side of the road began turning its mounted gun towards the new threat next to them. He felt his heart drop as the Alliance began setting their sights upon his unit, upon his men. Breaking cover, he rushed forward towards the enemy, unleashing his entire clip.

Noticing Falkor and his men closing in on them, the Alliance soldiers ignored their previous targets and returned their attention upon the approaching Dicade.

A deafening roar erupted in Falkor's ears. Not from the enemy before him, but from the tower the Dicade had claimed. He turned and watched as his men unleashed fifty caliber bullets into the Alliance before him. He watched as the bullets tore apart not only the wooden structure but also the Alliance soldiers within it.

Falkor's ears no longer rang with the sound of gunfire but instead rang with the sound of his men cheering as the Dicade soldiers climbed down the stairs. Though, he did not cheer with them as he lowered his line of sight upon the men who had died.

Silence once again filled the air as the Dicade soldiers followed his gaze, which was now resting upon the dead bodies of their allies. He began to speak. "These are but a few that were lost today. We will not forget their sacrifice. We will not regret their loss, for if we did, their sacrifice would be in vain. These, the fallen, are the true heroes of our time. With the greatest of odds against us, thanks to them, we will now be able to deliver our message. Let us not delay while the path before us remains open. Let us not delay, for, through them, this path was opened."

The men moved forward, disappearing into the woods.

CHAPTER FIFTEEN

Scerion stood in awe as bullets whizzed by his head. They were actually winning! The Alliance army before him began to flee. He looked to his left, and then to his right, as the town's population began cheering as the army began a full retreat. The snipers continued to fire, picking off as many as they could in the distance. Scerion spoke, and the crowd before him grew quiet, "Against great odds, we survived, we lived, and we won. Though do not be deceived, more will come."

"Despite that, I thank you all, for, with your help, I feel our true goal will be accomplished. News of what happened here today will spread across the world..." Scerion beamed at the thousands of men and women before him. At the thousands of starving civilians who pushed back the might of the Alliance, through pure determination alone.

"And with that hope, and with your courage, there now stands a chance to regain our once-great nation. Your sacrifice, no, not your sacrifice but your fortitude will echo across this land, becoming the story of inspiration and courage that all will wish to follow. For you did not hide in the shadows. You did not let those above you hold your fate within their hands. For you have become truly free."

In the distance, a flare began to rise, shining within the night's sky. Scerion pointed towards the flickering light and shouted as a smile spread across his face, "That flare is the symbol that our mission has indeed been accomplished. I will not hold it against you if you now hide. If you now strive to live, for one day, we will take this city back."

"Although, it breaks my heart to admit that today will not be that day. So, I urge you to either survive or to stand with me and fight. Fight for your freedom, for no matter what end occurs, know this, that today you showed your will to those who held you hostage." Scerion watched as a few thousand men and women walked forward, many picking up the weapons of the slain soldiers of the Alliance. But he also watched as many chose to survive, disappearing back into the decrepit buildings from which they came from. He smiled once again, knowing that they would fight another day, and exhaled in relief, knowing that their mission was complete.

Sitting down, he pulled out an old metal flask, taking a long, slow drink; until the sound of men marching in formation grew too loud to ignore. "For those who remain," looking behind him, seeing well over a thousand citizens standing ready to fight, "For those who remain, and for those who left, I thank you all. Without your help, we would have been laid to waste for nothing. I am proud to call myself a citizen of old. I am proud to call myself a citizen of this great city. I can now smile as I walk towards my freedom. I can now smile as I leave this place and become truly free. They come now to give you your freedom. Let's see if we can give them some of theirs too." The crowd roared.

Eston and Ashling watched their men move in formation. The first row of the Alliance bore bulletproof shields ranging from their ankles up to their shoulders. They advanced in unity, edging closer to the rebels with every step they took. As the rebels formed in their sights, they halted, and the men behind those bearing shields put their guns on the shoulders of the person in front of them.

The inhabitants and the Dicade fired upon the Alliance, their bullets ricocheting off of the thick bulletproof shields. The snipers began to fire, taking down the Coalition with precision from above. With each man that was shot down, the man behind him picked up the shield and held it in place, as the soldier behind him placed his gun on his comrade's shoulder, holding the Dicade at bay.

Pressing the screen on the table, Eston commanded, "The Alliance decrees you to engage. Serve the nations as it is commanded of you, as is expected of you." The Alliance soldiers fired as their bullets erupted into the crowd before them.

Scerion glanced next to him as a bullet struck his friend in the arm. He watched as his friend grabbed at his wound, then took a step forward in longing defiance against the Coalition. Returning his attention to the enemy before them, he felt a warm and moist liquid spread across his face. A scream erupted next to him, and as he looked back towards his fellow comrade, the soldier's arm was gone. Scerion wiped his face and looked down at his own hand in shock, for what he looked upon was blood, the blood of his friend.

He watched as a bullet penetrated another soldier's chest, and as the man began to fall, he heard a small pop. Before the man fell to the ground, his chest erupted, sending out fragments of bone and bullet into the crowd. All around him, he saw the untrained civilians begin to run as hundreds of bodies began to explode. He kneeled down, in an attempt to minimize the space he took up, as those in the Dicade army followed suit. Yelling over the gunfire, "They are using exploding rounds, put distance between one another." His men fanned out, returning fire once again.

⇥⇤

"My Eston, my child, you have outdone yourself again. Look at them run. Look at them flee." Ashling began giggling hysterically as a smile returned to his face, "They're just like kernels of corn, expanding in the fire, our fire Eston. The fire of the Alliance in which claims their very souls. Watch them Eston, watch them go, pop, pop, pop. They are all going, pop, pop, pop! One by one, one by one, exploding, there they go, watch Eston, watch them go, pop, pop, pop."

Peering at Ashling, Eston thought how he had never seen anyone go from such gruesome fierceness to such childish behavior in a trifling amount of time. He swallowed his vomit that now entered his mouth as he continued to watch hundreds die before him, yet again.

The Alliance soldiers now turned their attention to the building's foundation, unleashing their brigade bullets into its core, slowly carving out the beams that held up its fragile body. Within less than a minute, the building collapsed, killing the snipers that hid inside.

They refocused their fury upon the few remaining Dicade troops in the middle of the road.

Scerion looked around him; less than ten men remained. He stood and started to run towards the Alliance soldiers in front of him. The remaining Dicade followed suit, charging with him, yelling, as bullets rained into their flesh. The last words the Alliance heard echo through the air was Scerion screaming, "For our liberty and our freedom!" With those words, Scerion smiled as his body exploded, and he fell to the ground dead—with his comrades surrounding him. His blood trickled out from his body as he was finally permitted the freedom he desired, the freedom he deserved.

The Alliance soldiers broke formation and took after the fleeing civilians. Ashling's demeanor once again returned to a strong and calm manner. "I had total faith in you, Eston, for I never doubted the Alliances strength that I vested upon you. I will admit, I am impressed with how well adjusted you have become to the events that have just unfolded. I did not expect you to calculate that far into the future, nor have planned so many contingencies, all of which came in handy, it seems. Reaching into the relics of the old, combined with our techno-logical feats, and used in ways I have not seen before. I expected no less from a member of the Guardians of the Shadows, but even I am taken aback a little. On behalf of the Alliance, well done, my child, well done indeed."

He watched as Ashling vanished from the command room, his voice drifting to him. "Prepare yourself, Eston, for we will call upon you soon."

His shoulders slumped over as he observed the dead Colonel's body being drug out of the room. Eston, now alone, stared at the screens before him. He peered into the city's center, noticing thousands of dead bodies next to the stage where he once stood. He lowered his head as tears ran from his eyes. He forced his head up, fixing his eyes back onto the screens to confirm what he had done, what he had just received the highest praises for. For on their dead bodies, he had climbed a little higher onto the log; he had indeed caused a ripple no one would soon forget.

He continued to gaze upon the screen, noticing not only men and women but entire families dead. He looked upon a young girl, no older than six, whose eyes were stuck open with the expression of absolute horror; her hand was still clinging onto her dead mother's next to her. He vomited onto the floor, no longer able to hold back his own disgust.

Weeping softly, his voice broke every few words as tears flooded down his face. "How can this be for the good of the Alliance? How can this be for the betterment of mankind? No matter how we hide what we have done to this city, it is truly a massacre. Even if I cry one tear for every person I killed, I would not have enough tears in my body for all of them. Though I still shall try, I owe them that. I am but a tool, I said. Heck, I am but only a weapon, is what I should have said."

Eston stood up and turned off the screens before him, fixing his tie, not bothering to wipe the tears from his face. Taking a deep breath, he walked forward and declared. "For the Alliance, to put their needs above myself, an individual. To give the Alliance my body, mind, and heart for as long as I stand. Our nations, indivisible, with health and prosperity for all. I have given away not only my body tonight, for I have also given away my humanity."

CHAPTER SIXTEEN

Coretheen woke up peering at Damian, still lying on her chest. She smiled while twirling his hair between her fingers. With the caress of her fingers, Damian awoke, gazing deeply into her eyes, and gently laid a kiss upon her forehead. He stood up, stretching his arms out as she stared at him, noticing that for the first time, he seemed as if a profound calmness had come over him.

"Relax, Damian; you made me breakfast, now let me make some for you." She walked to the kitchen as she noticed Pikon and Kamon passed out on chairs across from one another with an empty bottle of rum between them. Beaming, she pulled out some cast iron pans and noticed some canned vegetables and fruit in the wooden cupboards. She drew out some powdered eggs and dried meat and laid them out. Then started the wood stove and allowed it to heat up while preparing the vegetables, fruit, and kneading the dough for a loaf of bread. Pushing with all of her might, she wedged an old wooden window open and watched as the sun danced across the mountains before her. A gentle breeze of fresh air tickled her face along with the song of a falcon that rang across the valley.

Within a few hours, Coretheen could hear both Pikon's and Kamon's laughter make its way into the kitchen. She pulled out the freshly baked bread and started to cook the eggs and meat, turning as both Damian and Kamon walked into the kitchen.

"Wow, Damian, you sure got yourself a fine lady, already cooking for you." Kamon said while grimacing.

"And as the cook," Coretheen snapped back light-heartedly, "I decide who gets to eat, not to mention who gets to clean up after we're done eating."

Damian and Kamon gazed upon every single cast iron pan and dish that was laid out upon the counters. Kamon hesitated, "How, how did you manage to use every single pan?"

"I think she did a fine job cooking for us," Damian smiled, "and a proper cook uses every instrument available to them to make sure the flavor rings true, as the Miss has apparently done."

"Well then, I see," Kamon began rubbing the back of his head, "I guess you got this game down, already sucking up…"

Before he could finish his sentence, she broke in, "Yes, he does, and Kamon, you better learn how to as well. For now, you're on the shortlist for the dishes."

"Aww, come on, Miss, I was just joking with ya." He moaned in agony.

"See that Kamon, you got to know how to work a lady properly."

Coretheen glared at Damian, and Kamon shouted, "Yes! Looks like with that comment, I am out of the running."

Walking over to Coretheen, Damian gave her a hug from behind and gently kissed her neck as she turned her head, returning his kiss. "Annnnd with that, I am back on the shortlist." Kamon sighed while sitting down at the table, lowering his head as both Coretheen and Damian giggled.

Damian sat down with Pikon and Kamon at the table as Coretheen smiled, listening to their stories of the past. "Pikon, I remember how scared you had that one private last year, after his acceptance into the Dicade; what did you say again? After he spilled his drink all over you?"

"Boy! You better know how to salute your leader, and no matter what I made you do, there is never a good reason to waste liquor." Their laugher continued as Coretheen once again took a deep breath of air and listened to the falcon's song ring out across the mountains. She brought in the dishes of scrambled eggs, freshly baked bread, sweetened peaches with freshly sliced strawberries, along with corn and some venison on the side. Damian stood up, helping her bring in the food.

Both Kamon and Pikon looked at her as Kamon turned his gaze to Damian. "You know Damian; she is a fine addition to our little group. She can definitely stick around for a while."

"I guess all it takes to lower your guard is cooking a little food." Coretheen declared.

Kamon took a bite, "Ma'am, if all girls cooked as good as you do, I don't think there would be any time left to fight."

"We all would be too busy filling our mouths!" Pikon exclaimed while shoving another bite into his.

As their plates became empty, Coretheen heard the falcon's song again. "That bird has been singing that song all morning. I wonder if it is as happy as we are?"

Damian's smile turned to a dead stare as Kamon stopped filling his mouth. "Coretheen, you're stating you have heard this bird sing before?"

"Well, yes, before I started cooking, I heard it. Its song echoed through the mountains while you all slept."

"Is that the only time you heard it?"

"Well, no, I also heard it when you three were reminiscing about the past, and of course, just right now." Before she could finish her sentence, all three of them rushed from the dining area. Damian burst through the door first, raising his hand to the sky as Coretheen followed them outside, confused. Damian let loose a loud whistle; within a second, they heard the falcon release its song yet again as he returned the bird's call.

She watched as the falcon descended with great speed towards Damian while Kamon began to explain. "There are few ways of transmitting information in which the Alliance is unable to confiscate it. In the days of old, people used to use pigeons to carry messages, without using any technology in existence. In essence, this is the same principle, though each major city of the resistance is given a falcon to carry information. They are trained to track one of us three, even here. I'll admit, at first, it was tricky to train these beasts, but their speed was necessary in order to exchange messages as quickly as possible. It is an asset that was worth every second of time and energy." Coretheen watched as the falcon started to dive towards Damian's arm and, in a split second, landed softly upon it, drawing a small amount of blood with its talons.

Damian, without even flinching, untied a small note from the falcon's leg as blood trickled down his arm. He didn't speak, and after a few minutes, he passed the note to Pikon, who in turn passed it to Kamon. She looked as Kamon's kind face turned to the ground. Peering towards Damian, she noticed that his free hand was now clutched in a fist as his jaw muscles clenched tight.

The air remained silent for a moment until Pikon grimly commanded, "I will procure us a new meeting place so we can plan for the future. We must no longer delay; this area will not suffice as commands here are limited. I am glad you all made it." Pikon then paused while looking towards Damian, "I now know the reason you were late." He turned his gaze towards Coretheen as her face began to turn red. "I understand why you had to protect something as rare as Miss Nerites. I will reroute our documents and the needed information to a new destination. Damian and Kamon, you will be informed as soon as an area is secured—so look to the sky on your journey back to the city; we will reconvene there shortly."

"With this new information, we must not hesitate, not even for a second. Damian, accumulate your runners and draw up whatever forces you can. Kamon, try to obtain extra funds if at all possible. I will have all of our benefactor's information waiting for your arrival. Let us depart." Damian and Kamon both nodded as Pikon began walking away.

She watched as he became smaller with each step he took, disappearing into the distance. She looked at Kamon, who was writing furiously on a piece of paper, then reattached the paper to the falcon's leg. Damian raised his arm, and the falcon took off, flying back to whoever sent the majestical creature here in the first place.

Looking at them, she questioned, "What happened?" Then put her hand in between Damian's arm and pulled his face towards hers, and urged. "Damian, please, tell me what happened. Damian, please, I need to know. I want to know."

The man before her remained quiet as Kamon sadly revealed, "It's Seattle. It is no more."

"What do you mean, it is no more?" Still looking at Damian, "What happened?"

"The Alliance destroyed it," Damian whispered to her softly as despair filled his voice, "they wiped its population from the face of the earth by cutting it off as if it were a disease. The few people left alive will soon starve, or worse, die trying to escape. It is only a matter of months before there will be no one left alive."

Coretheen sat down on the ground and begun playing with a weed sticking out of the earth, "Can we save them, Damian? Can we free them?"

"We can't mobilize that quick. We don't have the supplies yet, or even the weapons. If only they would have waited a year or two more. Maybe then we would have had a chance, but right now, how we sit, it only would be sending more to their deaths."

Coretheen started to twist the weed furiously between her fingers. "How many did the Alliance murder?"

"Of the current count, ten thousand, if not more." Damian looked at the weed Coretheen grasped between her fingers. "It's too hard to tell with our limited information. Seattle is blacked out. No one can leave or enter. Any resources they had were taken from them.

They are left in the dark to starve or feast upon each other, becoming mere animals within their cages." Coretheen tightly grasped the weed within her hand as he knelt down next to her. "To them, we are just as the weed you hold in your hand. They bend it in any direction they deem necessary, in the disguise of righteousness. Eventually, every gardener will deem the weed a nuisance and pull it out to save the prime of his garden the resources that lay beneath."

Looking at the weed, she spoke as sadness filled her. "Even flowers appear as but weeds before they bloom."

"Yes, Coretheen, they do." He said tenderly while putting his arms around her. "But both weeds and flowers bear beauty that only the observer can see. It is in the eye of the beholder that deems what is truly beautiful and what can be cast aside."

Coretheen tightened her grasp on the green stem within her hand, "In my eyes, it is the mighty Alliance that has a grasp on all of us. They are the weed that we will pull from the ground." She said while tearing the plant out of the soil, roots and all, throwing it onto the dirt.

"I am sorry, Coretheen," Kamon apologized, "after today, I now hold you as one of my own. This dire news that was delivered to us cannot be ignored. We shall hold it next to our hearts until justice can once again become law. Damian, I will soon speak with you and hopefully your kind lady too. I thank you for the meal you cooked, and I promise the next time you prepare such a meal, I will gladly clean up whatever dishes you used in its preparation." With a slight bow, Coretheen and Damian watched Kamon walk away, soon to disappear into the trees as Mr. Pikon had before him.

Damian offered Coretheen his hand. "My Lady, we too must set out, for I must notify our supporters of the fall of Seattle."

She grasped his hand tightly within hers. Then took her foot and crushed the weed she had torn from the ground deep into the soil, and whispered. "We will pry the Alliance from this soil, returning it into the ashes it rose from, and plant a new seed within the dirt. We will watch that seed. We will water that seed, the seed of hope, until it blooms, destroying the chaos of the Alliance.

CHAPTER SEVENTEEN

E ston opened his eyes, hearing a message ring overhead. "We will reach your destination of New Chicago within the hour." Then he attempted to close his eyes again, only to be plagued with the image of the young girl who had died only a few days ago. Her eyes were stuck wide open as her small fingers clung desperately to her dead mother's hand. He envisioned how scared the young girl must have been as her mom died next to her. How hard the young girl's mom must have tried to comfort the young child, before she too, drew her last breath. He opened his eyes as the images vanished from his mind. Pulling out his tablet, he started to watch TV.

Sadly, there was rarely anything interesting on since the Alliance took over the media. Most broadcasts were of new laws enacted for the betterment of the nations. Or when the next mandatory viewing for the population would take place, notifying the civilians of what was required of them. Today was no different. Today's broadcast showed the Alliance's victory over Ukraine and how the forces of the Alliance dominated the country. It showed the civilians walking in lines towards concentration camps, with tanks on either side of them, while Alliance jets flew across the sky above. A banner strung across the bottom of the screen, notifying the entire population that the next mandatory viewing was only a few months away. He turned off the tablet and requested a drink from an attendant as a message was broadcast across the plane. "We will arrive in New Chicago in fifteen minutes. Please buckle your seatbelt as we begin our descent." He looked out the window towards the beautiful city that he was allowed to reside in.

As the plane stopped on the runway, he stood up as a young, slender, and beautiful flight attendant escorted him off of the plane. He exited the plane seeing Mr. Lorne at the end of the terminal waiting for him. While he was walking up, he observed Lorne devouring a sub he had in his hand. Lorne exploded in speech, putting his hand on his shoulder. Eston did not even slow his gait as he continued to walk.

"Eston, I wish I could have been there. Ashling was quite proud of how you handled the situation in Seattle. He said it was even more serene than usual. He mentioned the Dicade presence, good thing you were there, ehh Eston? Ashling was beaming from ear to ear. I never saw the man smile like that."

He watched Lorne take another bite, continuing to talk without even chewing. "I knew you could do it, my boy. I am glad I picked you. I saw your potential the moment I laid eyes on you. I just wish I could have been there myself, Eston. I wish I could have gazed upon that city crumbling."

A speck of bread shot out of Lorne's mouth and landed on his cheek. He wiped it away with his hand and started to walk faster as Lorne continued to ramble. "I got us some food for the ride home. I just had to see you in person. I want a play by play account of the decommission. Eston, don't spare any details. I heard Ashling taped the whole thing; I want to hear it from the commander before I gaze upon his works." Lorne stated proudly while patting Eston on the back.

An assistant rushed to open the door to the limo for both Eston and Lorne. He sat down as Lorne collapsed across from him. A table was located between them with two large pizzas, breadsticks, and some nachos as Lorne continued to talk. "I had the pizza brought in from my favorite little place outside of Vermont, and the breadsticks are from this little Italian joint right here in New Chicago. The nachos, ohh, the nachos, they are straight from Mexico and prepared here, so they are fresh. Only the best for our young upcoming star of the Alliance, heh?"

He watched in amazement as Lorne opened the box and started to eat while offering him a plate. He never imagined a man could talk and eat at the same time without choking or even taking a single break to breathe. Yet, this large man in front of him seemed to have the skill mastered, not even allowing him to get a word in. He took a bite of the pizza, tasting how fresh the cheese was, how the sauce seemed to have been made from tomatoes picked right off the vine. He forgot how long it had been since he had eaten and quickly took another bite as Lorne continued.

"Eat my boy, eat. You deserve it. It's good ehh? Very good, it is made from the freshest of ingredients, grown from the richest of soils." Lorne lobbed a breadstick on Eston's plate, "The breadsticks are to die for, and the butter used is the richest in the Alliance." He took a bite as the bread itself seemed to dissolve in his mouth, filling it with a rich buttery taste. He looked at Lorne, who seemed to be enjoying every bite that he took, more than he himself did. Lorne became even more excited as to what was soon to come. Eston finished the pizza and breadsticks and took a bite of the nachos on the table as the limo continued driving.

Rubbing his hands together in excitement, Lorne urged. "Now that you've tried the great food, tell me your colossal story. Tell me how you conquered, and tell me how you became the brightest young star of the Alliance." Eston once again imagined the city he laid to waste how they would be starving to death at this very moment. He began to swallow his last bite as it was met with the bile that was wrenching up to his mouth.

Looking towards the gluttonous man across from him, Eston squared his shoulders and forced out a laugh as he began to speak. "What is there to tell? The might of the Alliance was under my wing, and simply put, I did not disappoint."

While shoving some more nachos into his mouth, Lorne laughed, "Come on, come on, let's not be modest; I want to hear the deetails you little devil, the deetails."

Eston thought to himself, after what I had done, I may yet be a devil hiding in human flesh. And began, "I gave my speech beginning in the usual manner of the Alliance, with the pledge of course. This is when I first saw the men bearing the symbol of the Dicade in the crowd. Through the wisdom you taught me, I quickly realized they were controlling the crowd skillfully with psychology. That is when I withdrew the merciful hand of the Alliance. The city was fenced in, using the usual fashion, and those scarabs of old became quite useful lining the beach."

"I had no idea you would deploy those old things," Lorne slapped his knee in anticipation, "how insightful and magnificent. Now Eston, I want you to start from the start, from the very beginning."

Eston looked down upon the floor of the limo, watching as a gnat landed on the food in Lorne's hand.

Lorne quickly put the food in his mouth without noticing, devouring the gnat without hesitation—just as quickly as the Alliance had devoured the city only a few days ago, then replied. "I will tell you the tale of not how many died, but a tale of how the brilliant Alliance won, saving those who still produce for the whole."

The limo pulled up to his apartment as he finished telling his account of the decommission of Seattle. "You did the Alliance proud Eston, saved many lives, and showed intellect beyond your years, beyond that of our own military operations unit."

He briefly looked down at the floor of the limo as the image of the young dead child appeared in his head again. He had left that part out. Hearing Lorne speak, he quickly made eye contact and forced another smile. "Your servitude has made me very proud, though not only me Eston, for the Alliance is proud too. We know your service will continue, for you are a true patriot of these great nations, Eston."

"For I, the patriot, live to serve, for the betterment of the Alliance."

Eston's eyes seemed cold and withdrawn as Lorne slapped him on the back. "We have great things planned for you, Eston, great things."

"I can't wait to help them unfold. You have been a true friend since the beginning, Lorne." His voice drifting as he forced yet another smile upon his worn and tired face.

"My boy, you have never done anything but make me proud since the first day I laid my eyes upon you. Soon Eston, very soon, the eight will convene again, and we will require your presence. For my boy, you are now in their ever-reaching sight. Now try to get some sleep. You look like you need it. Anything you need, Eston, just tell your assistant. He has been notified to get you anything you wish, and I mean anything, of course, at the expense of the Alliance. It is our way of saying thank you, the very least we can do to repay such servitude and devotion."

"Thank you, Lorne. I may take the Alliance up on that offer."

The door opened, and Eston stepped out, looking up at the giant skyscraper where he had half a floor to himself. His assistant grabbed his bags, "Whenever you're ready, Sir. I will lead you up to your apartment." He stood in the elevator as it rocketed up to his floor. His assistant spoke again, "Sir, is there anything that we can obtain for you tonight? There are no limits, Sir."

Eston looked up at the digital numbers on the elevator as it approached his floor and spoke, "Yes, there is actually. Get me the best-aged whisky you can find along with some sleeping pills for me tonight. I wish to feel refreshed when I awake to-morrow. Also, tell no one to disturb me, till at least evening."

He walked into his apartment while taking off his clothes. He took a quick shower, threw on a pair of boxers, and brushed his hair. He looked at his tired, worn eyes and whispered to himself. "If I can't manage a good night's sleep on my own, I will force it upon myself."

As if on cue, a knock on the door rang out, and as he opened the door, he noticed a young, thin blonde. "Sorry, Miss," he said, blushing. "I didn't expect a young gal to be bringing me what I need. Let me grab some clothes." Without speaking, the lady walked into his apartment, putting the whisky on the end table and a bottle of sleeping pills on the side. She poured him a cup of whisky, filling it to the brim, while Eston rushed for a pair of pants.

She picked up the cup of whisky and walked over to him, placing it into his hand while gently stroking hers across his chest. "Drink up, Mr. Tavernier, for I am here to help you sleep."

Eston took a long, deep, and slow drink, squeezing his eyes tight as he felt the liquor run down his throat. "You brought me what I need, thank you. You are now free to go."

The woman spoke again, this time putting her arms around him. "Yes, I did, but you do not realize all of what you need. Tonight, I am exactly what you need." She took a step back and started undoing her shirt as he took another long drink. He started to feel the smooth aged whisky take its effect upon his body, numbing his mind and his senses as he gazed upon her naked and slender form in front of him.

"Screw it. I don't care anymore." He muttered under his breath.

She slowly walked to the door and closed it. "You won't care about anything by the time I am done with you."

CHAPTER EIGHTEEN

D amian and Coretheen gazed upon their old city, the city where they first met. She held Damian's hand tight within hers while peering upon the crumbling skyscrapers.

"Coretheen, there will always be one thing I will thank this city for. It has lead me to you, and through you, the sky seems a little bluer, the water a little clearer, and the air a little cleaner. You are the fresh breath I needed in my life."

She looked up at Damian, "Then let us not delay to the city that has given us each other, even in the darkest of places you once told me a gem can be found. This city is our gem because it gave us each other."

The sun held high above them as they entered the streets. Coretheen's ears perked up as she stopped walking. Damian turning around, "My Lady, is something wrong?" Then he too heard the song of the falcon singing across the land. He let loose a high-pitched whistle while stretching out his hand to the sky. Within a few moments, the falcon dived towards his arm, landing with swiftness and speed.

Untying the note from its leg, he read it as she peered over his shoulder. "Convene where metal crosses metal, and the current of life still flows. Convene when the predators attack their prey and approach in silence, bearing the symbol of freedom." Coretheen looked puzzled. He shrugged his shoulders and stated, "Kamon is apparently up to his old fun again. Simply stated, meet at the old warehouses and railroad system down by the river, at night, bearing the symbol of the Dicade." He raised his hand after marking an "X" on the paper and released the falcon back into the sky. Coretheen gazed upon the bird as it began its ascent into the clouds, disappearing as quickly as it had appeared.

Putting his hand above his eyes, Damian gazed up at the sun. "It seems there is still a few hours before the sun will set; let us make our way to the old library, so we can inform the runners. They at least deserve to hear the news that I have returned to the city in one piece."

They started their walk towards the library; every few blocks noticing both men and women hiding, trying to conceal themselves from any soul that was visible. "My Lady, soon, the day will come that we will be able to police the streets peacefully. We will be able to protect all in our cities from the evil that lurks in the day and abolish the evil that hides within the night. Soon, all will be able to move freely as they once had. It will not be perfect, but at least the fear of becoming one's prey will be lifted from their shoulders, and only the burden of receiving sustenance and work will remain."

"That is a dream I cannot wait to see unfold." Coretheen grabbed Damien's hands tightly, "When I first met you, I never knew that safety was one of the greatest comforts in the world. I never knew what true peace was, what true happiness could be." She turned his head toward hers, giving him a quick kiss, then continued to walk forward without hesitating for even a single moment. Damian stood still looking up into the sky as she snickered, "Well, my knight, what are you waiting for, me to carry you?"

Damian laughed, briefly rubbing the back of his head. "What can you expect when such a beautiful lady gives you a gift, such as that? My Lady, at times, you make it hard to walk, let alone breathe just a single breath without you."

"I guess you'll just have to get used to it because I am not stopping any time soon." She joyfully threatened, walking back, grabbing his hand.

"That, my Lady, I can definitely live with."

After an hour of walking, Coretheen's gaze rested upon the old library, in which hundreds of ancient vines clung to the side of the building, piercing into the cracks of the walls. She mused, "At least the cracks serve a purpose."

Damian entered the building, then walked into the middle of the room. The air was still as the sun shined brightly through the skylight above them. The light refracted off of the glass, acting as a prism, creating small specks of rainbows that danced all around them. Damian reached out his hand, offering it to Coretheen. As she walked towards the center, his voice reverberated within the air. "Dicade, the strength of the many, above the few." The runners once again appeared around them, stepping out from the pillars that held the building strong.

"Sir, we are glad to have you back." Jacob stepped towards Damian smiling, "We knew you wouldn't abandon us, though we had no idea how long it would take you to return, and honestly, your arrival is much sooner than expected."

"I am here in front of you again, though once again, I do not bear good news. I am here to inform you that there has been another attack on one of our fronts. This attack weakened our forces to the west. New plans are being formulated against the Alliance, and for the time being, I want you to converge forces. It may soon be time to act, draw up all the trained forces in the area, till more orders are delivered."

"Sir, does this mean that we will soon take this city? Does this mean that the cascade that will lead to the decay of the Alliance is at hand?"

"Honestly, Jacob," he sighed, "I am not sure the Dicade are quite ready for this advancement, but if this decision is made between the President and me, we must be ready to move quickly. How is the current morale, Jacob?"

Straightening his posture, he proudly confessed. "It is better than it has been in years, Sir. The resistance is strong, and with your return, we will be even more invigorated. We are all itching to finally act and protect those that are victims; to unleash our fury upon those that claim our servitude."

"Good, Jacob, glad to hear it. Let us all hope that our dream can soon be unleashed upon the might of the Alliance. Though let us not act too hasty. This is the first city we will reclaim. With this city, we will state to the world that the nation of old is back and will rise as it once was."

Coretheen eyed the men standing next to the columns, noticing all eyes were now on her, the women standing next to their leader.

He glanced at Coretheen, seeing her anxiety and hesitation build. "This is Coretheen Nerites," Damian's voice boomed, "a new recruit who freely joined our ranks and is now a proud member. I am sure her unique skillset will soon unfold, providing us with great advancement."

He pulled out a chain and leaned forward, placing it around her neck.

Picking up the metal, she traced the engraved symbol with her fingers as Damian continued to speak. "Miss Nerites, if you accept, we will welcome you into our ranks, and you will be our equal, just as I am equal to all of you. For we all choose to serve this cause as we see fit, to release this world from those who are willing to steal one's mind and one's freedom." They gazed upon her, her clothes dancing with rainbows from above. "Well, Miss Nerites, we the Dicade, await your response."

Hesitating yet again, she looked around her. "I, Coretheen Nerites, am honored with this invitation bestowed upon me. I gratefully accept the request, and I promise to lay my life on the line for the Dicade, as they have risked their lives for me in these dark times. There is no greater cause than I can imagine than delivering this world from the darkness that consumes it. Although I am weak, I will fight by your side and give any use that I have in my body, for I am proud to be all of your equals, the true light in this world." The men, one by one, came up to Coretheen and shook her hand.

She raised her tremoring voice. "Thank you for your service, your faith, and your support for the brighter future we all long for, that we all hold close to our hearts."

"We are entering the planning phase," Damian whispered to Jacob, "and I want you to be my prime runner. If you need to contact me, we will be at the warehouses near the old railroad tracks by the river. I want you to come every night, before dawn, to see if we have any new messages that need to be delivered across the land. Make sure your symbol is visible, so no resistance is met. Only come at night, alone, make sure no one is following you. Change the route you take every evening and never take the same route twice." Jacob nodded and started to turn as Damian grabbed his arm, "Jacob, I trust you with the whole might of the Dicade, with the last light we have in all of our eyes, I place our faith in you."

Without saying anything to Damian, Jacob nodded once again, then turned and walked up to Coretheen. "Coretheen, it is a pleasure to have you join our ranks, and I look forward to seeing you again in the future."

The light of the sun faded, concealed by the clouds on the horizon, as the men began to depart. Damian looked at Coretheen, "The sun is setting. Let us not delay. For as the sun sets, the risk of a negative encounter increases, and tonight we do not have time for such inconveniences."

The sun's edges went black, and the stale night air became thick with the stench of rot. Coretheen grabbed Damian close to her as the darkening sky filled with screams. She closed her eyes, remembering how those screams once belonged to her too.

"There is no reason to be afraid. No harm will come to you on this night. Sadly, I cannot say that about the others." He comforted. "The past is behind us, and the future is what holds the hope of this city. We will not falter. And soon, the screams of the innocent will be replaced with the screams of those who do them harm."

They walked hand in hand near the old railways as the river rustled a few hundred yards away. Behind an old building, a man approached, and the click of a shotgun could be heard, followed by a well-formed voice declaring, "State your purpose."

"We mean no harm, for we are part of the strength that will soon become many. Part of those who go against the ones who enslave us." Damian and Coretheen turned as the man peered at the symbol stretched across Coretheen's neck. His eyes soon rested upon Damian's cane.

"We welcome you, Sir, please follow me." The man sternly spoke. Damian grabbed her hand as they were lead to a warehouse only a short distance away. The man gestured them to enter as the door slowly creaked open.

Coretheen walked ahead of Damian as he quietly spoke to the man. "Notify the men that I will have a runner approach before dawn, every night, starting to-morrow. He is not to be harmed and has permission to enter freely." The man nodded and disappeared back into the dark.

They entered the warehouse and were welcomed with the warm smile of a friend.

"Damian! I am glad you arrived safely. We have al-most compounded all the information we need; Mr.

Pikon is still yet to arrive." Damian looked around as at least fifty men were scurrying to get the area prepared.

"I see this area is well defended, Kamon." He smiled as they both grabbed each other's wrists, shaking one another's arms.

Kamon continued, "And Coretheen, it is a pleasure to see you bear our symbol. I welcome you, and I am glad that we have you in our ranks."

"I am glad to see you too, Kamon," she blushed, "but I didn't forget your last promise either."

"Aww, come on, Miss," Kamon snickered, "I was hoping you would have forgotten that by now."

"I will never forget that promise," she said, giving him a sly smirk, "and actually, I think the dishes are still there waiting for you, Kamon."

"And you, my friend from old," Kamon glanced over at Damian, "I thought you're supposed to stick up for me. Heck, we protected each other from many foes of the past, and here I am being bullied by a woman, and you won't even come to my rescue."

"Now, Kamon," Damian retorted, "if you can't handle a young lady's wrath, I don't think you will make it much longer in this world."

The three of them laughed as Kamon admitted, "I guess you're right, as usual. We better get some rest, for as soon as Pikon gets here, there will hardly be time to breathe, let alone sit. There are a couple of cots over on the west side of the building you can close your eyes on."

He gave a slight bow, "We are much obliged, as usual, Kamon, thank you."

Damian and Coretheen laid down in a cot next to each other. He reached over, grabbing her hand in his, and closed his eyes as the cool night air took him.

CHAPTER NINETEEN

Eston awoke with the afternoon sun beating upon his back. He rolled over to see what time it was and noticed the young naked woman lying next to him. He looked upon her slender body, her tanned skin until his eyes rested upon her face. His chest tightened as if there was a snake wrapping itself around his heart, squeezing, slowly strangling it, until there was no longer blood coursing through his veins. She couldn't have been more than sixteen years old. He rushed to the bathroom, quickly getting dressed as the room began to spin.

Bending over the sink, he squeezed the counter as hard as he could, attempting to stop his hands from trembling. His face alive with anger, he looked up at the mirror and held back his tears while whispering, "They sent me a child? The Alliance sent me a child? How could I have not seen it yesterday? How could I have been so clouded?" Hearing footsteps behind him, he turned, once again peering at the naked girl before him.

She walked up behind him and put her arms around him. "I told you I was just what you needed. Didn't you have a good time last night?" He stiffened as she continued, "You could arrange to make this a nightly occurrence. Wouldn't that be nice?"

He pushed himself off the sink and grabbed her hands, screaming, "How could you? How could I do this?"

She stopped speaking, taken aback by the man before her; she squinted, seeing something she hadn't seen her entire life.

"You're just a child! How can you live your life like this? How can you let yourself be used as others wish? How can you just be a…" Eston stopped as he was about to say, a tool…

Holding his breath, he knew he had no right to finish that sentence after what he had just done for the Alliance. He, too, was just their tool, to be used as they deemed right. He looked down upon the ground, letting go of her wrists as his hands dropped to his side.

She looked up at the man before her, with a new gleam in her eye. "I see something rare in you, Mr.

Tavernier. Something I never expected to see in those serving under the Alliance. I see goodness."

"If you knew me better, you would never say that." Eston tightly closed his eyes, attempting to hold back his tears.

"You're wrong!" She exclaimed. "For two years now, I have been used for this reason. I was found in the scum of the streets and sold to the Alliance for this very purpose. I am not the only one, either. To be honest, most nights aren't too bad. Better than the streets, at least. Here I get food; I get clean water and things many others would never get out there. Back then, I feared daily for my life, and as I feared," she hesitated and took a deep gulp, forcing herself to continue as she closed her eyes, remembering the past. "And as I feared, many unspeakable acts took part against my body." She raised her hand to Eston's face, "Though you showed me this morning that despite a lack of control for a moment in time, your true self still leaks through under the mask you're wearing. I know one day, my use will end for the Alliance, and I will be cast aside as if broken, but till then, I must continue. I must continue forward, for what other choice do I have?" She slowly walked back to the bedroom and started getting dressed.

Before the door closed to his apartment, he heard her voice drift to him, "I owe you my thanks, Eston, for my hope may one day return. That is if there were more people like you within this twisted world." With those words, the door closed, and Eston bent over the sink watching his tears slowly find their way to the drain.

His mind shot back to reality as a knock on his door resonated through his many rooms. He quickly looked up, noticing the dried tears on his face. Wiping them off, he moved out of the bathroom, seeing that the sun was already setting. After making sure he was presentable, he walked to the door and opened it as his heart sank.

Immediately straightening his spine, Eston squared his shoulders and fixed his tie. "How can I serve the Alliance today?" His eyes glanced down at the one before him, the one who bore the pin from the Guardians of the Shadows.

"The Alliance requires your presence tonight, immediately." Eston gave the man before him a quick nod and followed him to the car waiting below.

He sat down in the back of the limo as the windows became tinted once again, disrupting his vision of the outside world. Though this time, there was a mass next to him no one could ignore, and it came with a giant slap on his back.

"Eston, my boy! How was last night? Good, ehh?"

Taking a deep breath, he forced a hollow smile upon his face. "Lorne, last night was divine. It was the rest I needed."

"You deserved it, that's for sure. As far as the Alliance is concerned, you can have whatever you want. That is, as long as you keep up this streak, you're on. That special gift last night, I picked it out just for you, Eston. I knew you would like it."

Eston watched as Lorne started to laugh. He watched his fat as it pounded down against his thighs with each breath he took. He swore he could feel the suspension of the car breaking with each exhale he made.

"My boy, I had the pleasure of that young jewel too. I have never gazed upon something so full of youth and so very fit. Mmmmm, she is definitely one of my favorites."

He stopped moving, imagining the child underneath him. He wondered how the poor girl survived a night with a man like Lorne. His eyes became sad as he forced another smile on his face, followed by a giggle, masking his grief for the young girl. Lorne slapped him on the back again as Eston clenched his teeth to keep his irritation from showing, "Ahhh, Eston, you got to enjoy the fine things in life, and she is definitely fine."

Amusing himself, he pondered, "I am shocked that with a man as great as you are, that she didn't suffocate under your immense mass."

"What was that, my boy?" Lorne paused.

He opened his mouth, but before he could speak, Lorne continued without grasping what he had said. "My boy, that is what separates us from those uncivil rats we call civilians out there. We enjoy the fine things, and they don't have the aptitude to comprehend them."

He sighed in relief as Lorne's rambling for once sided in his favor. The car began to roll to a stop, and the windows once again became clear, allowing him to see the tunnel where his nightmare first started. He gazed towards the door, noticing Ashling standing in its way with a sly smile plastered across his face, and on either side of him, two guards stood, bearing the pin of the Guardians.

"On behalf of the eight, I welcome you back into the shadows. Let us not delay, for today; you do not wait on us. For on this day, we have been waiting for you." Ashling turned, walking through the dark doorway.

Entering the room, he peered at the screens surrounding him, already lit with the shadowy figures. The iron tree in the middle of the room started to spin as its roots stretched out of the floor.

The eight silhouettes spoke in unison, their voices becoming as one. "We the eight, in accordance with our laws, have summoned you here to bear the fruit of the nations under the Alliance." The trees' roots started to rotate slowly, further exposing themselves out of the shimmering marble floor as the stone crumbled before him.

His heart fluttered and squirreled within his chest as he looked towards a light being emitted from one of the blossoming buds of the iron tree—a light he had never before seen—a light like no other. For as this light was emitted, the room did not become lighter. It became darker. This light appeared to engulf all the energy around him. Leaning forward, he noticed that it was no light at all, but the opposite. This source consumed light; it was but a swirling vortex of blackness that emanated true darkness from its core. He watched its swirl, its dance, drawing in the light, trapping it, and then extinguishing it from existence.

He raised his line of sight as the lights began to flicker, then dim into an unnatural twilight. The shadows on the screen now appeared as but white silhouettes of the true images of their true selves. He turned his head towards Ashling and noticed his eyes were glowing white, causing his spine to reverberate all the way to his soul.

The eight Guardian's voices roared, "Reach forward Eston Tavernier, reach into the darkness and claim the Alliance's gift." Eston looked at his hand, slowly moving it forward, reaching toward one of the dark vortexes that blossomed from the tree before him. As his hand approached it, the vortex broke apart and slowly swirled up his arm to his eyes. He wrenched his head back and grabbed at his eyes as pain rippled throughout his entire body.

Falling to his knees, he heard Ashling's voice gently calling forward. "Relax Eston, relax my child, for we are merely providing you with the true sight of the Alliance."

As the pain slowly subsided, he opened his eyes and gazed around the chamber. Ashling's beaming white eyes remained. As for the screens, they once again showed only images of shadows before him.

The trees' roots slowly began their retreat back into the marble floor as Ashling began to explain. "We have implanted genetically modified cells into your eyes, made specifically for you. They are connected to the Guardian's computers through a unique wireless signal that they generate independently. You may now access its mainframe, on a moment's notice Eston. Attached to this gift of ultimate knowledge, you can now see those bearing the mark of the Guardians."

Eston looked towards Lorne as he saw something under his skin swirling where his heart was supposed to be. No, it wasn't his heart, but around his heart. Peering closer, he watched as black roots slowly weaved themselves around Lorne's soul. He quickly looked down upon his own chest and grabbed at his shirt, as the same black roots were entwined around his very own heart, around his very own soul.

Ashling started to laugh as he attempted to soothe him. "My Eston, my child, do not worry; it will not harm you. For it is only the symbol we all bear as we move forward across this world we claim. No harm will occur to you, for you are a true patron of this society, a true patron of the Alliance."

Taking a deep breath, Eston closed his eyes, but instead of the darkness he wished for, he saw hundreds of blinking screens. He opened his eyes quickly as Ashling continued, "In time, you will learn how to navigate it. Though, that is something you must learn on your own as your cells adapt to the newly imprinted genetic code."

Regaining his composure, Eston gradually stood up, his voice breaking as he spoke. "I thank those before me for the gift and trust that I have been imprinted with."

"Under the Guardians of the Shadows, a new name will be given to you." Ashling revealed, "Your gift is the gift of sight. You will now be called Oculi Tenebrarum, known to the Guardians as the eyes of darkness. Your trial of shadows is now complete, as we, the eight, have embraced you under our wings."

"We the eight, welcome you, Oculi Tenebrarum, our newly founded General of the Shadows."

Eston walked to the center of the room, gazing up at the iron tree, "With my body, with my mind, I will learn and use this gift you have given me to pierce through all things, both in the light and within the darkness. I will be the air beneath the wings that protect me. Lifting the Alliance a little higher with each movement I make."

With another smile, Ashling nodded towards him in approval.

Eston felt as if all the light in the world had been absorbed by the Alliance. He never grasped how far the Alliance's technology had grown and what they were truly capable of, till just now.

"Thank you, Eston. Now let us advance to other avenues that still require our attention."

CHAPTER TWENTY

Coretheen gazed up at the peaceful night sky. A red hue stretched across where the sun had set, outlining the decaying city in the color of blood. She climbed the stairs to the top of the old warehouse and looked down upon the river as the thick black water flowed through the night. Every once and a while, she would notice a small swirl in the river reflecting the blood scorched sky, only to vanish as the deep red was pulled underneath the water's surface a moment later.

Her hair started to blow across her thin, stretched face as a harsh wind pounded her body. The water's current rushed forward as a chill swept throughout her, causing her to clench her arms tightly across her chest.

Peering up to the sky, profuse ominous clouds began to form, consuming the moon, leaving only a faint glow of light left over the river. A loud screech pierced her ears, echoing throughout the city as a steel foundation collapsed into the river upstream. Coretheen watched the steel structure twist and turn as it was pushed by the current.

Closing her eyes, she took a deep breath and whispered, "Even the foundation of this once great city is crumbling under the force of the Alliance." The sound of the rushing river faded, and she opened her eyes as the wind against her cheeks slowed, then dissipated completely. Pale light from the moon shone through, leaving her imagination to only guess what was hiding within the shadows. The black water stood motionless as if being replaced by obsidian glass that had been poured into the river. She looked up at where the moon had been hiding, as it cast an ominous midnight green upon the world around her.

The rooftop began to vibrate as she returned her gaze to the water. The entire rivers' surface appeared as if dark molten metal was coming to a slow boil. The dense liquid slowly turned as drops began to break free, stretching into the air, only to fall back into the abyss of the river seconds later. Yet, the only sound she could hear was that of her own heart pounding within her ears as she exhaled into the silent scene before her.

She closed her eyes tightly and opened them again. Staring in disbelief as hundreds and thousands of drops were gently drifting into the air, slowly floating towards the sky, defying gravity itself. The riverbed began to recede, revealing what hid beneath its surface.

Squinting, she peered closer as a smoothly rounded outline slowly began to unveil itself within the liquid. Hundreds, no thousands of similar shapes became exposed as more drops rose to the sky. Gazing towards the pale white objects below her, Coretheen watched in horror, falling backward as the realization of what was underneath her hit. She let out a loud scream as she began to sob, "There's so many, so many poor souls, so many bones that once bore hope; that once breathed fresh air."

Her mouth went agape as she screamed in terror again, "Its, it's not water at all, it's, it's all blood, so much blood!"

With a thunderous crash, millions of gallons of blood fell from the sky from where it had been suspended within the air, landing back upon the corpses below. Once again concealing their existence from the world around them.

In the shadows behind her, she sensed a man standing just out of sight. Coretheen turned on her knees as the outline of his body slowly began to become visible. She stared at his face, consumed with shadows—seeing only his mouth move—unable to hear what he was saying.

She looked down at her hands as they shook uncontrollably. Her eyes stuck wide open in fear, drying from the dense night's air.

The man before her whispered again. His voice was finally cutting through the scorching heat. "Be quiet young lady, and listen, for how can you hear if you do not listen? How can you act if you cannot see? How can you feel if you cannot hear the pleas of those around you? Be quiet young lady and listen, for the dead are crying out to you. Who will answer their cries? Be quiet young lady and listen, for the dead are crying out to you."

Coretheen heard a loud screech and turned her head as the steel structure scraped against the seawall. She quickly looked to where the man was standing, now nothing but another shadow in the night. She placed her hand on her rapidly beating heart, looking at the water as the current was now rushing once again. She raised her gaze to the moon, now shining its light down upon the city. The clouds were now in the distance, and the red hue that once dominated the city had receded with the sun. She blinked, her eyes still sore from being wedged open, and then turned to look back at where the man had been standing one last time.

With a longing glance towards the river, she rose up and started to climb down the stairs. As she reached the bottom of the stairs, she gave the river one long last look, "Was it real? Was it a dream? No matter if it was or wasn't, I will hear their cries. I will listen to their suffering, and I will answer them with all the strength I have." Coretheen raised her shaking hand in front of her eyes, clenching her hand into a fist as hard as she could.

CHAPTER TWENTY-ONE

Kamon slammed a book of files down upon the table as Coretheen walked back into the warehouse. "We have been here for almost a week." Now grunting with anger, "Page by page, book by book, document by document, what was the point of coming back into this decrepit city if we can't even figure out how to solve the problem?" Kamon continued to mumble under his breath, "Noo, walk to a secret place for a week, then walk back. Why did we even bother leaving that beautiful place? I was enjoying my time, but nooo, the Alliance had to destroy a city and go ruin it all. First, the compound, then Seattle, what's next? So here we are stuck in this blasted city of ruins, not even gaining an inch of ground."

Damian's face lit up as he peered at Coretheen, giving him a reason to ignore Kamon as he ranted like an insane man. "Ahh, you have returned, my Lady. Please come and rest."

Walking over to the table, Cortheen's eyes settled upon the documents spread out across it. Curiously looking closer upon them, she saw numerous forms, transcriptions, invoices, and shipping reports on the national lines.

"Do you think we will be able to manage Damian?" Pikon questioned. "We are already behind our needed budget, and our businesses can no longer falsify their documents and margins to allow a surplus of income. Not only that, it is becoming increasingly harder for them to hide under false tenses from the coalition, and they are starting to come under review. Many are being decommissioned as productivity and profits have decreased under the heavy taxes. The Alliance's new agenda is harshly hitting those few companies not run by the coalition—even those that resemble a slave encampment can't keep up with the high demand."

Coretheen interjected while grabbing a piece of bread off Damian's plate as he briefly smiled at her. "Well, I had some experience with my dad's business when I was a kid. I even attended university for the purpose of taking it over one day. I could take a look at it if you don't mind. Who knows, a fresh set of eyes could be of some use."

"Young girl, before we waste our time, can you proclaim your general idea?" An elderly man glaring over the documents queried.

Damian returned the glare, although his was not directed towards the documents on the table but at the man above them. "That is not the way a gentleman would inquire, nor is it a polite inquiry in itself."

"No, it's ok, really." Coretheen defended. "Let's see. If you transfer all of your tangible income to buy materials and finish your weapon quota before the businesses are decommissioned, then you could ship the materials to the manufactures to increase production covertly. This would be a much more proficient method. In my opinion, having them produce a minimal quantity of excess weapons while falsifying their documents and shipping reports is a slow way to compile anything. It is much better to grasp what each individual company is good at and assist them in acquiring materials to produce their products, in turn expediting the desired outcome."

Kamon, whose tensions were still running high, sarcastically snipped. "Ohh, yes, Damian's dear lady, you make it seem like it is that simple. Even if it were, it wouldn't and couldn't solve our problems." Kamon gestured his hand toward the table, "Though if you think you can manage, be my guest. Dig through this vast pile of paper and make money appear from nowhere."

Damian's gaze rested upon Pikon, requesting permission.

Looking upon Damian's eyes, Pikon sighed, noticing the urgency within them. "I guess it couldn't hurt; someone go get the rest of the records and time tables for this young lady."

Coretheen took a deep breath and exhaled while staring into Damian's eyes. Those calm blue eyes of his spoke to her. They egged her on. Those quiet eyes had faith in her, and those very eyes who had saved her in the past now grasped at her soul. As their eyes became locked upon one another, there was no need for him to speak, for she knew he had confidence in her without him uttering a single word. She could see in those eyes that he trusted her. She knew that her chance had presented itself, and it was time for her to grasp that very chance.

Taking one more long, slow, and deep breath, she breathed out any doubts. Her anxiety faded, allowing her mind to relax, allowing her mind to focus on the task at hand. Calmness set in, and as her mind cleared, she thought to herself, "This is how Damian must feel before he engages a foe, allowing his mind to use all available knowledge at hand."

Kamon soon returned, laying the records out on the table. They both watched with inspiration as the young lady pulled up account after account, scribbling numbers down on pieces of paper for hours. Once and a while, a hum was heard, followed by, "If we take financer sixteen D, who you'd usually use the funds for consumable goods, and transfer his funds to financer seventy-five A; eighty-three A; and one hundred eleven A, who produces food—they could give us the excess. All three have unused land, so we could have a surplus of food reaching up to ninety percent. This would allow us to cut forty percent of our current food expenses and better provide for our reserve, feeding tens of thousands more men. Of course, we would also increase the amount the Alliance would receive to avoid suspicion."

"There is so much more we could do than just that if we expanded the collaboration between all parties. Financer ninety-eight D could receive his ore from financer sixty-three O at a higher price and use financer eighteen T for the transfer, allowing them to collaborate a cost increase of a minimum of five percent. In turn, this would generate four billion a month in extra revenue to stockpile ammunition for years. We could send them soldiers over the next few months to help them mine for ore. Then have eighteen T transfer the excess ore from sixty-three O to manufacturing division twelve, under the proclaimed notion of returning empty crates. When in reality, it would be full of the extra ore they had already mined."

"The manufacturing division could use the excuse of decreased productivity, under the new Amendment, and the redistribution of their current equipment before their decommission, to explain their stall in production. This would provide for the manufacturing of eighteen thousand guns past the five thousand promised for a three-month period. At their current production level, we could expect an increase of light tanks and artillery up to thirty a month—that is, if we provided the material to allow them to operate twenty-four hours a day."

Damian's head started to drift as his eyes became heavier; he looked at the clock, knowing that the sun would already have well past risen. His head began to nod as sleep was overcoming him when she yelled, "I think that's all I can do. If all of them are willing to co-operate, I think we can improve our overall proficiency by approximately three hundred percent."

"Umm, Miss Nerites," Kamon curiously and shockingly conveyed, "there is by no means you could have freed up that much of our resources."

"Interesting, you decide to be proper now, huh?" Coretheen chuckled, "Essentially, if the financiers, manufactures, and producers approve of my plan— with the extra materials we provide them—they can increase the goods we receive. This, in turn, would free up our resources, for we will be providing them with the resources they need for their increased quota, not only to us but maybe even to the Alliance to avoid suspicion. You will no longer be wasting money buying stale food and left-over scraps to obtain what you need."

"Essentially, we are still spending 400 billion a year, but if we get the items at cost, we change that 400 billion into an estimated 1.2 trillion worth of goods, instead of just a monetary value as before. We can do all this while weakening the Alliance due to an artificially and self-adjusted increase in prices between our financers. When in truth, the increase in price across those willing to cooperate will be secretly providing us with enough reserve to start a proper resistance, though, on paper, the cost increase would appear to be real to the Alliance as they distribute their funds. The total Alliances GDP ranges roughly 110 trillion a year. We are looking at about a one percent increase to the general inflation artificially. It should go unnoticed, at least till we accumulate what we need."

"Well, Kamon, I think it's worth a try, don't you?" Damian whistled, "Heck, the progressive Alliance of Coordinated Governments yearly revenue is reported to be 75 trillion a year. Although, most of that is overhead, and the remaining usually goes to those in charge of regional districts and the house majority leader. I see it as the only way to take a grasp of what was taken from us, for the Alliance does receive almost all profits."

"I don't see any other choices," Pikon confirmed, "let us start the collaborative process. Miss Nerites, I would like you to stay and help oversee the communication between the companies that are willing to defy the Alliance. Damian, I need you to summon your men representing each one of the businesses and communicate the plan as soon as they are updated on their tasks. Keep the information disclosed at the very minimum needed to get the job done. I'll send runners out to inform them to expect a revised plan accommodating the essential advancement of our time table. How many men are in your region Damian?"

"Currently, Sir, we have 12,500 ready to mobilize here, with approximately 45,000 in reserve waiting for proper training. As of now, we can only feed an extra 1,000 men a cycle, and to complete the standard training cycle, it takes six months. Reports have been received of 25,000 trained within the east region and 100,000 in reserve. The reports are not as accurate out west Sir, most cities are fenced off, and resistance measures are barely able to hold 2,000, with only 10,000 in reserve. Between the north and south, we can prepare 14,000 to mobilize and maintain 155,000 in reserve. Shall we mobilize Sir?"

"Send a message to each Lieutenant General in every one of our cities." Pikon directed, "We will hold off mobilizing for eight more months and hold off training all of our reserves for four more months. By then, we will have enough supplies to train the reserves and to feed everyone. During those months, increase recruiting."

"Kamon, I need you to take Nerite's plan and begin collaborating with the businesses. See if it is plausible to stockpile enough food for 500,000 men, for three years, within a six-month time. See if we can create a three-month period of inflation at a rate of one percent. Then continue that falsified rate until we hit five-point six percent a year. Giving us an income of 6.16 trillion from general inflation and another 1.2 trillion in total goods, totaling 7.36 trillion. Work with all the financers and those still able to support us. Have a general rise of prices equally on all products, showing a fixed inflation across everything. Use the remaining funds to increase manufacturing production. Make sure that the Alliance is unable to put any blame on our essential financers and warn those that are not essential that a trail to their destruction may be needed. Notify them that we will provide shelter and warning prior to their decommission if this becomes necessary."

"I will contact Japan, Australia, and India," Kamon affirmed, "to see if they can spare any food, heavy artillery, or at the very least, manufacturing capabilities. I will tell them that we may finally be able to fight the Alliance from within their own nations. At the very minimum, we can create a distraction with guerilla warfare till we can claim an area to ourselves and increase manufacturing."

"Very well, Kamon, it seems a solid plan is forming. Damian, after preparations are made, we need to make a statement. It will be risky, but we need to show an act of retaliation against the Alliance to draw in new recruits. Not only will this increase our reserves, but it will pull attention off of the foreign frontlines, which will drastically increase the chance of aid. We must be successful. Kamon, I want you to collect information and potential targets we should strike. Coretheen, you are a bright girl, indeed; let us get this moving as quickly as possible. You are all dismissed." Damian smiled at Coretheen as Kamon started pilling the documents into the boxes, his excitement growing with each box he filled.

CHAPTER TWENTY-TWO

"Manus Furtim Proditione, we have summoned you here in relation to a persistently growing problem." Ashling confessed while taking a long and slow glance at one of the eight screens before him. "As of recent, it has come to our knowledge that the Dicade has spread its foundation out to the west. This being the case, their hindrance now seems to bear more weight than their use."

The one Ashling was looking at, the shadow he called Manus Furtim Proditione, replied. "There is a great general that the President of the Dicade has put his trust in. His goals are vast. His movements are quick. He calls upon the masses, and they answer him of their own accord. He moves the Dicade without my knowledge, and with such support, to interrupt him would be unwise. I do not know of all of his movements, for he commands a vast amount of his own runners in secret, to build their cause. I have learned his name, a true general and even truer leader; his name is Damian Gardge."

"Damian Gardge, is it? Well, that is an interesting name. One that I have not even heard whispered in the streets. He is truly an interesting specimen, then?"

"He is interesting, very interesting. His presence inspires hope, even into the souls that have become lost. His gaze captures one and inspires them; even I, at times, have become entranced by his demeanor, his movements, and his very presence."

"Is that so?"

"Yes, Ashling, it is. As of recent, there have been great advancements in their cause; for they have been notified of Seattle's decommission."

Ashling quickly sent Eston a glare and roared, "The Dicade's blood was spilled upon the ground, and their bones were crushed into the dirt under our very feet! I personally witnessed their full demise as Seattle was encased in steel."

"Nonetheless, a message was delivered to their leaders, and this has spurred them into action, advancing their time table immensely. Not only this, but a new face has emerged. A young lady with the name of Nerites is helping them coordinate resources. It seems her skills of structural organization could have significant repercussions on the Alliance."

Ashling put his hand to his chin as his voice drifted, "Hmmmm, Nerites, you say? That is interesting. I wonder if it is the same bloodline?"

"I thought the same, and even through all my research, I can honestly claim that I do not know. Though, what I do know is that the Dicade will pose a real threat if we allow them to grow for more than a few months, especially if those that still oppose the Alliance offer assistance."

The room grew quiet as Ashling pondered until the shadow spoke again, "I recommend advancing the eradication of those that hinder our future advancement."

"Their hindrance may indeed become more of a problem than their worth Furtim Proditione. I was hoping that we could draw out those few civilians, those few companies. And that, that certain someone whose mind seems to reign independence and freedom."

"I understand Ashling, and I felt that time was drawing close, but the risk seems too great now." His voice was rising as it echoed within the hall, "Most of our goals have been accomplished. Almost all of the citizens that would rise up against the Alliance have been revealed, thanks to the Dicade. All businesses that oppose the Alliance have been identified through their assistance to the Dicade. Those civilians that choose freedom will be destroyed as they breathe their last breath. And for those that still have free will, those we will crush and shatter, breaking that very will. Even if a few manage to live, it will not matter, for they will have no leader, which is, if any, remains at all. The last of this nation's wealth has been accumulated. We will now acquire it and use it to expand our territory, and if that certain someone is still alive…"

Ashling snarled, "That is a big if." His eyes were piercing with rage so fierce that the very screen he was staring at seemed to tremble.

"True, but even if he does decide to crawl out from beneath the dead and show his face, he too will be of no threat anymore, for he will have nothing to call upon. Even a seed cannot grow without nourishment from the dirt it has been planted in."

Ashling nodded as his eyes pierced into the darkness, "Leaving only the slaves who will obey the Alliance, even if it is to their own death. They will give up one another's life just to live a little longer in my world. In a way, this will play to our advantage. You are lucky, Eston; unknowingly, this serves the Alliance greatly, for, in turn, this will free up a great deal of our resources. We will strike on all of their known fronts. We will broadcast their demise, showing our might to the whole world. We will portray them as a mild nuisance and show them the full force of our army. The world itself will quiver under my footsteps."

"I will keep you informed as the weeks' progress."

The eight silhouettes rang out in unison, "In accordance with our laws, we the Guardians of the Shadows have reached the conclusion of this meeting."

Eston watched the screens turn black as Ashling began walking up to him, their voices still ringing within his ears.

Grasping his tie tightly within his hands, Ashling pulled Eston close, placing his mouth within his ear only to release a whisper that was viler than any scream could have been. "You are lucky, my child, for your next mistake, will not turn out this pleasant. This much, I guarantee."

"Aww, come on Ash. You know the boy did marvelously. You said so yourself." Lorne defended as Eston was thrown to the ground.

"These great nations," he rose, directing himself toward Ashling, "of the Alliance of Coordinated Governments..."

Ashling slowly twisted back towards him. His fierceness and anger growing with every word he spoke until his eyes bore deeply into Eston, who was now only a few inches away.

"The one who the shadows call Oculi Tenebrarum. Who was given the eyes of the Alliance to judge. Who was given their eyes to weigh what is right and what is wrong. Given their sight to see the world as it truly is."

"Are you insinuating that your lack of attention on your task is my fault?"

"Ash, come on," Lorne pleaded as he paced back and forth, "I'm sure the boy doesn't mean it like that."

Clutching Eston's neck within his hands, he peered into the eyes of his prey. Applying more pressure, slowly, gauging the one before him, gazing into his eyes while the seconds passed until he could feel his prey's pulse beating within those very hands. A peace filled him, as he knew Eston's oxygen supply was diminishing further with every beat of that heart.

With the last breath within his lungs, his voice broke free from their confinement as his vision blurred. "I, a dedicated piece of clay, bend to the will of the Alliance, which of course, is your will Ashling."

Releasing the grip on his neck, he took a step back, his eyes seamlessly piercing into Eston's soul.

Fighting the urge to rub his throbbing throat, Eston smiled, gave Ashling a slight bow, and acknowledged, "For you Ashling, are the essence of the Alliance itself and your will, will be done."

"My boy, why didn't you state that from the beginning." Lorne waddled to his side, slapping his hand across the back of Eston's head. "Gesh, lad, you gave me a heart attack. What? Do ya not need me anymore? Do ya not like your old Mr. Lorne? Trying to kill your dearest friend, who has done everything for you?"

Still holding his bow, Eston clarified, "I was merely stating to the king of this world. That I, his servant, for whom he's bestows this gift upon, will abide by all that he requires of me."

"That's my boy, always thinking about the Alliance." A smile returned to his thick cheeks as he began rubbing Eston's head, furiously, "See Ash! He means no harm. All a misunderstanding."

Looking at Eston, Ashling began examining him as he slowly rose to meet his eyes. "So it seems, though Eston, do not test me. These are not but games, and all tasks assigned, no matter how large or small, should be held in the highest regard. Do you understand?"

"The tasks of the Alliance are always the highest priority for any true servant of the coalition. That being said, Ashling, no greater pleasure exists than to serve."

"Lorne, return Eston to his home, for we must begin to formulate a strategy. We shall meet later tonight."

He turned around, pausing briefly, "And for you, Eston, although I do see worth in you. Although I do see intelligence and use, do not think that use cannot be replaced with another brilliant young mind, as easily as I can cast you aside."

"As I voiced before, my use is whatever you deem it." Eston assured, "For if I have no use for the Alliance, then what else is left of me?"

Ashling began walking through the door as his body was consumed by the darkness of the tunnel, his last words echoing from within the shadows, "The answer, my child, is that nothing will be left."

"Well lad, that was a little tense. What did they use to say? Ahh, that's right, that the air is so thick you could cut it with a knife. I guess we better do what he says and get you home. Shall I arrange the young lady to meet with you and relive some of that tension?" Lorne began jabbing Eston with his elbow. "Ehh, my boy? What do you say?"

"Tonight Lorne, I feel I better work on some plans that may be of some use to the Alliance. I appreciate the offer and the kind thought; but, distractions are not what I need when there is so much left to do."

Lorne put his hand on Eston's back, leading him towards the limo. "That's the spirit! Put that mind of yours towards furthering the Alliance, and maybe one day, you will be one of those shadows on the wall."

CHAPTER TWENTY-THREE

F og danced over the train tracks as the chilly night
air clutched at his body. Pushing himself harder
with every step, he jogged between the thick rails for
the frigid air encased not only him but also tormented
the Dicade soldiers.

With the fogs next swirl, the Dicade broke formation
as the figure before them became revealed. Two trained
their sights on the one approaching, adjusting their
crosshairs with his every step. The other two broke off
towards the river's edge, flanking behind the man before them. The remaining soldiers walked calmly down
the middle of the tracks, towards the approaching man.

His eyes falling upon the two men before him, he
picked up speed. Feeling his fingers grow stiff from

the cold, fiddling them within the confinements of his pocket until they clutched a small piece of cloth.

With that movement, the two soldiers rushed forward.

Despair briefly filled his eyes, his muscles worn, tired, as weakness was the only strength that remained. His eyes fell to their feet as he began tracking their movements with ease, first to the closest one. The man to his right released a wide punch. Raising his arm to guard, the second soldier rushed forward and clutched his arm tightly within his. He turned, letting the second man catch him off balance, forcing his weight upon the man still holding his arm while he ferociously kicked the other man to the ground. With that kick, the balance of the one who held him was lost, and they tumbled to the dirt below.

A deep bellowing laugh echoed within the night as the two flanking soldier's eyes fell upon the man on the ground and upon the man who grasped the Dicade flag tightly within his hand.

"I am the personal runner of Damian." He rose, speaking as he straightened the fabric between his hands, "I request an audience with him immediately." Jacob wiped the dirt off of his clothes and offered his hand to the man he fell upon.

"Kid, you definitely got some moves." The man on the ground grabbed Jacob's hand within his, confessing, "They almost remind me of Damian's, though still a little sloppy."

"Or," he mused, "are you just getting a little lazy being stuck on patrol duty?"

"That could be a possibility, but your observation skills are mediocre at best."

"How's that?" Jacob clarified, "I saw both of your men flanking. Didn't you notice my hand on your gun when I fell?"

"Yea, and didn't you notice the two snipers sighting your head within their crosshairs?"

Jacob looked at the ground shyly.

"Yeah, that's what I thought. You're a runner, and runners are supposed to be a pro at reconnaissance, even if this area is under our control for the moment."

The men guided Jacob down the tracks as he scanned the area. Eyeing the warehouses ahead of him, he started spotting snipers, counting a minimum of fifteen. He noticed many men bearing the Dicade symbol in the guise of the homeless and the hungry, which wasn't far from the truth. He stopped counting after he reached fifty.

The gates to the rusting warehouse screeched open as he gazed upon the one who had personally found him many years ago. The one who brought him out of the darkness, Damian Gardge. The four men escorting Jacob broke formation, returning the way they came from, ensuring that all who ventured into the area were discouraged from advancing.

"Jacob, I have been expecting you, and I welcome you. I apologize, but the time is once again urgent, as there is much to be done. The time for us to act is here. It is time for us to draw up our forces, for we are now ready to begin their armament. The coordination between all our supporters is essential. This task, I grant to you. Coretheen has created a different message for each and every one of our supporters. The messages have to be delivered quickly and secretly. Not one can be missed, for if not all comply, our plan will be seen by the Alliance who watches from above. So, I ask you to collect your best runners and have each one of them deliver their package and return it with their company's seal. You may use ATV's and any gas that is required for these missions. Time is the issue here, not resources. For, in this case, any time that is lost, ensures that resources are lost."

Jacob's eyes reached past Damian and fell upon a lady holding a box far too large for her arm span.

"Hi Jacob, it is nice to see you again. I am sad to say I got a large load for you, but both Damian and I agree this will be the safest and quickest way." She explained.

His mouth hung open as Damian continued, "We must collaborate between all of our supporters. This is the final step before we strike and a very necessary one."

"Yes, of course," Jacob acknowledged, "that's not it at all, Sir, for I am honored to be placed in such a high position of trust."

"There is one envelope for each runner. Each envelope is to be delivered with the corresponding list." Jacob peered at the envelopes, noticing a number on each one. "This list will tell you where each envelope will be delivered, based on the numbers you see on the outside. Each runner will deliver their message to our allies. Our allies will use their book cipher to decode the message, and they will follow the directions precisely. Jacob, you will use your own book cipher to decode the list we are giving you. Each code is unique and ensures that you do not send a runner to the wrong area. Upon delivery and decoding, ensure that each runner receives the mark of approval before they return. Do you understand, Jacob?"

Silence filled him, as all he could manage was a single nod.

"Now, the hard part. Jacob, this task has to be accomplished within two weeks. If needed, have the runners send confirmation by falcon."

Taking the large box, Jacob no longer hesitated, determination rising in his voice. "I will not delay, Sir, and I will report back to you in no longer than two weeks from tomorrow."

"I am glad to hear it. I will not wish you luck because luck is based on chance. I will not wish you anything, Jacob, because wishing is a measurement of uncertainty. And I have no uncertainty, for I know this task will be accomplished through you. Depart with speed and stealth against the prying eyes of the Alliance."

With those words, Jacob turned as four members of the Dicade surrounded him and ran off into the night's thick air.

CHAPTER TWENTY-FOUR

Closing his eyes, Eston looked upon the Alliance of Coordinated Government's banner. The capital swayed in the back with faded stars and striped lines over the buildings. One star for each nation under the Alliance, and in the middle, he saw a single blinking line.

He opened his eyes and yawned, "How am I supposed to sleep if every time I close my eyes, the only thing I see is those who I'm supposed to worship?" He got up and started pacing in a circle around his apartment, complaining to himself. "It has been four days since I got this so-called gift." Putting his fingers up into the air, making quotation marks, "And yet, this glorious gift continues to deprive me of the sleep I need just to function. Does the Alliance expect me to be able to think without sleep? Apparently, sleep is a luxury; they do not even allow their servants to acquire. Heck, this thing should have come with a manual."

He fell down onto his bed, "I wonder if the fat one has some unique property that the Guardians gave him?" Eston started to laugh, "Of course they did. They gave him an enlarged stomach that can consume and digest nutrition faster than the Alliance spreads across this world."

Eston closed his eyes. His thoughts were straying to the first time he saw the congressional buildings. At that time, the sights he gazed upon seemed impossible—beyond his reach; now that he was here, it lacked the luster he had once envisioned. He felt a small tug behind his eyes, pulling them back. He focused on this weird sensation as he grumbled, "Great! Now they have gone and screwed something up inside my head."

He began to hold his breath as the tugging slowly transformed into pressure; he could feel the blood pulsing throughout his eyes with every beat of his heart. Suddenly the room went black as he was cast into the darkness, unable to see anything, not even the blinking line.

The pressure continued to build until images began to flash, flashing as fast as lightning striking the ground. His mind raced as his pulse seemed to become faster with every second that passed. In between each and every beat of his heart, the images became clearer, more consistent, till he was able to make out the capital buildings he was thinking about less than a minute ago. Eston relaxed, and the banner of the Alliance returned. He forced himself to concentrate on his heartbeat. He forced himself to feel the blood rushing through his eyes. He concentrated on that pressure, the pressure building within his head until the feeling his eyes were going to be pushed out of their sockets was the only feeling that remained.

His mind strayed to the flickering screens the night he received this nuisance from the Guardians. Instantly profiles came into view, each with a code name like he himself had received. He pictured Lorne as his profile was immediately displayed. He read on how Lorne found him. How Lorne tutored him in aspects of the Alliance and how Lorne recommended him as a representative. He could see all those Lorne had brought into the Alliance, each as impressive as the last, with only a few that had been accepted into the Guardians.

Eston thought about himself as his own file quickly appeared. He read through his encounters, his missions, and the decommissioning of Seattle. He read about his swiftness, his strategical readiness, along with Ashling's statement of how he had never seen anyone use the Alliance's capabilities with such precision and insight. The Alliance had never advanced a member of

its ranks as quickly as Eston had risen, since its formation, granting Eston the title of Brigadier General.

Now almost becoming second nature, he thought
about Ashling, and immediately his profile was opened.
He spoke out loud after releasing a sharp laugh. "Ha,
so your name eludes even the Guardians Ashling?" To
his surprise, the only thing under Ashling's file was the
speaker and true leader of the Alliance of Coordinated
Governments. Eston opened his eyes, looking at the
room in front of him. "A gift indeed, imagining a face,
thinking of a name, and receiving instant results." He
turned to look at his clock, "Only a few minutes, huh? I
must have read at least fifty pages; my brain apparently
can react quicker than my eyes can." Then he threw
himself back, falling onto his bed, as a sense of euphoria
erupted within him.

Closing his eyes again, he began to dive into the
files of the Dicade, first pulling up their President.
Kamon, President of the Dicade, and Pikon, the director of all military forces. He smiled. "Well, I see the
President of the Dicade has a huge history of education
ranging from Stanford, Oxford, and MIT for applied
mathematics. Also, having both doctorates in law and
psychology; now that is a deadly combination indeed."
He continued, "Pikon, you are the true muscle of the
movement, with a history of military experiences at Fort
Leavenworth and a doctorate in computer engineering,
programming, and philosophy. No wonder why the

Dicade forces are so rigid, allowing them to maneuver secretly and efficiently. They do have a background brewed for destruction."

"What was that last name?" Suddenly the file opened up, "That's right, Damian Gardge. Damian Gardge, General of the Dicade, has a vast number of independent runners and army personal that answer only to him. Helped form the underlying network of the Dicade, whose movements are unknown even to the Alliance. It is considered one of the biggest growth factors of the Dicade, expanding their network and resistance in secret, under the premise that the fewer people who know about the underground network, the better they are protected, until their day of mobilization." Eston continued reading. "Damian Gardge is considered a key aspect of the strategy of the Dicade. History unknown to the Alliance."

Exclaiming as wonder-filled him, "Well, this one is interesting, not much on him at all. Even to the vast eyes of the Alliance, this one remains an unknown card, hiding within the dealer's hand."

A low pitch ring rang out next to him. "I can only guess who that would be, especially at this time of night." The images began to flicker again as his phone's home screen became visible with the word Lorne on it. "I can even connect to my wireless devices without lifting a finger! Controlling it as if it were a part of my body, another extremity in which I govern." Eston looked at the green button that read answer, turning on his phone's speaker.

Immediately he heard Lorne's voice coming from his phone still sitting on his desk. "My boy, great news! The time has come for your assistance. Time to show Ashling what I have always seen in you. Time to wash away any doubts that he has in you. Washing them away as quickly as one would swallow cheap whisky." Lorne laughed, "Ha, you get it, my boy; you swallow cheap whisky in an instant." Eston shook his head as Lorne continued, "The planning has begun, and Ashling has already invoked his emergency power, stating the secrecy of these projects necessities no congressional vote. He has declared a congressional recess for a minimum of a month till these urgent matters have been resolved. You should get the message any minute now, relieving you of any current obligations. The extinction of those who oppose us takes priority, which will allow us to create a truly peaceful world for all those who serve the Alliance. Ashling hasn't invoked this power since the battles that claimed the nations of Europe, who had opposed the Alliance in the first place."

"I am glad to hear it," Eston responded, "and I can't wait to send my regards, and thanks for this amazing gift the Alliance has given me."

"Glad to hear that you are on your way to mastering it, lad, you'll need it! Don't thank us with words, show the Alliance how much of a use you are, my boy, and expect a car to be there in the morning. Sleep well."

"I definitely need some of that." Eston yawned, "But..."

Lorne interrupted him, "I know, I know, how can one sleep in such exciting times? Undeniably these are exciting times, and to think, we are both apart of it. Just keep making me look good, Eston, and I'll make sure the Alliance will give you more than you can ask for. Now, get some sleep, and I'll see you tomorrow, huh, boy?"

Eston, now looking at the ceiling, "Will do Lorne, you too." Lorne must have hung up as he heard the dial tone erupting from the speaker next to him. He stood up and ended the call by pressing the button on his phone.

CHAPTER TWENTY-FIVE

The thick night air felt as if water was flooding into his lungs with every breath he took. He had to keep running. He had to keep pushing himself, for as soon as the sun broke over the horizon, he would have to wait another day to reach Damian. Having been running for days now, spreading his runners across the land, he had yet to rest himself. For secretly delivering one envelope at a time to a trusted runner was in itself a vast task.

He was hoping that Damian already received numerous replies from the falcons that flew high. As for the rest of the letters, they were tightly strapped to his back. His two weeks time frame would end with the rise of the sun, and he strived not to disappoint. Excitement built as he pushed his body to move a little faster, a little harder, as he jumped over a fallen pillar from a collapsed building. With every step, he pushed himself to the very brink of his limit, humming an old rock song he and Damian used to train to. He could feel the world was indeed about to change. The rustling of water trickled into his ears, and he took another deep breath, pushing himself to his breaking point, as the taste of blood entered his mouth.

Jacob reached into his pocket, pulling out the Dicade's small flag, and placed it on his back. He did not lose a step as four members of the Dicade began jogging next to him, escorting him to the warehouse. Looking to the east, he watched as the light of the sun started to lick the clouds with its rays. Stopping within a few feet of Damian, Jacob raised his eyes and looked upon Pikon, Kamon, and Coretheen—who all stood out front, ready to greet him.

Raising his head, he exhaled forcefully and claimed, "The task has been accomplished." as the sun's light rose above the edge of the river.

"Just in time, now let us get inside before the cover of night is no more." Kamon said while beaming.

"Well done, Jacob, I had faith in your abilities, and you did not disappoint." Damian assured.

Kamon's smile still stretching across his face, "Son, I cannot believe you pulled that off."

"The funds have already started to compile, and we are storing resources beyond our imagination." Pikon paused with amazement before continuing. "It seems with the messages you delivered, you spurred on a sense of hope and dedication, increasing their production beyond what we had perceived even possible."

As the five of them walked in, Jacob collapsed at the nearest table, pouring the contents of his backpack out. "Counting the messages delivered by air that you should have already received and those I carried with me tonight, all the companies have sent their acceptance and agreed to comply with their tasks." They watched hundreds of envelopes fall onto the table and floor. "Every single one of them responded. I have been told that they all bear the marks of acceptance, Sir."

Kamon whistled as Pikon acknowledged, "Impressive indeed. This is going smoother than even I could have imagined. Kamon, I think it is time to move up our timetable. It is time to act. Let us draw the Alliance's sight on us. It is time to make the world aware of our presence."

"Yes, of course," Kamon affirmed, "and with good news, I heard word from Australia."

Pikon responded quickly, though taken aback a little, "And what was their response?"

"They sent word that if we show them the force of our might—in just one city within the heart of the Alliance's holdings—they will support us with manufacturing, arms, and any funds needed to draw the Alliance's attention away from the fronts of their war."

Damian pulled Coretheen close to him as Pikon continued, "Then it is time. What are the potential targets Kamon?"

"Pikon, there is only but a few within striking distance. First of all, there is the representative's congressional building. Second is the Alliance's media broadcasting tower. Thirdly, another target that seems appropriate is the Alliance's Defensive Intelligence Strategical Positioning Service, though their defensive structure would be hard to overcome as it is their main base of operations. Then of course, lastly, there is always the residential district of those that claim to serve the people."

Pikon put his hand up to his chin for a few moments in thought. "Damian, what is your assessment of the targets?"

"Breaking the barrier of New Chicago alone will be quite a task. It will require either great stealth and thought or an immense force. I think stealth, in either case, is the preferred method. This will limit our chance of encounters, ensure an easier entrance, and overall improve the chances of escape and success. This, with my regards, would rule out the defense compound and that of the representatives, which will be heavily guarded at all times by the army of the Alliance. The only truly viable option, in my opinion, would be that of the Alliance's media center. This would not only showcase our forces and our capabilities; it would also allow us to show our disgust with the current rule. We could broadcast our own message, form a political statement, and at the same time show a strategic force against the Alliance, a perfect package. This is the most logical course and also the one I would suggest."

"I agree with your analysis Damian. I want you to begin the planning, select some men, and I want a timetable by the end of the night."

Turning, Damian instructed. "Jacob, after you get some much-deserved rest, and after the sun sets, I have yet another task for you. I want you to select the twenty-five best men in this town and have them prepared for battle as soon as possible. They will be briefed here when a plan is finalized. Eat as much as you require today, sleep as much as you need, and give your muscles a break; then return with the best force you can muster. One more thing, Jacob, I also want you to be a part of this force. I'll need someone who thinks as I do, who moves as I do. I have trained you in the past, and there is no one as perfect of a fit as you are. For Jacob, I will be personally assisting in this endeavor."

Jacob embraced Damian's arm, "I am glad I will be able to walk in battle next to you, to finally do something that is worth our cause."

Walking up behind Damian, Kamon shouted, "Like I am going to let you have all the fun!"

"Is the President going to come off his high chair and enter the battlefield?" Damian sarcastically retorted.

"I was the one who found you and gratefully accepted you." He began to laugh, "Anyway, I am telling you an order. This task before us will be a tall one to climb. With the short amount of time we have, you will require my set of skills, and you know it. We will need your fighting prowess Damian and your strategic facets for battle. My skills are not only that of organization and connections, or did you forget that Pikon and I set up this resistance? We kept it from the Alliance's prying eyes for many years. Pikon is capable of getting around any of the Alliance's surveillances and breaking into their wired networks. And as for me, do you forget what I am capable of? Not only do I still maintain my fighting skills, as you have seen before, but I also have that one skill set even you do not have. That skill set is…"

"And what is that Kamon," Damian quickly interrupted, "Other than the potential to waste the Dicade's resources on propaganda? Now I understand why you picked the Alliance's media as a target. It was to advertise yourself across the world's airways. This whole time, was your only goal to perpetuate your image indefinitely, Kamon? I should have known it from the start. That is why you insist to come along in our crusade against the Alliance of the so-called, Coordinated Governments."

"Hmmm, so I ask," he snapped back, "did you recently learn how to break sequences of codes and deciphers using zero-knowledge proofs?" His sarcasm only grew with every word. "How about interactive proof systems using models of computation and polyno-mial-size? Do you even know the basic components of quantum computation for interactive proofing? I doubt it. Even if Pikon could gain you access to the proper means and technology behind the Alliance's walls, you would have already failed."

Damian rubbed the back of his head while looking at the ground, "Geesh Kamon, when you put it that way, how am I supposed to respond?"

Kamon's face was now turning red as he continued to spew spit towards Damian. "Noooo, we just magically get all of our information Damian, they just deliver it to us in plain English? Heck, Pikon doesn't even need to extract it from their central network. They actually have a carrier specifically for the resistance of the Dicade. Of course not! All the information we ever get our hands on is eventually broken down by me or someone I taught. Even you, Damian, were taught in basic cryptography, by who? Yea, that's right, me; you have never once been able to break one of my codes. Wait, what happens when you get stuck? That's right. You have to send it to me; you always send the real challenges to who? Me."

"Boys, boys, settle down," Coretheen stepped in, "there is no need for all of this."

Kamon snapped back, "Now look what you have done. You got your lady after me again. You never knew how to play fair. I am outnumbered all over again. Pikon. Pikon! Get over here. I need someone who's mind still sits on top of their shoulders. Ahh, I swear love makes one impractical."

Damian, not missing a step, "At least if I am impractical, it is a temporary insanity, other than a permanent mindset, like yourself."

Coretheen protested again, "Boys... Boys... Boys! Come on..."

"Permanent? If that is the case, it is because you drove me here in the first place. You put more stress on me than the whole Dicade forces, combined!"

"Kamon? Damian?" Her voice growing louder.

Damian took a step closer, "You're just jealous, Mr. President."

"And why would that be, ohhhh, great General?" Taking another step closer, leaving only a few inches between one another.

Coretheen, now yelling, "Both of you, stop, now!"

Kamon and Damian both turned their heads towards Coretheen as Kamon bellowed, "Now look, there you go again, getting me in trouble with your lady."

She continued to yell, her fists now at her sides and her head was leaning forward as she screamed, "Kamon, I am not his lady! Don't make me go and cook a meal for every single one of the Dicade's soldiers, in our entire army, then make you uphold that promise you made." Damian began to chuckle, "and for you, ohhhh, great General, you hold that chuckle, or it will be the last time I ever, and I mean ever, cook for you again!"

Both Damian and Kamon burst out laughing as they looked at Coretheen's face begin to turn even redder, her eyes squinting furiously ahead of her. Kamon attempted to speak, pausing between words to laugh, "Damian, I told you that she would threaten me with that."

"Indeed, you did." He said while wiping off a tear rolling down his face.

He pointed at Coretheen, "You should see the look on your face."

"My Lady, it is a very precious view."

Coretheen opened her mouth while exchanging looks with both of them.

"See Damian," Kamon said while still pointing at her. "I told you this would be fun. I told you that if we played it out just right, we could cause her to stir, just like when we first met. Hmm, Miss Nerites?"

A dark glare was released towards Damian. He drifted his gaze towards the ceiling while rubbing the back of his head, attempting to appear innocent. She looked toward Kamon, who was barely containing himself, giggling with every word while slowly exchanging his weight back and forth between his feet. No longer being able to maintain her composure, she rushed at Damian.

Damian quickly turned around as Coretheen attacked with a barrage of slaps to his back. Then he darted behind a table as she turned her gaze upon

Kamon and lunged forward, unleashing her fury upon him.

Kamon started to laugh again and yelled, "Ahh, the fury of your lady."

"I am not his lady!" She snapped back while chasing Kamon around the table.

"Damian, don't just stand there," he implored, "restrain her."

"Why should I put myself in such a dire situation?" He said as a smirk stretched across his lips.

"To protect your President, of course!" He pleaded while running around the tables. "Pikon, help, help, were being taken over by a vengeful force! Pikon, help!"

"What kind of President cannot even lead his own generals to protect him? What a shame for the Dicade, to fall to such a young and violent force, no matter how formidable." Pikon shook his head while looking down at the ground, "And to think that your time was so close, almost coming to hand."

"Aww, come on, Pikon," Kamon whined, "be my true master in arms, the true director of all of our forces. Come save the President, come save me so that we may fight another day." Pikon began to laugh as Kamon continued to pant, "Pikon, come on, Pikon? Pikon!"

Coretheen stopped slapping Kamon as she came closer to Damian and roared, "Sneak attack!" barraging Damian's back with slaps once again.

"Come on, my Lady; don't get angry. We only came up with the idea last night. Not to mention, it was all Kamon's idea."

"I see... We have a traitor in our mists." Kamon glared at Damian.

"No wonder why your army doesn't beckon to your call, Mr. President," Pikon sighed, "for you can't even control your own generals, how sad."

Kamon and Damian started to laugh.

Coretheen scowled at them but couldn't help but to give in to their joy and began laughing with the rest of them. Soon, all four of them were sitting down on the floor, trying to catch their breaths.

"I have not laughed like that for many years." Pikon said while standing up, "I truly needed that relief. Though we better not delay anymore, for we have much left to do, and our timetable is shrinking."

Kamon yawned, "Yeah, I guess we better. Anyways, if I don't get to work soon, I'll never get some sleep."

"Damian and Coretheen, that means you too," Pikon commanded.

As Kamon joked, "Yeah, no smooching on the job."

"I wouldn't dream of it."

"You wouldn't huh?" Coretheen said as a hint of a smile tugged at her cheeks while she blissfully threw a quick jab into Damian's shoulder.

The four of them broke out in laughter again.

"Since we met, so much has happened. So much has taken place, yet, I couldn't imagine a world without all of this." She looked up at Damian. "Without my new friends, my new cause in life, the hope that everyone inspires in me, and of course, without you, Damian. I want you to be careful when the day finally comes for you to strike when the day comes for you to claim our freedom."

Coretheen stared at Damian's eyes as a fierce determination engulfed them, and gold spread forth from his pupils as he spoke. "The time to sit idly by is over. The time to act has come. I once spoke to you about when it would be time for us to strike, how I had to learn, how I had to anticipate their movements before I could act. Coretheen, I finally feel that I have learned what I needed to know."

He paused, clutching his cane tightly within his hand, as he looked down upon its symbol. "This task is too important; there is too much riding on this day. This act will spread upon the world, reverberating across those souls brave enough to wish for change, to wish for hope. And with this act, they will stop wishing. They will come out of hiding, and when they do, they will reach for their freedom. They will grab that freedom with their own hands. The world will once again see the importance of true freedom, and having once lost it, they will cherish our gift. The gift to do what one wishes, when he wishes to do it."

Smiling, she peered into his eyes. "For that Damian, is a dream worth fighting for."

"No, my Lady. For that is a dream worth dying for."

CHAPTER TWENTY-SIX

Eston Tavernier woke up every morning, walked to his window, then peered down upon the freshly paved streets of New Chicago. The sun stood still above the city as he stretched—taking his time—for the city now waited on him to move. These cities were rare, few, and only the most esteemed and significant souls resided here. He took a deep breath, gazing upon those underneath him, for he was significant, he was essential, and he now knew what was best for those below.

He had to appear proper, so those beneath him had something to look up at and admire upon. Those below him had to understand that the Alliance knew not only what was best for them but also who. And who was best to lead them, were of course, in the ranks he stood.

Staring across the city, he smiled, arrogantly stating, "For the wind itself sways to my whim."

He walked over to his mirror and turned on his light. He noticed the stubbles of hair protruding from his face; he needed to keep a smooth face. He found himself shaving at least twice a day. For if he was not clean-shaven, then those that were inferior to him would not be able to appreciate his face, the face of the one who held their lives within his hands. He slicked back his short blonde hair with water, looking at his smooth face and admiring his protruding cheekbones. Maintaining a clean cut was important, for even a week without a trim could result in him becoming closer to the de-caying scum below. He brushed his teeth, noticing that his white luster seemed to fade. He had to remember to go see his dentist soon because his friendly smile and attitude made the civilians more compliant with his wishes. He reached into his closet and pulled out his suit. A suit given to him for his hard work and com-mitment to the Alliance, and without thought put it on, knowing that he deserved it for all of his hard work—despite it costing more than most would make in a year. Appearances must be kept up, for he had now made a name for himself. He had made the water ripple, and he was now the one sitting on top of the log.

He grabbed his overcoat and looked at himself, not hesitating as he unbuttoned his cufflinks, for he too was a hard-working member of the Alliance, and he wanted everyone else to know it. For he had already rolled up his sleeves, and he had already gotten the dirty work done. He told others it was an important aspect of being a part of the Alliance, to serve, no matter how mundane or gruesome the task.

Pulling out his agenda, he threw it aside and shrugged. "People's agendas now move around me." He looked upon himself, noticing that he had gained a few pounds. "No one but Ashling himself could get rid of me." Besides, he thought he looked healthier as he flexed in the mirror. "I deserve the extra food. The Alliance owes me." Peering into the mirror once more, he smiled pompously and stated, "Hi, I am Eston Tavernier, and you will approve this message."

A knock was heard at his door. "Yes?" Eston queried as his door opened.

Instead of where his assistant once was, a soldier from the Guardians of the Shadows now stood. "The shadows require your presence."

Eston turned around, looking at the man before him. "Of course, they do." And walked through the door ahead of the soldier, impatiently demanding, "Come young one, for I have much to do."

Standing on the elevator, he could feel every floor they passed, hearing the winding of the magnetic stabilizers as they shot down to the lobby. With the ding of the elevator's doors, he looked upon the car before him. The limos' doors were already wide open, waiting for his arrival. He positioned himself in the back, and they began to pull away. Although this time, the windows didn't go black, obscuring their route. He smiled as his importance was further validated, then opened a bottle of brandy and took a long slow drink while looking upon the empty streets.

In time the familiar shape of an octagon began to rise in view before him, recognizing it as the Defensive Intelligence and Strategical Positioning Services compound. He smiled as he noticed the familiarity of the setup, resembling the image of the once-mighty Pentagon. Positioned around its borders, he could see missile defense structures, knowing one would be on every side of the octagon. Only one open road to the compound existed, and the entire road leading up to it had tanks on either side, creating a massive wall of deadly steel.

The car slowed, and as he stepped out, he gazed upon the side of the compound. He had read about how massive it was, but seeing it in person sent chills throughout his body as he gaped at its vast walls rising eight hundred feet above him. Eston put his hand on the cool wall. It was formed out of a solid piece of metal. This metal did not shine. It did not glimmer. In fact, it carried no reflection at all.

He closed his eyes, pulling up the octagon's file. Then whistled, as the wall itself was made out of two plates of titanium carbide and insulated with microscopic iron spheres. In between the two-massive metal plates, a single piece of hardened superconductive copper was positioned. If either an energy strike or a missile strike hit the building, an electrical charge would surge between the two plates on impact, melting the copper and disrupting the attacker's projection. It created a reusable and almost perfect defense as the surface and copper re-hardened. The towering structure was even impenetrable to electrical magnetic pulses. He opened his eyes and looked towards the top of the compound, seeing jets equipped with vertical takeoff mechanisms, just in case a defensive air operation was needed at a moment's notice.

The giant wall slowly retracted back, opening large enough to allow a massive vehicle to enter. Soldiers rushed forward, bearing the pin of the Guardians of the Shadows. He stood with eight men surrounding him, guns at the ready, as one of the soldiers grabbed his shirt. Eston stared at the man before him, then closed his eyes while calmly elucidating, "You're merely a soldier, who beckons to the will of those who prosper for the Alliance." He quickly located the man's file based on facial imaging and continued, "Remove your hands from me, Jonathan Delaware, second battalion of the shadows. Do you not recognize those you serve?"

The men looked confused as Eston pulled out his coin and showed the soldier. "Sir, of course, Sir. Sorry Sir, it is protocol." The soldier began to quiver.

He grabbed the soldier's hand and twisted it off of his clothes. "There are no protocols when dealing with me; remember your place next time my presence is made." Eston looked past the troops as a laugh bellowed from inside the compound. He threw a quick look of disgust towards the sound, for the man it came from was devouring a turkey leg. With each bite he took, he could see the skin being ripped from the meat as grease dripped down his chins.

Swallowing without chewing, he somehow still managed to speak. "My boy, you have arrived. I see you have acquired the voice of a true commander. That is good. We have much to do. Come, let me show you to our wing of the building."

"Of course, Lorne, my friend, show me the way into the future."

"The beginning of the future, my boy, the beginning." He chuckled as his multiple chins flopped on his chest, "So much left to reach for, so much left to grasp, so much excitement left to see. Now come, Ash is waiting for us."

Eston followed Lorne as he stepped into the elevator, and the metal squealed under his weight. Lorne, taking another bite of his turkey leg, waved the last soldier off that was escorting them. As the door sealed shut, the elevator became consumed in darkness, revealing the roots that were twisting around both Lorne's and his heart. A voice echoed from the speaker above, "Oculi

Tenebrarum and Unus Quisnam Dux Ducis Ater. You have been given acceptance to wings one through seventy-seven, as true servants of the Alliance." Closing his eyes, he brought up Lorne's given name, seeing it meant the one who guides the dark.

"Lad, I see you're starting to get the hang of our gift." Lorne continued chewing while wiping off a piece of meat that had managed its way down to his chin.

"I am just beginning to grasp the vast amount of uses it may have, Lorne. If this is the gift Ashling gave me, what gift did you receive? Even more, what gift does Ashling himself possess?"

Lorne pondered for a second, "Hmmm, my boy, that is an answer I can't divulge. I was told that your sight would stretch far, reaching even the most hidden aspects of the Alliance. Though... though, the few things that are not listed under your sight are unknown to anyone, except Ashling himself. Each one of the generals, under the Guardians, does indeed have their own aspects of gene modification. I can honestly reveal that Ashling possesses something, something that no one alive knows. I truly believe that he is the only one who knows his unique ability. I will say one thing," the elevator doors opened, "that the gift you received has never been used or tested before, and its potential is unknown, even to Ashling himself. Lad, you see, the modification develops and evolves uniquely in each person."

Eston grew silent as the weight of what Lorne just disclosed settled upon him. The Alliance themselves do not know the reach of his sight; he was truly given great power.

"That is true, Lorne." Ashling's voice reined in as he walked up to Eston, shaking his hand. "Although only those truly gifted will be able to use the gift that we have given them and be able to adapt to it appropriately. In certain cases, the increased stimulation on the cortex of the brain can lead to one's death. I am glad this was not the case with you, Eston. On behalf of the Alliance, I welcome you into our central operations. This area, in particular, is only allowed for those devoted to the Guardians of the Shadows. All the Alliances information, transactions, strategy, and even technological developments are stored and researched in this compound. The floor plans that are available to the public show that this compound only ranges forty floors above ground. Underground there are well over a hundred floors. As I am sure you already discovered Eston, its perimeters are nearly impenetrable to any force."

He stared upon the room before him. Every single wall, desk, and even the floor itself portrayed images of the Alliance's forces around the globe. He closed his eyes and quickly saw he was located on subfloor G-66, with interactive screens on all the surfaces, connected to the world's quickest quantum computer. The same computer he had access to remotely, through his eyes. The computer gave the Alliance a strong edge over the rest of the world. It was able to break almost any code and hack into any technological infrastructure connected to either a satellite or an open internet system.

He opened his eyes as Ashling continued. "Today is the day that we affirm the Alliance's future," Eston looked upon the room, seeing hundreds of soldiers rushing to complete their assigned tasks. "All you see is at your disposal, Eston, but first, let me tell you about the Dicade. Let me truly open your eyes to the importance of what is ahead of us."

"My leader, whatever you say, will not matter. Not that I do not heed to your words, but for the single fact that I will obey the Alliances needs over any individual, including myself."

"I know you will not fail me, Eston. Those who reach for a purpose that their heart supports will also allow their hearts to guide their minds, and in doing so, they uncover avenues that they would have never even contemplated before. I need your full heart in this effort, Eston, so watch and listen closely, my child."

"Of course, Ashling," bowing as he explained, "but I realize that the Dicade's movements are just another tool. They were used to draw out all those in the country that go against the Alliance's wishes, against your wishes, Ashling. Their use is to allow a peaceful nation to rise after those who are willing to cause chaos are removed, reigning in true peace for the betterment of all those who serve under the Alliance's name. No matter what the cause, some horrific acts must be carried out on the few, for the betterment of the whole."

"Yes, my child. That, in a sense, is true," Ashling explained. "Their evil was required. Their demise is certain. With their demise, peace will set in, and we will become truly prosperous as the wars across the world will finally come to an end. No longer being distracted, we will put the full force of the Alliance against those who still oppose the greater good of this world. Though, that is not the only reason the Dicade must be destroyed. They not only acquire their money by drawing resources from businesses that go against the Alliance. The Dicade's hands reach into the soil of this earth that we protect. They consume the population, disrupting production and devouring resources for a cause of personal interest. The Alliance thinks as a whole, and although thinking of one's self is a grave crime that the Alliance does not tolerate, the Dicade do much worse. The Dicade control lives. They run a black market of trade in all categories. They even capture and sell children, allowing their purchasers to use them for whatever they wish. The Dicade lures out the innocent by inspiring hope and promise; then, they take those who have been accepted into their so-called movement and make them slaves. They are even willing to sell their slaves' bodies, anything, in the name of profit."

Eston gazed upon the screens lining the entire room, seeing men capturing innocent families, forcing slaves to do unspeakable acts, and even selling children; their eyes consumed with fear. He swallowed hard as he noticed that in each picture, men proudly wore the symbol of the Dicade.

"They use it as a pass to do anything they please, no matter how gruesome." Ashling placed his hand on Eston's shoulder as he solemnly explained.

He swallowed hard again. He knew the Alliance was not perfect, for they too allowed some oddities within their nation, but they were different. Their people were not forced to do the deeds that the Alliance wished from them unless it was for the greater good. The Alliance does not want to kill. They just no longer provided for civilians that lacked a purpose for the grand scheme of the nations they served. If the civilians wished to be productive, they were then taken care of by the Alliance, and for the good of the Alliance.

Ashling continued, "When in need, they confiscate not only resources but also organs for the more privileged ranks of other countries, just so they can live a little longer. In the Alliance, we do not allow these vicious acts. We condemn them."

Eston looked upon the screens, noticing a small boy lying on a metal table with blood dripping down his legs, forming a puddle on the ground. The small boy's eyes were stuck open, his skin now blue, his hands and legs tied, with his abdomen peeled apart. The wound was jaggedly cut without any precision or care, and many of his organs were missing. The ones who did this had no regard for the immense pain the child must have gone through. Eston clenched his fist, thinking of how he, himself, had brought death to families under the Alliance. Although when he had done it, it was unknown, nor was it the purpose of his endeavors.

"I hope this truth will give you the motivation you will need Eston to destroy the Dicade, along with the inhumane acts they carry out to fund their wasteful and evil intentions." Ashling glanced over at Eston as he looked towards the boy on the screen, his fury growing stronger with every second that he peered at the image before him. "I know you do not support all of our avenues, though you understand their necessity for the Alliance. I heard of your immense grief after gazing upon the dead children within the crowd in Seattle. The Alliance would never do this intentionally; even you yourself were just trying to protect those who served the state, despite what was unknowingly hiding within the crowd. We cannot let those who use children as shields survive any longer. This is the time for war against the Dicade. This is the time for us to exterminate the insects that plague us. This is the time for them to perish under our boots."

Lorne put his arm on Eston's back as Ashling's smile grew wider, now stretching across his face. Still looking at the ground, Eston clenched his fists tighter, then slowly rose his head towards the ceiling, speaking softly, "Let us not delay, for the time has arrived for the loving hands of the Alliance to cover the world."

"Once again, my child, I couldn't have put it better myself."

Lorne slapped Eston on the back, shaking his shoulder. "That's the spirit; let us wash away the scum of the earth that hides within the cracks."

"Ashling, what has already been done? What has not yet been accomplished? What does the Alliance need of me? For not only do I belong to the Alliance but so too does my heart."

Ashling stretched his hand out at the screens, "A cease-fire has begun across strategic points, allowing us to draw forces back to our continent. The Air Force, Navy, and Marines are returning as we speak. And they will soon be ready to be deployed against the Dicade. The Alliance is only leaving defensive forces on our fronts, which require minimal manpower."

He looked upon the fleets of warships returning to North America, carrying hundreds of thousands of men, with thousands of fighter jets and tanks positioned along their decks. Above the warships, cargo planes and bombers flew overhead, stretching into the distance. Ashling continued, "Between the forces already positioned in proximity to the fenced-off cities, along with those withdrawing from the front lines, we will have more than adequate forces for a full-fledged assault. We have enough manpower to seek out every single Dicade personally. Once this is accomplished, we will no longer have to keep such a strong military presence here in North America."

"We will have the nation's military might waiting to strike across all encampments of the Dicade, destroying them within a single night. Then we will resume our campaign against those that still oppose us across the world."

"What do you think, Eston? Good, ehh." Lorne queried.

"With all this in motion, my speaker, what else is left for me? How can I be of use?"

"What do I require of you?" Ashling looked towards Eston. "What we require of you, my child, is the most important task. We require the acquisition of the true leaders of the Dicade. For without them, their foundation could be rebuilt. We need your insight to capture them. That way, we can draw information out of them, giving both them and the public the true justice they deserve."

Eston closed his eyes, bringing up the known positions of the Dicade and the last known position of their President. He then recalled one of the meetings with the Eight Shadows of the Guardians. "Manus Furtim Proditione, interesting." He quickly researched its meaning. He was taken aback, though he knew he shouldn't have been too surprised. The meaning of Manus Furtim Proditione was the key. He smiled, looking at Ashling, "My leader, I have formulated a plan, but I will require the assistance of Manus Furtim Proditione, the one that spoke before us."

"Good, my child, good. His hands will be freed to serve the Alliance. What is it that you wish of him?"

He stood up straight as goosebumps shot down his spine. "Come Ashling, for I will show you the demise of the Dicade." Eston walked forward as both Ashling and Lorne followed him into the center of the room.

He closed his eyes, taking control of the screens around him, as Lorne dropped his food upon the floor, and Ashling started to laugh hysterically, slowly raising his arms from his sides. "Yes, my child, that will do." Ashling's pale eyes gleamed with life as his laugh reverberated off of the sheer walls surrounding them. "That will do very well, indeed. You have done well, my child of the shadows, very well. Past all expectations imaginable."

CHAPTER TWENTY-SEVEN

Damian dragged his finger against the bulletproof vests in front of him. Then he looked at twenty-five of his best soldiers standing in formation. Jacob had indeed found the finest that they had to offer. Most of the men standing before him were in control of their own squads, all capable of extinguishing an enemy independently, if necessary. It was difficult for them to acquire this many vests, but many of the region's Dicade donated to the cause. Every one of them had memorized the plan of attack from every angle, knowing the terrain and the blueprints of all the essential buildings.

Feeling a gentle hand reach across his back, he turned to look at Coretheen, smiling as she spoke.

"Pikon and Kamon should be here momentarily. This is going to be dangerous, isn't it?"

Damian solemnly nodded his head.

Kamon walked down the steps with Pikon behind him and gestured for Damian to come over. "Damian, tomorrow is the night we will show our voice to the world."

"Tomorrow will be the first night, our first true step, towards reclaiming the freedom of this once great nation." Damian affirmed.

"With you and me working together, Damian, we will be undefeatable. The mission will be over before the Alliance's main forces are able to respond. By that time, the lies of the Alliance will be exposed across the nations, as the civilians tune into the Alliances scheduled broadcast."

"The plan is solid." Pikon broke in. "Our message will reach across the nations, but for us to be successful, we will need to add one more member to the task force tonight."

"And who might this be, Sir?" Damian nervously questioned.

Pikon took his thumb and pointed it at himself. "I can't let you two have all the fun, now can I? I want to take part in this as much as both of you do. We have been waiting on this day for a long time now. If we are successful, we will mobilize and take this country back. Support for our cause will spread across these nations, spreading quicker than this earth can draw in a few drops of rain within its dry soil after a drought."

"Sir, I cannot let all of our leaders march recklessly into enemy lines." Damian put his hand on Pikon's shoulder, "We have to think about the future. We have to have someone remain in case we succumb to the Alliance."

Coretheen looked upon Damian, wrapping her hand around his. "That day will not come, Damian, for this has to be successful. All of you—my family—has to return to the Dicade so your dream can be planted, sprouting across the nations of the world."

Damian peered at Coretheen's eyes, seeing tears forming. "No matter, I am in control of this operation, and I think it is unwise to put all of our leaders in an attack that might not be successful, despite the research and planning that was done."

"Trust me, Damian, I agree with you." Pikon confirmed, "It is not wise to send everyone into New Chicago for this mission, but without the success of this mission, the Alliance will just sweep the attack under the rug. Not to mention, if you are captured, the information the soldiers will disclose about the Dicade, despite their best efforts, will devastate us. Then it will no longer matter if I come or not, in either case, for they will find me within the day's end. Damian, you know as well as I do that if I come, the odds of success increase significantly."

He sighed, "They do increase, Sir. But…"

"Damian, there is no other choice; this is our first strong push against the evil that claims this world. With this act, the nation will see everything; our manpower will jump tenfold, and support will flood in from across the globe. We already have the supplies, thanks to Miss Nerites. It is time for me to put my life on the line for something that I believe in. I want that chance, just as you two do. I want to use the free will that God has given me to finally do some good and unleash it upon this world."

"Well," Kamon shrugged, "when you put it that way, how can I put my own wishes above yours? How can I claim that my will, outweighs your own? Damian, Pikon, and I formed this resistance. It is time we unleash its might upon the world. After tonight's victory, riots will break out across the nations. Then we will mobilize, taking back one city at a time, till there is nothing left that the Alliance holds. You knew from the beginning, Damian, it would take all three of our skills to pull this off. How would we actually get inside the city without Pikon's skills in the first place?"

Damian looked at Pikon, sighing once again. "I guess it cannot be helped. It is true that with Pikon, getting into the Alliance's broadcasting station will be an easier feat to undertake. Who am I to rate one's freedom above another's?"

"It isn't like I am a pushover or something Damian." Pikon grinned, "I can carry myself quite well in combat."

Kamon stood tall, beaming at the men before him. "The might of the Dicade and their three great leaders will combine forces, smashing their fury upon the Alliance of Coordinated Governments. Striking them and vanishing into the thick night air quicker than they had appeared."

"For even a single drop of water, combined with others, can form a rough river that smashes the mightiest of rocks apart. Have all the troops ready by tomorrow," Damian ordered, "for as the sun sets, we attack!"

Kamon threw his fist into the air as a smirk spread across Pikon's face. "We will be ready, my great general. I have many things to get in order, as I am sure you all do too. Let us get some rest."

Coretheen watched Pikon walk away as she turned her sad eyes to meet Damian's. "You do not deny Kamon's wish to strike against the Alliance, nor deny Pikon's wish either. Yet, will you deny my wish to join you in battle?"

Damian grabbed her other hand, pulling her closer to him while wiping a tear from her eye. "My Lady, every single member of the Dicade wishes that they were here today. Every single member of the Dicade wishes they could act on this monumental first step against the Alliance, though the truth remains that a small force can infiltrate our target quicker. The larger our forces become, the slower we will move, and the easier we will be spotted. A point is reached that too many bodies decrease how efficient we will be. Our only advantage against the Alliance is speed and accuracy. When we strike, they will be taken off guard. The soldiers positioned there are not used to combat, and chaos will follow with uncertainty. This is the only reason that we will have a chance. For within this chaos, our mission will be accomplished, and we will fall back to our base with minimal resistance. If they do follow us, they will be picked off by our snipers along the route." He watched as her tears started to trickle down her cheeks. His heart ached, for her sadness and worry not only expanded across her face but consumed her entire body.

"Damian, I cannot sit here and do nothing. I sat my whole life, watching everything collapse around me. I watched my father leave, and my mother die. I will not have the last image I see of you be that of your back, shrinking into the horizon."

He wiped another tear from her face and kissed her gently. "I could not function or act properly, knowing that you were in danger, knowing that I must protect you with every step I take." Then he held her tightly within his arms.

Kamon's excitement faded as he sorrowfully looked upon them. "Miss, I know how you feel. I think all of the Dicade know how you feel, in one way or another. We will return, and when we return, our family will only grow bigger, till there are more of us than drops of water within the oceans. The four of us will always stay together; you have nothing to worry about, Miss."

With those words, Coretheen could no longer hold back her sorrow and began sobbing. "Can you promise me that with one hundred percent certainty? Can you, Kamon? Well, can you?"

"No, but any of us would give our lives to save his."

"But, he would too!" Coretheen yelled.

Damian looked gravely at the ground, whispering softly, "That I would Coretheen, for sometimes you have to give a life, to save a life, and who am I to judge which one of those lives hold more value?" Coretheen squeezed Damian while continuing to cry into his chest.

"Miss, we will come back. He has me to protect him anyway, huh?" Kamon walked behind her, putting his hand upon her shoulder. "We have to come back, not just for you or me, but for everybody who counts on us, for the sake of the entire world."

"If the chance is so high, then I am coming with you!" She cried out, her voice consumed with emotion.

"My Lady, not all things are possible in this world. This just happens to be one of them."

She pushed him away, her voice rising in frustration. "If this is one of them, then I will just go and confront the Alliance all by myself." She grabbed one of the guns off the tables and started to make her way to the front of the warehouse.

Damian stared at the ground, unable to speak.

"Damian, are you just going to let her go? Let us be honest with each other Damian, are you going to be able to fight knowing that she is here crying for you? Are you going to be able to act, not knowing if she is chasing behind you into the enemy's grasp? Well, Damian, are you?"

He continued to look at the ground as Kamon yelled. "Coretheen, as your President, I give you permission to assist us in spreading the message of the Dicade across the nations of the Alliance."

She stopped, dropping the gun to the ground, and slowly turned around as Kamon continued.

"The President of the Dicade has spoken, for your will is just as great as mine."

Damian lifted his head towards Kamon, anger flaring into his eyes.

Kamon, remaining still, returned his fierce glare.

Taking a step forward, he punched Kamon across his face.

Without attempting to block it, he fell to the ground, spitting out blood. "Damian, you speak of hope. You speak of love. You speak of a truly free nation, like what was once before us. I know that the more you have to protect, the harder you fight, and the fiercer you become. With Coretheen at our side, your mind will see all, acting quicker than ever—for all those you wish to protect the most will be at your side. That, in essence, Damian, will put all of your soul into this battle, allowing us to claim the victory that we need, that we deserve."

A tear now ran down Damian's cheek as he nodded to his friend on the ground. Reaching out his hand towards him, "No, Kamon, not that we deserve, for we make our own destiny, and we will claim our own freedom."

He took Damian's hand and stood up as they embraced each other. "And after we claim that freedom, we will unleash it upon the world, as the Alliance's leaders flee before us."

They turned towards Coretheen as she fell to the floor and began to cry again; although this time, they were not tears of sadness, they were tears of joy.

"Thank you, Kamon." He said, now smiling. "I send you my apologies."

Hitting Damian in the shoulder, he professed. "See, I told you that love clouded your judgment."

"You might just be right, my friend. You might just be right."

CHAPTER TWENTY-EIGHT

Ashling walked around the iron tree, speaking softly and firmly as one of the screens came to life. "Manus Furtim Proditione, I am glad you could make it under the circumstances. Are all of our affairs in order?"

"They are. The Alliance will unleash its fury upon the Dicade, and their forces will dwindle under our power and might."

"I am glad to hear it. Now, to more important matters, what of Eston's plan? Is it also ready for deliverance, my shadow of darkness?"

"Yes, Ashling, it is ready, as you requested. It took some maneuvering, but it will not be a problem. We will ensure that their destruction is carried out. All the

T's have been crossed, and I's have been positioned. Everything will go as expected."

"Good, my true faithful follower. I know you will not fail me, for, without you, the goals of the Alliance would have had far greater hindrances." Ashling assured, "I will not hold you from your duties any longer. Go now, for our time is shortly at hand."

"In accordance with our laws, under your will Ashling, I take my leave for the day of the Dicade's destruction has finally arrived."

The screen went black.

Ashling once again slowly paced around the iron tree. "The day is soon to be at hand? No, the day will soon belong to me. The pests of the world will crumble under my iron boots. Their bones will crack with every step I take. No one will dare go against my wishes again. God himself will oblige to my requests as I release Hell upon those who dare rise from their knees."

He walked out of the room, briefly turning at the doorway to gaze upon the iron tree slowly expanding across the chamber. Smirking, he shut the door, listening to the cold iron roots scraping across the marble floor. "For my will, will be done. For my will, has finally come."

CHAPTER TWENTY-NINE

Smiling with approval, Damian gazed at the force in front of him, with Pikon and Kamon standing on either side of him. "Twenty-five of the best soldiers that the Dicade has to offer, each in squads of five." He watched as they applied their bulletproof vests and stocked their ammunition. Picking up his own bulletproof vest Damian applied it to Coretheen as Pikon strapped his on.

Coretheen looked upon him as he clutched his cane in his right hand. His thumb rubbing the symbol of the Elpis engraved upon it. Today was a hopeful day indeed. She looked upon the force in front of her, knowing that its entire power could not equal the one she had next to her, Damian.

Her heart beat fast. Not in fear but with excitement, for she longed to see Damian move again, as she had the first day they met. She stared in wonder at how his back was straight, how he held his body in a wide stance. Then looked up at the soldiers, all in uniform except for two of them, except for Damian and Kamon. "Damian, why do neither you nor Kamon wear a vest?" She pondered.

"We both decided there is something more important to us," he said kindly while glancing over to her, "and that is to protect two very important people. My Lady, my vest went to you; Kamon's, on the other hand, went to Pikon."

"Don't you worry, Coretheen," Kamon burst in, "both Damian and I work best without our movements being restricted."

"The vest does limit my movements." Damian grabbed Coretheen's vest, pulling tightly at its straps. "And could indeed provide more of a hindrance to me than an advantage. Kamon is right, do not worry—for no matter what scenario unfolds—Kamon and I truly do better without being constricted and confined." She peered down at her vest, noticing how it was large for someone her size, as Damian offered her a handgun. "I want you to stay by Pikon, no matter what, my Lady. Our squad will be protected by Jacob. Both you and Pikon must remain safe, no matter what obstacles appear before us."

Coretheen simply nodded as she watched Damian make his way to the armory, picking up a long rifle within his hands. He raised it to his eye, seeing that the barrel was straight, and then slung it across his back. She watched him handle an assault rifle, then put it down as he made his way to the handguns and picked up a Glock 23, placing it within his holster.

He dragged his finger over a set of throwing knives and mumbled to himself, "These were crafted with care and precision." Then began strapping the knives across his chest and legs.

"They are." Kamon agreed, pulling a large knife out from the groove of his back as he scowled with delight. "I cannot wait to return this knife to the Alliance. It has been so long since they have seen it, and I think it is finally time that I was pleasant enough to return it to them."

Coretheen gazed upon the knife. The very same knife she had seen Kamon claim when they were attacked at the Dicade compound long ago. She watched him toss it back and forth between his hands while laughing. Then proceeded to the armory weighing his choices between the weapons, as she had just seen Damian do. Looking upon the soldiers around the room, she noticed that most of them had selected assault rifles, other than the slim few who had chosen a sniper rifle.

Standing in front of his men as the warehouse doors slowly began to open. Damian's voice resonated, not only within their ears but within their very souls. "Do not bear the symbol of the Dicade tonight; for on this night, we wear black, being but shadows within the Alliance itself."

Coretheen gazed upon the sun rising against the river, streaking the sky with the color of blood. She whispered under her breath, "Even the heavens know that blood will be spilled on this night." She turned her gaze at the one before her as he continued to speak.

"We move in silence, as if fog setting upon an unknowing enemy, covering up their filth, the filth of the Alliance. For fog does not ask for permission. It consumes without hesitation, obscuring everything within it. We will move with swiftness entering their city. The city that they boarded off from the true citizens of this country. Instead of their message plaguing the ears of the population, the world will hear the truth. And with that truth, they will be liberated from the evil that the Alliance claims is rightfully theirs. So, let us move forth within the night. Let us be but the fog. Let us rid this city of the filth that cowers behind the very notion of the many, over the few."

With that, Damian started to move forward as the sun's light shone upon the world, shining as if it was the for the very first time.

CHAPTER THIRTY

Staring with wonder upon New Chicago, Coretheen sat down, massaging her sore legs as the remaining Dicade made their way through the thinning tree line behind her.

The city lights caught her eye, making her forget about her aching muscles, as she became paralyzed by the sight before her. "How can there be this much beauty within something so evil? I have never seen so many magnificent colors in my life." She stared in amazement at the giant obelisk of the republic, rising high above the city. "These buildings, they are Gods' kaleidoscopes, his colors dancing within their wonders."

Embracing her hand within his, Damian began instructing. "Jacob, I want your squad with me. Squad

Alpha, I want you to move up the east side after we penetrate the border. Beta squad, flank the west side. The last two squads are to cause a distraction by the congressional buildings—if you see units attempting to flank our position—though I pray this will not be necessary. If the broadcast is successful, I want you to move towards the entrance of the Alliance's media branch. Then wait to ambush any of their forces that move back towards the broadcasting tower."

"Tonight, every one of you will be grasping at not only each other's freedom but also the freedom of millions of people oppressed under the iron rule of the Alliance. You do this of your own free will and of your own accord. For not only is it my wish, but it is also your own. I thank all of you for being here with me tonight as we march towards the center of Hell itself. Do not fear the flames, for these flames carry no heat. They only devour the hopeless who wander mindlessly without purpose. We are not the hopeless, for we have a purpose. Let us move forth against those who choose to serve without question; against those who will soon become fatalities of their own ignorance."

With those words, Damian and Kamon rushed forward together as Pikon grasped Coretheen's arm. "Now is the time we watch Coretheen. Now is the time we move. For tonight Miss Nerites, tonight I will protect you. And Miss, I intend to keep my promise." She looked at Pikon and nodded, knowing she must do as Damian wished, for he had done what she had wished—watching as they moved towards the city that stretched out before them, quickly closing the distance to the perimeters thick wall.

Pikon stood up, rushing forward, following behind the Dicade troops as Coretheen hesitated. She hesitated not in fear but in surprise, for he moved almost as quickly as Damian had. He turned, impatiently waving her forward. "Miss Nerites, now is not the time to delay."

Approaching the vast city's border, Damian put his hand against the wall and whispered. "A solid slab of Tungsten Siliconite, their resources are impressive." Then glanced at Kamon, who begun to analyze the perimeter.

"It's at least twenty-five feet tall, and there's bound to be some Alliance dogs patrolling the area."

Tossing his gun to a soldier, Damian gestured at both Kamon and Jacob. He took a few steps back and threw his cane over the wall as they clasped their hands together. He broke out running towards them, and as he reached them, he planted his foot within their hands, leaping up as they launched him towards the sky. As his fingers came in contact with the walls smooth top, he pulled himself up. Using the momentum from the jump, he twisted his body sideways at its top, as if a pole vaulter maneuvering himself over a bar.

Landing on the other side of the wall, he rolled, spreading the force of the impact out across his shoulders and back. He turned around as four soldiers of the Alliance stared at him with surprise and watched as that surprise quickly turned into confusion, spreading across their pompous faces. He began to stagger forward, limping with every step he took. The two soldiers in the back raised their weapons, and as he slowly moved closer, the other two began their approach.

Slowing his hobbled gait, Damian lowered his line of sight as a rope landed between them. The troops turned their attention to the new object between them, and with that look, he gave them one of his own. Raising his head, a sly smirk stretched out across his face. The men in front of him began to raise their guns, but it was already too late.

Damian lunged forward, pulling out a knife in each hand while rapidly closing the gap between them. Then dug the knives deeply into their necks, releasing the trapped oxygen from within their lungs. Without breaking momentum, he continued to move forward, turning his back and rotating his hip towards the two remaining soldiers as their dead comrades fell upon them.

The combatants stepped back in an attempt to avoid their falling comrades. Their gargles still echoing within their ears; the muse of arrogance disappeared from their faces and was replaced with a new expression, the expression of fear. Fear from knowing that their own delay would be the cause of their demise, but most of all, fear from the beast that was positioned before them. Damian fiercely grabbed beneath one of the soldier's vests, digging his hip into the enemy while turning, throwing the man onto the ground six feet away. He swiftly positioned himself under the last soldier's readied rifle and clutched the rope resting on the ground. Wrapping it around the soldier's legs, he pulled hard while rising, causing the man to lose his balance. As the man began to fall forward, Damian wrapped the rope around his neck and grabbed a knife from his belt; then gave the line a quick tug as his comrades pulled the slack out of the rope and begun their climb. He gave the Alliance soldier a quick glance as the man slid towards the wall, grabbing at his neck frantically while tears ran down his face. Then he turned and threw his knife into the remaining combatant's chest, who was now attempting to stand.

Kamon landed upon the moist sod. Looking at the three dead men, then glanced at the one barely alive, clutching desperately at his own neck as the Dicade used his body as a counterweight. He briefly grasped Damian's shoulder in approval as the rest of the Dicade began to form a perimeter.

She swallowed hard as she watched the last member of the Dicade disappear over the wall. "It is now your turn," Pikon encouraged, "I will go last to cover your back."

She grabbed the rope ahead of her and looked at the massive wall rising above. Taking a deep breath, she planted her feet on the wall and leaned back onto the rope, letting her feet bare most of the weight. She moved forward, slowly pulling herself up, and as her arms began to burn, she whispered, "I have to reach the top. I have to continue with Damian, to see this to the end, to be by his side, and to follow my new family into the darkness—unleashing their light upon the world." She reached for the top of the wall and pulled herself slowly over the edge, then peered down below her, frantically scanning for the one she longed to see.

She exhaled in relief as her eyes settled upon the man standing at the end of the rope. A man with a gentle face. A man whose eyes were fixed on her. Swinging her legs over the edge, she started to lower herself down until she felt strong but gentle hands grasping at her hips. With that grasp, she let go of the rope as he lowered her the rest of the way to the ground, and as Coretheen's feet touched the soft grass, her eyes settled upon the four dead men. She worriedly peered into Damian's eyes, the eyes of the one she put all her trust in.

Returning her worried stare with a smile, Damian gently kissed her as a voice roared behind him.

"Damian, remind me not to get caught by you when I am on your bad side," Pikon said, landing behind her.

Walking towards the dead soldiers, Damian swallowed hard, pulling his blades out of their flesh. He watched the blood drip off the blades, then cleaned them off upon the dead combatant's shirts. Sheathing the weapons, he reached over to pick up his cane laying upon the dew-covered grass. Then glanced over at Jacob, untangling the rope from around the dead man's neck. The rest of the squad began to drag the bodies toward the buildings, hiding them inside whatever crevice they could find.

"Men, you know what to do." Damian commanded, "Move forward into the night, do not let them know of our movements, for surprise is the only advantage we have. Move swiftly, before the Alliance's broadcast ends."

With those words, she watched as the men disappeared into the darkness, leaving only Jacob's squad left out in the open.

After briefly looking at the streets ahead of him, Damian began examining the layouts he had taped to his forearm. "At this time, all of the civilians should be off the streets, preparing to watch the scheduled broadcast of the Alliance." Turning and looking at Coretheen, "We must move quickly. We must not pause, for we still have a few miles left to travel before we can claim our goal." He pointed ahead as she followed his finger towards a metal needle stretching far into the sky. "You cannot slow; you cannot tire. I know you can do it, my Lady." With those words, he dashed forward as Kamon nodded at her, then he too took off into the moist night air.

Coretheen nervously followed Damian until his hand raised soundlessly into the air. With that signal,

Kamon and Damian split, moving to opposite sides of the street. Grabbing Coretheen forcefully, Pikon threw her behind a car as Jacob's squad divided. Two of his men raced between the buildings as Jacob, and another positioned themselves behind a vehicle.

Placing her fingers upon its cool metallic surface, she peeked over the edge of the car, anxiously watching as lights began moving on the crossroads ahead. Her world began to fall, and as it fell, it was met with pain: pain from the rough cement scraping across her chest.

Whispering into her ear sternly, Pikon pinned her against the coarse ground. "Curiosity is not our ally tonight, do as I do and as I say, for we do not have the luxury of wasteful movements."

She edged herself forward. Peering between the car's tires, her heart began to beat rapidly within her chest. She watched, her unease building by the second as the vehicle continued to move silently across the intersection in front of her, surrounded by the soldiers of the Alliance.

The vehicle gradually came to a stop in the middle of the crossing as a thick red beam shot out horizontally over the street. She watched Kamon shake his head as Pikon pushed Coretheen lower, grumbling in aggravation, "They just scanned our heat signatures. Out of all the possibilities, why a scout vehicle?"

Looking towards Damian, Coretheen watched him move out of cover, out of his safety, and into the view of the enemy. She watched as he picked up a glass bottle and began to walk down the street as Kamon followed suit on the other side. The vehicle began approaching them as three soldiers departed towards Damian, while the other three moved towards Kamon. She turned, glancing behind her while another red beam swept over the streets.

Punching the cement, Pikon growled while dragging Coretheen further underneath the car, "Another scout vehicle! It seems that lady fate has withdrawn her warm hand."

She watched as its six wheels slowly rolled by, closing in on Damian, and as she clenched her teeth in aggravation, she knew that she was helpless—being only able to watch what was about to unfold in front of her.

"Citizens," the speakers blared, "declare your reason for not witnessing the scheduled broadcasting of the Alliance. The law dictates, under section forty-point two, that all citizens must attend the viewing. This is not an optional request."

Lowering his head, Damian started to sway as he walked down the empty streets, his voice slurring with each word. "The Alliance? Tonight? Aww, man, no wonder why my rep let me leave so early. I thought it was a chance for me to get a little action. Come on, give a guy a break, would yea?"

Knocking the empty bottle from his hand, the soldier grabbed his shirt.

Damian sluggishly raised his head towards the soldier as Coretheen watched his blue eyes become ablaze. She watched how his muscles seemed to reorganize themselves within his body as he prepared to strike. She watched him move his left leg slightly back and put his weight upon his right hand, grasping his cane in preparation for what was to come.

"The Alliance does not allow excuses or justifications for any actions! This crime will be sorted out by the judges, based on your importance. I hope your representative deems you imperative to his cause and crucial to the many civilians he watches over."

Taking a slow deep breath, Damian glanced across the street, seeing that the troops had Kamon against the wall. Then visually confirmed that the second vehicle had passed where Coretheen was hiding.

Pulling Damian closer to him, the soldier sardonically growled, "Do you not comply with the wishes of the Alliance?"

With that pull, Damian rolled his ankle, allowing himself to fall forward. The soldier pulled him up, now clutching him with both of his hands as the others complained. "Another worthless drunk to deal with. You should be thrown out of this city, with all the rest of the useless humans who plague our world."

With those words, Damian pierced his fingers into the soldier's eyes while latching the curve of his cane behind the other's neck, pulling him into his comrade as they fell to the ground. The first soldier let out a penetrating scream while grabbing at Damian's hand as blood poured down his face, only causing Damian to tighten his grip, digging his fingers deeper within the man's flesh and orbital cavities.

With that scream, the six soldiers in the street broke forward, running towards Damian, as Kamon pulled out his knife, cutting into the femoral artery of the one who was questioning him. The man grabbed at his leg instinctively as pain ripped throughout his body.

Kamon turned the knife in his hand, driving it up under the other combatant's chin, lodging it deep within his brain. Then he glimpsed down at the man clutching his leg, swaying as his blood freely flowed upon the street. The last soldier pulled out his pistol as Kamon let go of the knife, now lodged deep within his friend's grey matter. Quickly collapsing the man's wrist, Kamon grabbed the gun and turned it into the soldier's chest.

Coretheen watched the white in the man's eyes turn into fear as he began punching Kamon furiously.

The gun fell to the ground as his grip loosened from the physical barrage against him. Ignoring the force and the pain, Kamon dug his fingers into the soldier's carotid arteries, blocking the flow of blood to the man's brain.

She watched as the life slowly faded from his eyes while the man helplessly tried to tear Kamon's hands off of his neck. She peered at that man, one last time, as his eyes slowly rolled to the back of his head, and he fell to the ground dead.

Fixing her attention back to Damian, with his fingers still lodged inside the assailant's eyes, her ears rang as the man shrieked out in pain.

Turning sideways, Damian used the soldier as a shield against the incoming troops and returned his attention to the men rising behind him. Grasping the shaft of his cane tightly within his hand, he swept the rising warrior's knee, causing him to flip back onto his face. Then spun the cane in his hand and lunged forward towards the man raising his rifle, as blood oozed out of the soldier's eye sockets. Hooking the warrior's wrist with his cane, Damian flung the troop's arms up over his head.

The soldier stepped forward, attempting to maintain his balance.

A smirk stretched across Damian's face, for with that step, he had put himself within striking distance. He jumped into the air, with his fingers still lodged inside the other soldier's skull, using him as a counterbalance while he fiercely kicked out the warrior's knee. A crack rang out across the street as the man's leg snapped to the side. Pulling his fingers out of the combatant's eyes, Damian clutched his cane tightly within his hands, then brought it down upon the man's head. The soldier shot to the ground as blood arched off his cane, and another crack reverberated down the streets. Landing softly upon the ground, Damian kneeled and grabbed the man's neck, who was now grasping frantically at his eyes, whimpering with every breath he managed to take.

Coretheen's heart dropped as the realization hit her; Pikon was no longer at her side. A blurred image burst past her, and with that image, their words echoed within her head, "Any of us would give our lives to save his, we will come back, not just for you or me, but for the sake of the entire world."

Jacob rushed forward towards the six troops closing in on Damian. Wrapping his arms around one of their necks as one of his squad members tackled another one to the ground. The remaining troops turned around as two more of Jacob's squad members rushed out from between the buildings, taking down two enemies in an instant.

A sense of relief briefly filled Coretheen as the remaining troops of the Alliance raised their hands in defeat. As her heart settled, she quickly scanned the streets in an attempt to locate both Pikon and Kamon and allowed herself to breathe a sigh of relief.

Two combatants rushed out of one of the vehicles as Pikon managed to open its doors. She watched as he moved without fear as he moved with experience, without any emotion, seeming to be moving to achieve only one thing; to move forward. She watched him take out a wired guillotine, quickly wrapping it around the first man's neck in mid-run as he kicked the second man back into the vehicle. Blood trickled around the wire, digging deeper into the man's neck with every one of his movements; until Pikon released his grip, allowing the man to be released from the agony of his life.

She watched as Pikon disappeared into the vehicle and glanced back towards Kamon, seeing him climbing out of the second vehicle, wiping blood off of his knives. A scream erupted as she wrenched her head back towards Pikon. Closing her eyes tightly against the sound she was all too familiar with, the sound of a man choking on his own blood. Although with that fear, with that memory etched inside her brain, she remembered something else, something stronger, more powerful than that terrifying sound.

Damian's voice drifted in from the past, "Your arrogant perseverance has ended. You will fade as those before you have, as you led them into the darkness." With that, she remembered her strength. She remembered his strength, and she remembered how that fear had brought her this hope, how that fear had brought her Damian. The image of Damian reaching for her hand flooded into her mind as his voice echoed from within her memories, "Don't be afraid, for I will not leave your side. Stay close, my Lady. Don't be afraid."

With that scream, the two soldiers who had their hands up reached for their weapons as a gunshot pierced through the night air sending Jacob falling to the ground.

The gunshot rang within Coretheen's ears as her focus returned to the present.

Two knives instantly flew through the air, one penetrating deep within a soldier's temple—the other puncturing the last soldier's windpipe. Damian and Kamon converged on Pikon, as he explained, "I disabled the vehicle's alert prompt to headquarters. Although I doubt this commotion, along with that deafening shot, will go unnoticed for long."

"This just got a whole lot harder," Kamon said, grumbling with frustration.

The fierce blue fire seemed to shine brighter from Damian's eyes as the other's anxiety only grew. She watched as the gold by his pupils slowly spiraled outward while he walked towards the soldier, still holding onto his eyes desperately.

"Now, Mr. Warrior of the Alliance." With every word he spoke, the fire in his eyes only grew fiercer, "I see the markings on your uniform, and they indicate all the sin of this world in which you support. Do not deny you are indeed the one who leads this surveillance and scouting convoy. Now, I will reveal to you what I require," he continued while giving a slight bow, "and you will comply with my wishes, for they are required of you."

"You slaughtered my men," he professed while spitting at Damian, "what makes you think I will help you? What are you fuc..."

Damian grabbed the man by his hair and began slowly dragging him towards the vehicle Pikon was sitting at. The soldier grasped at Damian's wrists, trying to relieve some of the pressure on his hair roots while wailing as blood streamed freely down his face from his once useful eyes. Throwing the man against the vehicle, he questioned, "Self-proclaimed warrior of the Alliance, shall we try this again?"

The man in front of him nodded furiously.

"We have disabled the vehicle alerts that were sent from the scan, and it was not delivered as a threat. Though, my Sir, I am sad to inform you that your companion's shots will consequently still draw some attention, and this is very unfortunate for you."

The man in front of him began to laugh.

"I am very pleased to enlighten your mood, for the pain you are experiencing must indeed be immense. As I was stating, Mr. Warrior of the Alliance, I need you to answer the radio's call, which should be coming any minute, and let's say, hmmm... Let's say it was a misfire at some stray. And, and that punishment has already been carried out. Shall we?"

"And as soon as I do, I'm dead anyway." The soldier laughed again in an attempt to mask the excruciating pain ripping throughout his body, "If not by you, by the Alliance."

He sat down next to the suffering warrior, resting his back on the vehicle as Kamon broke in, "You are just a dog who beckons to the Coalition's whim in hopes of receiving a new treat. Why not do something that's dignifying, for once in your life?"

"Yes, that may be true." Damian softly placated the soldier, ignoring Kamon's response. "Indeed, I see the dilemma that has presented itself to you. But, obliging to our wishes will benefit you most of all, I can assure you of that."

The soldier grimaced while wiping off the blood streaming down his face. "And how's that?"

"For it will help you most of all, hmmm?" He paused, letting the question condense within the thick air. "In fact, I will let you choose your own outcome, your own resolution to your predicament. You can choose to die peacefully, by my hand. Or you can choose to remain here, waiting for the sun to rise and for the Alliance to find you. During that time, I am sure you can think of many situations that you could report that would... umm, let's say, signify your course of action."

The soldier began chuckling as his voice filled with sarcasm, "Ahh, what an option you have given me. So many great choices to pick from," he laughed again, "give me the transponder."

"Now, now, my Warrior of the Alliance, no heroics here," he reminded, "for this is not the time to test my patience."

Spitting towards his voice, "I can't wait till the Alliance finds you, so they can use your bodies as their personal toys. You are all fuc..."

Damian instantaneously took out two knives and pierced the combatant's skin, wedging the blades under the man's knee caps. His shrieks cutting through the nights' air as Damian slowly pushed the blades deeper, one inch at a time.

Kicking frantically, he grabbed at Damian's hands while pleading, "Stop. Please! I... I, I'll do it. I will. I, I promise, anything, just make it stop!"

"Why do the men of the Alliance always speak such profanity?" He curiously conjectured, "For what purpose does this serve, other than to show your own ignorance? In any case, I send you my regards. I send you my thanks. For I now know you will carry out my wishes, without any deviations or flaws. Sadly, I will leave my blades in their position to ensure your full cooperation in this task I have assigned you. You understand, don't you? It isn't that I don't trust you; I actually have the uttermost faith in your capabilities, but as a member of the Alliance, you are used to aaaaa, a certain, shall I say, motivation behind your actions. I will not deny you this accustom that you have grown used to."

He patted the soldier's head as the radio buzzed, "Lieutenant, this is dispatch. We had a report of gunfire in your area. Respond immediately."

Damian handed the soldier the radio as he grimaced, "Yeah, one of my idiot soldiers had a misfire. He freaking got afraid over a stupid, um, stray dog. On the bright side, it seems there is one less scavenger roaming our streets. Don't worry; I'll be sure to teach him a lesson when we return to base."

"Affirmative Lieutenant," dispatch crackled in, "have a safe night."

The crackle cut out as the man threw the radio aside, "If you only knew."

"With the uttermost respect," he ensured, "I send you my thanks, warrior of the Alliance. This will hurt extremely, but I promise you your legs will regain their previous potential. Sadly, I cannot promise that same positive outlook for your eyes." As he pulled the blades out, the man unleashed a scream that penetrated into the night's air once more.

"Now, without delay, I must know your choice. For I am a man that actually keeps his word; that is as long as the terms are met with respect and in a timely manner." The soldier smiled, raising his head towards the sky as Damian confessed, "I am glad you're able to find enjoyment from the options you have available."

"I wish I could watch your face when they rip the guts out of you. Watch as you realize that your attempts against the Alliance were even more worthless than that of your own bowels; that is after the Alliance has slowly ripped them out of your stomach and laid them out upon your chests. I wish I could see that look of defeat. I wish I could see your souls crushed as any chance of hope is leached away from those eyes of yours."

"Sadly, that is impossible, my kind Sir, for I do fear you will never see again."

The soldier growled as if second nature, "fuc...,"

Before he could finish the word, Damian cut into his throat and sighed in frustration. "Now, that was truly unwise on your part, my dearly belated warrior of the Alliance. I did not wish to make this choice for you, but I am growing tired of warning those under the guidance of the Coalition to speak well in the presence of a lady." Sighing again as he shook his head. Coretheen watched the color begin to fade from the soldier's skin, and as his skin became paler, the fierceness in Damian's eyes began to retreat. She watched his face relax. She watched his muscles return to normal as he picked up his cane from the ground and made his way to Jacob, placing his hand upon his shoulder that was bleeding.

"I think the bullet went through," Jacob assured.

"Good, I am glad to hear it." He said as a calm and gentle smile returned to his face.

"Sir, I am sorry I let that shot get off. My men and I should have been more attentive to those we held."

"Our cause is all the same," Damian guaranteed as his voice rose with encouragement, "I will not hold any single man who marches next to me at fault. We carry each other, and that means the fault is shared between us all. Nonetheless, we will move on. What has gone astray has been mended." He looked toward Pikon, questioning, "Can you send the scouting vehicles back on their previously scheduled routes?"

"Of course," Pikon reported, "these things pretty much run on autopilot anyway. Just give me a second."

Nodding, he began walking towards Coretheen, who was still positioned behind the car. He reached out his hand towards her, his calm gaze settling upon her. "My Lady. No, not just my Lady, but also my fellow Dicade. Will you continue to walk with us, despite witnessing the horror before you?"

She looked up at the man before her, seeing him once again as she first had, his arm outstretched towards her. She reached out, grabbing his hand within hers, and as she stood, she proclaimed with a ferocious determination. "The true horror of this world is claimed not by you, but by the Alliance who strangles those below them, using their dead comrades to climb a little higher." Damian smiled as the last body was loaded into the vehicles, disappearing into the night as quietly as they had arrived.

"That should be it," Pikon affirmed, "let's hope that we don't get any more unplanned company."

"We better not," Kamon said while wiping the sweat off of his forehead. "That last batch wore me out."

Damian turned towards Kamon smirking, "That's what sitting on the sidelines and getting old does."

"If I recall right, which I do," Kamon snapped back, "I took my three down before even one of yours were out of the action."

Damian opened his mouth as Coretheen interjected. "Boys, I know how you love to compare each other's masculinity at moments like this, but am I correct in stating that we're on a time limit?"

Looking up at the stars, he rubbed the back of his head, "Yeah, I suppose your right, my Lady. Kamon, shall we?"

"Without delay, my faithful friend, without delay."

Coretheen closed her eyes for a moment, then smiled as they moved forward into the night. Towards the tower rising high in the sky before them, knowing that she would follow those hopeful eyes, wherever they went.

CHAPTER THIRTY-ONE

Eston looked over the screen as the time neared. The broadcast would soon start. He closed his eyes tightly, reminding himself that this was for the better. That the people of the Alliance needed this for their own survival, for this was the beginning, the beginning of a new world. This was the beginning of the rekindling of civilization, bringing about slow and steady prosperity to the people of the Alliance. He looked over to Ashling, who now stood in the middle of the room leaning over the desk. He watched as his hands slowly squeezed the corner of the desk as the timer counted down to the start of the broadcast.

"My child, the time is almost at hand." Ashling exhaled, "The might of the Alliance is ready before us, ready to strike our eternal enemy down." He raised his arms, slowly turning, beholding the images of all the screens around him. "To strike down those that betray the Alliance. To arrest all those who go against the needs of the many. To show them the true justice that awaits them." Ashling's smile grew larger with every second that passed.

"Soon, the Alliance will enter a new age of prosperity for all." Eston declared, hopefully.

Loren laughed, "With Ashling at its head and us standing on his right side, my boy!"

"We deserve it for serving the civilians of these great nations, under the guidance of the Alliance, so faithfully."

"Yes, and for that, both of you should be proud, to truly be a servant towards the Alliance in body, in heart, and in your soul. For true leaders hold all the strings of the world." Ashling smirked, stretching his hands out over the troops on the screens below him marching in formation.

Coretheen felt her breath being forced out of her with every step she took. Every minute walking felt like an hour. She felt as if her lungs were being constricted by a ton of dirt, weighing down upon her, only growing greater with every step she took. She paused, looking ahead as Damian and the others continued to move. She briefly rubbed her shoulders and chest, feeling where the bulletproof vest slammed down against her body with every step she took, and that wasn't even the worst of it. For her legs, her legs throbbed under the weight of the armor, being far more of a strain than she would have ever realized.

Pikon stopped ahead of her, glaring as their time only decreased.

"I just can't bear the thought of taking one more step. If I do, my legs will split in two." Knowing how important this task was, she released a soft whisper, "Maybe Damian was right, maybe I shouldn't have come. I am more of a burden. I can't even keep up with them, let alone do anything but hide when a threat shows its face."

No longer hearing footsteps striking the pavement, Coretheen looked up, seeing Damian staring at her as the broadcasting tower rose behind him. His stare was not one of contempt. Nor was it one of disgust or hatred. It did not show strain as their window of opportunity quickly shrank with every minute that passed. As she looked at him, she noticed that his eyes showed understanding and encouragement, and those eyes gave her strength.

Coretheen felt blood rush throughout her entire body. And with that, she took a deep breath and tightly closed her eyes.

When she opened them, she did not see the towering buildings of the Alliance. She did not see the great lights illuminating the streets, greater than any show of nature. Nor did she see the Dicade standing around her. She looked past them, towards Damian, towards those eyes.

What she did see was the buildings turning into the trees that Damian and her swiftly ran through on their way to the cabin. The tower in the distance was the obstacles that Damian lifted her over, without slowing, and with such strength that nothing seemed to fatigue him. She was not a burden to anyone, for she was his companion as he moved throughout his life, as he was her companion. She was no longer wearing a bulletproof vest, for its weight was now the wet clothes that the rain had soaked. She began running towards Damian's smile, grabbing his hand, pulling him forward towards the obstacles in the distance. For no obstacle could stand between them. Their footsteps pounded the pavement and what before seemed like hours now only seemed like minutes.

"My Lady," Damian gently said while slowing his pace.

With those words, her illusion dissipated, and the trees returned to buildings as her vest once again dug into her skin. The tower now raised high above her, sitting on top of a skyscraper. She gazed upon the fresh sod encircling the building ranging at least one hundred meters in diameter. Spread across the sod, she noticed multiple pieces of commemorative art, showing the feats of the Alliance's army.

One, in particular, struck her hard. She looked upon its iron figures showing a soldier handing food to a child, wiping a tear from his face. She read the words engraved in its thick cold iron, "The many outweigh the needs of the few." The soldier, representing the government, stood on a rock. And on that rock were the symbols of businesses that were taken over—the same businesses that were crushed under the weight of the Alliance. She looked upon her family's crest, the symbol of their company, proudly displayed on that same rock. Their company, being stepped on by the soldier's muddy boots, the Alliance's boots, claiming it as their own.

Damian touched her shoulder as his voice caught her attention. "Coretheen, can you please do this for me?" Speaking softly as he watched tears fill her eyes, "Please, stay back with Pikon till the perimeter is secure."

She could do nothing else but nod in agreement.

Removing the map from his forearm, he applied the blueprints to the networking and broadcasting rooms of the skyscraper ahead of him. He took out a bird whistle and blew it in two short successions. Within moments he heard one reply from the east and another from the west. The Dicade were in position for attack. He squeezed Coretheen's hand and nodded at Pikon, who took ahold of her and retreated back a few hundred yards.

Once he could no longer see Coretheen, he closed his eyes and slowly began taking deep breaths. With each succession of breaths, his respirations slowed. He quickly opened his eyes, analyzing the battlefield in an instant, formulating a plan based on the possible scenarios that could unfold. He saw four guards at each entrance. The blueprints had five entrances, equaling a minimum of twenty men on the outside, with more guaranteed to be inside. He assumed that once an attack was made, all entrances would be locked down immediately. He noticed a patrol car circle the building with only enough armor to provide protection from standard gunfire.

He pressed his wind-up stopwatch during the vehicle's next pass, noticing a five-minute window. No matter where it would be, he knew it would respond in less than two minutes. Still enough time to give him a slight edge if he could position the patrol car exactly where he wanted it disabled.

"At least we got one good thing, no patrolling dogs from what I can see." He revealed, "Though, they do have this whole area scoped with thermal cameras. Thankfully for us, the guards are probably too busy paying attention to the broadcast that just started."

Kamon put out his hand towards him, and as Damian grabbed it, he spoke. "Damian, since I met you, I never once considered you as a subordinate, even in a military sense. Your skills first showed through within the harsh streets of old Chicago, as you defended the people who resided there from becoming prey. I knew it from the very moment you organized your attacks— wasting no movements, analyzing multiple factors, and formulating a plan within an instant—if not tens, no hundreds of moves in advance. That is a gift that, no matter how much I try, I will never be able to accomplish. As I watched, I knew too well what could have been lost. I came to your side being fully aware that it was not you who needed me but the Dicade who needed you for their existence; how I needed you, Damian. Since that day, I have taught you everything I knew about leading and so many different skill-sets other than just fighting. You absorbed every single piece of information, and to my shock, surpassed me in almost every category."

"That is why no matter how you moved or how you expanded your cause, I did not question you; but supported you in any of your decisions. For the men follow you, Damian, just by gazing upon you. They follow you, Damian. Not me, you. And I do not regret that for an instant. I always considered you a friend, an ally within this harsh world. You are in the truest sense, family, Damian. I am glad to be by your side as you lead the Dicade, no... as you reclaim the world that was lost."

"Kamon, without you and Pikon, the world would have never stood a chance. It would have fallen piece by piece till all the pawns were dead, leaving an opening for the king to claim the entire planet. I know you well,

Kamon, and to me, you are the true leader of the Dicade. I have only ever known your ability, your actions, and your wishes. Those wishes are also my own, and they are what inspires all who follow me, who follow you. You are the one who secretly organized businesses, both nationalized and private, to support the Dicade. You are the one who grants the people the freedom to fight for something they believe in. You give them hope, and you will give them freedom."

"If the Dicade has a heart Kamon, you are it. I am your faithful friend. I am your companion, and you are my family. As we walk across this dark world, I am glad to help you unleash the light upon it. The light you have trusted in me to spread."

"All here in witness," Kamon said, beaming, "I, the President of the Dicade, now promote Damian Gardge to a five-star general. Second in command in all matters, only behind Pikon and myself."

The members of the Dicade saluted him as Jacob put his hand on his shoulder, smiling. Damian stood silently as the patrol unit passed them again.

"In my whole life, Damian, I have never made you speechless this many times within such a short span."

"And I have never had so many great things in my life happen," he confessed, "so many close friends, no not friends, but family support me as I walk through life with them. I happily and honorably accept it, Kamon."

Kamon laughed, "Well, Jacob, return this man his rifle!" Jacob grabbed his rifle from one of the Dicade soldiers and handed it to him. "Damian, let the men see what you are truly capable of, having no reserves with the task at hand, bearing your full concentration."

Putting bullets into his rifle, Damian glanced down at his stopwatch as it ticked past the six-minute mark. "Then let us not delay the destiny that we will make for ourselves on this very night." With those words, Kamon's and Jacob's squad readied their weapons. "In forty seconds, we will take out all four dogs of the Alliance, in one strike."

"And as they are dogs who serve their masters unconditionally, they will die as such, for they are just but animals in the night!" Kamon roared.

Strapping his cane across his back, he looked at his stopwatch one last time as Jacobs's squad aimed down their rifles. He whistled as the mark crossed seven minutes, and with that whistle, four-gun shots erupted. Damian and Kamon launched forward across the fresh sod, closing the gap quickly between them and the tower. Reaching the entrance, he plastered his back against the cement outcropping while Kamon guarded the east side of the property. An alarm began to sound as thick metal plates closed off the entrances to the tower.

Seeing Alliance soldiers swiftly coming around the building, Damian raised his gun, rapidly killing two of them as Kamon unleashed fire towards the east. The armed forces dashed for cover as the patrol car roared around the bend. Peering at the fifty caliber guns mounted on the truck less than forty meters away, he looked towards Kamon as their cover had now vanished. Fire erupted, not from the vehicle before them, but from Jacobs's squad.

The turret turned towards Jacob as his squad dived for cover. Taking out a flare, Damian struck it against the ground and threw it into the air. With that signal, gunfire burst forth from the other Dicade squads as the Alliance's armed forces were caught in the open—expecting the only danger from the south. The vehicle, now being shot at from all directions, began its retreat, as the snipers started to pummel the vehicle with fifty caliber bullets. Damian smiled as one of the snipers hit the driver, and the car slowed to a stop. He watched as a squad from the east quickly blocked the vehicle and extinguished all life within it.

Pikon and Coretheen began running towards the door while the other members of the Dicade took defensive positions, and as they were running, Damian and Coretheen's eyes locked onto each other. As their eyes locked upon one another, a peace filled not only her but also him too. With that peace, another sensation began filling them both, rising within them. A sensation that resonated between them as a yearning, yet warm love fell upon them, connecting them no matter what obstacle was between them.

Pikon's commanding voice broke their stare, reminding them of the task at hand. "We will have to move quickly, for I am sure the Alliance's military has been notified of the attack." He speedily accessed the electronic clearance computer, meant for verifying those permitted to enter. Clasping his hands together, he excitedly exclaimed, "I wholly doubt they ever contemplated that the computer meant to give access to those entering, would be the one flaw in their system allowing those they wished to keep out entrance into their inner depths."

"Then again," Kamon mused, "I doubt they thought anyone would have the guts, let alone skill, to break into their great secluded city."

"I think they never truly prepared for a small-scale attack," Damian offered, "thinking their advanced notification systems would give them plenty of time to mobilize."

"The Alliance soldiers in this city have become lazy as real threats have become extinct. Even as we speak, the army probably considers this a mild inconvenience." Pikon explained while typing furiously.

Joyfully punching him in the shoulder, Kamon's sharp laugh echoed within the air. "I doubt the ones inside think that. So, hurry up, Pikon, before we have more to worry about."

"They are probably just waiting for back up, hiding behind their thick metal doors. My part is done; all you have to do is break the access code." He stood up and moved over, allowing Kamon to take reign.

"The Alliance knows how not to progress, that's for sure. They are still using the same encryption codes from seven years ago. Heck, I think even you could break this one, Damian. I can easily use their own computer against them by controlling the quantum decoherence. That's it, got it."

"Good job Kamon," Damian said as he nodded in approval, "that was your quickest yet."

The patrol car slowly rolled to a stop in front of the door as Jacob stepped out. "Got us some mobile cover, Sir."

"Beta squad, I want you to cover the outside," he ordered, "Alpha squad, along with your squad Jacob, you are both to move in with me. Pikon, I want..."

"I know Damian; you don't have to worry." He interjected.

"My Lady," he said while gesturing at her to get inside the car with Pikon.

A roar erupted across the city as Damian quickly looked up, seeing a red flare flashing above. The other squads had begun using guerilla tactics to distract the enemy at the Alliance's representative building. "Let us hurry, for now, our time is truly limited, for every minute wasted more of our companions become endangered." With that, Kamon entered the code, and the thick metal doors rose.

The timer on display approached zero as the screens across the room illuminated exhibiting businesses, cities, and underground holdings of the Dicade. Hundreds, if not thousands of Dicade encampments flickered across the screens. Walking into the center of the room, Ashling grinned, "Today is the day that the resistance will end. No one in this country will dare rise from their knees, and the traitors who do will die tonight."

Looking at the screen on the table, Eston brought up the national broadcast that was about to begin. "Today is a great day for the Alliance." The newscaster reported, "The rebels who call themselves the Dicade have been spreading their filth across these great countries. On this very day, that filth will be washed clean. This group claims they are your freedom, they claim that they are justice, but I ask all of you watching do these images look like freedom? No, they are the most heinous acts that these nations have ever witnessed."

He watched the same images flash across the screen that Ashling had shown him not even a month ago. He looked away from the screens as the taste of vomit returned to his mouth. "From drug trafficking to slave trading, even organ harvesting on small and helpless children, these are the acts that bear the Dicade flag. These acts, these horrifying acts plaguing our cities, will come to an end tonight. No longer will you fear for your lives and cower, for the protecting arms of the Alliance are here for you. They are here for everyone."

"We will wipe out those who support the movement of the Dicade, vanishing their very existence within a single night. Although we do ask for your support and patience on this bloody eve, for before the sun rises, the Dicade will be wiped from this earth, and peace and prosperity for the civilians of the Alliance will begin!"

"On this special occasion, you will see your beloved Alliance free you from this horrifying plague. So, let us go live, for I have been told the commencement has already begun."

Eston watched the live feed, showing tanks closing in on a dug-out tunnel, and as they zoomed in on a Dicade flag, gunfire erupted.

He could hear Ashling laughing in the background as his voice reverberated around the room. "That's right; this is all because of you. Without you, these people could have been spared; you just had to resist, but even the most intelligent insects get terminated if they infest where I live… where I preside as king."

He watched as Ashling's eyes focused into the distance as if talking to a force only he could see.

His laugh grew louder, filling the entire room. "And soon, very soon, that will be the entire world."

CHAPTER THIRTY-TWO

The thick metal door to the tower rose slowly, and as it did, bullets erupted from underneath it. Damian and Kamon swiftly ran from the entrance as two soldiers of the Dicade legs were torn apart by the projectiles. With every inch they fell towards the ground, bullets rained into their flesh, ripping them apart, piece by piece. The shots stopped as the door finished rising. Damian stared at the two men in front of him, their clothes now dyed red with their own blood. Hearing Coretheen screaming as Pikon yelled, "I shut off the power. I shut off the security systems; why the heck didn't we take cover?"

"Crap, how can we be so stupid?" Kamon proclaimed as his face began turning red in anger.

Damian slowly exhaled, looking at Kamon, as Kamon returned his stare. Then he once again slowed his respirations, replaying the scene in his head, tracking where the gunfire had originated from—calculating the point of origin from the bullets imprinted on the patrol car behind him. He pulled out his flare gun, loading a white phosphorus flare.

Turning his gaze briefly towards Coretheen, confirming that both her and Pikon were still alive within the armored patrol car, he then proceeded to load two more rounds into his rifle. He did not talk, for no words were necessary. He took one more look at Kamon, who now nodded in agreement. Closing his eyes, he shot the illuminating flare into the entrance, seeing a bright light enclosing around him, piercing through his eyelids. Without hesitating, he pulled his rifle to his shoulder while counting down from thirty inside his head. The light began to flicker faster, and as the time approached thirty seconds, he ran through the door with Kamon following behind him. The flare's light dimmed as he opened his eyes, already pointing his rifle to where the first Alliance soldier would be positioned. Whispering to himself, "Four left, fifteen meters. Four right, fifteen meters. Two center, at twenty-five meters, all armed with automatic rifles."

Damian let off four shots, taking down the four soldiers to his left. He quickly repositioned his gun, shooting four more shots to his right, and ended in the middle, firing his last two shots in the clip. The ten soldiers hit the floor in quick succession, no longer than a second from the first man to the last. He dropped his rifle and pulled out his handgun while running into the lobby. Passing the ten soldiers whose grey matter was now spread out across the walls, he crouched by the marble wall, swiftly turning to his right while firing four quick shots, landing two center mass in each readied soldier around the corner. He watched as two more men fell to the ground, as Kamon turned left, unleashing his fire.

He ignored the footsteps of his fellow Dicade, rushing into the tower behind him. Nothing else mattered; except destroying those who inspired fear into the ones he loved. For he had to extinguish that fear, the fear within them, within everyone.

Looking at his forearm, he began running through the lobby, with Kamon following closely behind, firing a few shots as Jacobs's squad positioned themselves to hold the rear.

Damian continued to move forward. Taking a sharp right, he fired a barrage of bullets into four more Alliance combatants moving towards the lobby. Bringing them down simultaneously, he dropped his Glock as it ran out of ammo.

Approaching the door to the stairs, he pulled out a knife within each one of his hands, grasping them as he stabbed a guard's leg as he took his first step through the doorway. The guard started to fall as he wedged his second knife under the man's jaw. Feeling the man's moist blood pulsating down his hand, he grabbed the soldier, preventing him from dropping, and clutched the dead man's assault rifle. He took aim at the three troops coming down the stairs as they fired into their once alive ally.

Damian fired back, unleashing his clip into their flesh as the door closed behind him. He quickly glanced down, watching as the blood began pooling onto one of the steps, only to proceed to trickle down to the one below it.

The door opened behind him as he reached back, grabbing his cane, swinging it shut. A loud crack was heard as his shaft connected with the gun of the enemy behind him. While pressing down on the fighter's gun, he wedged his knife into the soldier's chest as Kamon came up from behind, breaking his neck in a single movement.

"Glad you finally caught up. Where's the rest?" He questioned.

The remaining Dicade approached the stairs, as Jacob explained. "We lost one of our men in the lobby, but the lower level seems clear." Hearing footsteps echo down from above as more men began their approach.

He stared back towards the lobby as both Pikon and Coretheen were running towards them. Fear struck Damian's face as he watched a soldier taking aim from behind. He frantically reached for his gun, realizing too late that he had discarded it moments ago when it ran out of ammo. He reached for his knife as the combatant began to fire at Coretheen.

Seeing him reaching for his knife, Pikon crouched down, sweeping Coretheen's leg.

She began falling as bullets whizzed inches above her head, and as the bullets flew past her, they pierced into another. Into a Dicade soldier standing in front of Damian, killing him instantly.

Taking aim at the man behind them, Pikon released a bombardment of bullets into his flesh.

Looking up at Damian from the ground, she rubbed her shoulders until her gaze landed upon his eyes. She gazed upon those eyes, seeing something she had never seen before, as he stared between her and their ally, who was now dead in front of them.

"So-sorry, I thought it was clear," Jacob explained.

"These things happen," Kamon assured him, whose eyes began to water. "We don't have the luxury of time to observe the whole floor. We are all taking risks tonight, and it is no one's fault. We knew not all of us would return."

Coretheen stared at the man in front of her, gazing deeply into his eyes as she pushed herself off the ground. And as their eyes met, gold began radiating outward from his pupils, spiraling, consuming his fierce eyes in their entirety. She watched as he took a long, deep breath, placing his cane upon his back. Then with one last look, he rushed towards the enemy.

She stared in wonder as Damian scaled the stairs before her. She watched as he lunged forward, grabbing the stairs in front of him with both of his hands, pushing with his feet, launching himself up eight steps at a time. Only to land upon his feet, repeating the act again and again. Coretheen was not the only one who stood still, memorized by the man before them, as every member of the Dicade was frozen in awe.

Not once had Coretheen seen him this fierce, not from the day she first gazed upon her savior, nor even on this very day. He moved as if a panther through the jungle, digging its claws deep into the dirt, gaining traction before lunging itself forward upon its prey. She watched as his muscles and limbs bent, reacting in ways that seemed inhuman, as his speed and swiftness only increased by the second.

Six Alliance soldiers raised their guns from the floor above, pointing their sights directly on Damian.

His eyes focused on their hands, watching their fingers carefully massage the triggers, and before they pulled them, he leaped into the air. Pulling two knives from his thighs, he threw them at the troops before him. Watching as they landed within their flesh, stumbling forward in shock.

One grabbed his chest, looking down in horror while the other knife pierced through his comrade's neck.

Only to fall over the stair's railing, plummeting down to his death. With that, the remaining troops unleashed their hate-filled fire towards the beast before them.

Grabbing two more knives, Damian leaped over the side rail towards the flight of stairs above him. Bullets exploded everywhere around him, and as the broken concrete peppered his flesh, he threw the knives. Each knife penetrating the chest of one who protected the true evil of this world. One who supported the spread of fear and hatred. Grabbing the lower edge of the rail above him, he pulled himself up while flipping, bringing his legs down upon the knives, driving them deeper into the enemy's hearts. Losing his momentum, he grabbed the handrail once more, pulling himself forward and back onto the stairs.

The two troops began to fall, clutching the knives wedged within their chests as Damian crouched behind them, grabbing one of their sidearms, rapidly firing into the remaining enemies' skulls. Both bodies fell to the ground as he calmly stood up and began walking up the remaining flights.

Coretheen felt two strong arms grab her shoulders, feeling the world fall around her, as she once again made contact with the cold ground. A loud thud shook the floor, and as she opened her eyes, she gazed into the eyes of a dead soldier lying in front of her; his bloodshot eyes stuck wide open in fear.

"Sorry about that, Miss," Kamon helped her to her feet, "but in another second, you would have met the same fate as the one before us, crushed under the gravity of the situation."

She glanced at the man once more, blood leaking out from every orifice of his body.

Letting go of her, Kamon readied his gun, "Men, are we going to let Damian do all the work for us? Stop staring. Let us be of some use to the man before us, our Damian Gardge!"

"Yes, Sir!" they yelled while taking off after him as their hope, their inspiration, and their light rose within them all.

Reaching the top floor, Damian glanced down at the blueprints. The floor was a giant circle, encased entirely in glass. Positioned within its center was the base of the broadcasting tower, connected to the building's foundation. He waited for Kamon and the others to catch up, knowing that behind the door, more troops would be waiting for their chance to draw out their crimson life. And that no matter which direction he went, without support, his rear would be left open to an attack.

"Sir, what's our plan?" Jacob said as the remaining squad members arrived.

Closing his eyes, Damian played out every scenario he could imagine. "Kamon, I want you on the right side of the door. I will be on the left. Jacob, I want you to take a rope and attach both ends to the rail on this floor. Make it long enough so the two of you can stand on it. I want only your guns showing as we open the door.

Keep it high enough to maintain a line of sight once the doorway is cleared."

"Remember, stay clear of the doorway when Kamon opens it, for I'm sure the entire entrance will erupt with gunfire. I want the remaining men behind me; hold the rear as Kamon and I move north, keeping a tight formation. I want Pikon and Coretheen in the middle, that is, after the hallway is cleared. Jacob, once we begin moving, watch the base of the tower for any combatants."

"Damian, I borrowed this from one of the filth below," Kamon smirked while offering him a handgun. "It's not completely full, but it almost has a full clip."

"Thank you, Kamon, my friend." He said while giving him a quick nod as the fierceness within his eyes began to retreat. "Everyone, remember to keep our formation tight as we move forward, almost as if making a capital E. Now let's get going, for we have no time to waste."

Gazing upon Coretheen, whose hands were tightly clutching at the sides of her vest as she bit her quivering lower lip, Damian spoke. His voice was settling upon her, comforting her as if a warm blanket on a chilly night. "My Nerites, my Lady, our task is nearing the end; remain brave and strong as I have always known you to be. I am glad to have you at my side, even in the most dangerous of situations. For, in the end, my Lady, my Nerites, you were the one that was right, not I." He grabbed her chin, raising her head up to his, and softly kissed her lips.

"This could break even the strongest of men, Damian. Though I do not fear for our freedom is in reach, and most importantly, you are in my reach." And as she grabbed his hands, he released his gentle grasp upon her face.

"Sir, we are in position," Jacob informed, "and we are awaiting your command."

Damian watched as Pikon led Coretheen down the flight of stairs. Then he took his position on the left side of the door, holding a pistol in one hand and his cane in the other. With the nod of his head, Kamon yanked the door open.

Bullets ripped through the doorway as Jacob raised his gun over the edge above him. He made certain his gun was anchored, ensuring it would not stray towards his companions, then pulled the trigger—emptying his clip through the entrance.

Raising his head to see into the hall, as Damian and Kamon fired blindly into the enemy, Jacob noticed four downed soldiers and a few more diving for cover. He put his assault rifle hard against his shoulder and started firing, mowing down the remaining men. Then rose a little farther, yelling, "Clear!" as they fell, littering the floor with their dead bodies.

Simultaneously, Damian turned left while Kamon turned right, bursting through the doorway. Kamon rapidly shot three Alliance soldiers as Damion turned, taking down two more. Then they both moved north as the squad closed in behind them.

Noting no men, Pikon and Coretheen ran through the entrance, moving to the center of the formation.

"Pikon, when we get there, I want you to start breaking into the network and set up an interface to broadcast." He commanded while continuing to move. "Kamon, break their algorithm and see if you can find anything beneficial that we can use against the Alliance."

Hearing footsteps pound against the marble floor ahead, Damian's muscles tensed as four men appeared around the bend. He and Kamon quickly rushed forward.

Taking out his cane, he crouched as he swept the first man's legs, continuing to move forward as the man began to fall. Swiftly placing his gun under the second man's neck, Damian rose. Pushing the soldier's gun up with his free arm as he pulled the trigger, releasing a fountain of blood towards the ceiling as his pistol's slide locked open.

Releasing fire upon the oncoming troops with precision, Kamon covered Damian's flanks, allowing him to return his attention to the man behind him.

He watched as the man rose his rifle, taking aim at Kamon, taking aim at his President, his family. Hurling his empty pistol at the man before him, the combatant instinctively raised his arms, attempting to block the incoming projectile. With that move, a smirk stretched across Damian's face as he was granted the few seconds he needed. Pulling out a knife, he threw it at the enemy, watching as it pierced through his eye, plummeting deep within the man's brain.

Gunfire broke out as he heard glass shattering. Glancing towards the tower, he watched as Jacob's squad slew another force outside. "We good?" Damian quarried.

"Were good Sir."

"Resume formation then." He demanded while sending a quick nod of approval to Kamon.

Eston watched Ashling's smile widen as the destruction of his enemies unfolded in front of his eyes. Peering as Ashling slowly turned, attempting to take in all the images at once. His lips were only stretching tighter with every image he saw. Glancing over at Lorne, he watched as Lorne shoved popcorn down his throat, not even pausing to breathe, let alone chew. Then allowed his eyes to wander up to screens before him as Lorne's voice broke through, "What a magical sight."

"Indeed, it is a majestical sight, Lorne." Rubbing his hands together quickly, like a praying mantis getting ready to devour his meal. "Yet, the final gift is still to come." Ashling's voice drifted over the room, his eyes still fixed upon the screens before him.

CHAPTER THIRTY-THREE

Glancing at the blueprints, Damian rushed towards the door leading to the broadcasting control room. Signaling to Jacob to secure the entrance, he burst through the doorway.

He stopped running, as his gaze drifted upon the screens positioned within the room, while the rest of the Dicade ran past him. His sight settled upon them, the screens before him, and as he did, anguish struck not only across his face but also at his heart.

"The rooms clear." Kamon chuckled, "There is no one here. Damian, I can't believe it! I think we actually have luck on our side." Kamon began looking around, noticing the Dicade soldiers stopping, staring at the screens around them. He looked up, as he too became frozen by the images before him, while Coretheen and Pikon ran into the room.

"No, this is not luck at all." Damian ensured, "They are streaming live from the field, explaining why they are not here tonight."

Coretheen glimpsed at Damian's eyes as they began to water. She looked up at the screens as grief flooded her. For the images before her were indeed horrific, but for Damian, she could only imagine how he was feeling. She let a tear roll down her face because she knew that he would not, and embraced him within her arms. "I am sorry, Damian, I am so very, very, sorry."

Throwing a knife into the center of the screen, Kamon collapsed, "But... How? When?"

She looked up as the cracks began to spread around the knife as if a spider was slowly weaving a web. The Alliance had cast their web upon them, as they now entered into a world of solitude, a world of darkness. She stared between the cracks, reading the message scrolling across the bottom of the screen, as Pikon turned up the volume.

"The secret rebel group, now known to us as the Dicade." The reporter stated, "Who were spreading their plague across these fine nations of the Alliance, is now being captured by the army of the world. They are known for causing great misdeeds, not only against the Alliance but against its civilians. Their moral conducts are crude, corrupting hundreds of businesses under the threat of their own lives while laundering money and resources across the globe. The Alliance will draw these traitors out with a single swoop. Let us go to a live feed as the Alliance cleans the filth that has tormented our nations."

Damian fell to his knees, dropping his cane to the floor while looking up at the screen. The cane began rolling as the symbol of the Elpis faded from view. The screen flashed from one scene to another, showing compound after compound being wiped from the earth. As the screen flashed again, Damian saw a business district being raided, forcing the workers out into the streets. A soldier tore the Dicade flag-off of a man's back, then pushed the rest up against the wall, firing into their flesh without a second thought. Then it flashed to the Alliance handing out food and clothes to the civilians, as Dicade soldiers walked in long lines to the train cars. Civilians began throwing rocks at his men—his friends, at the Dicade—his family, as they were forced into the cramped cars.

Kamon stared at the screen in disbelief as anger built within his heart. "The Alliance, spilling their lies once again. This time they have gone too far, attempting to strike the Dicade from existence." Then out of frustration, he threw his gun onto the table in front of him.

Watching image after image flash onto the screens, Damian kneeled as he became speechless. Helpless, but to watch the scenes unfold in front of his eyes. The

Alliance's army was now running through tunnels. Tunnels that he recognized as the old New York subway system. He watched as the Coalition surrounded thousands of Dicade members. He watched as his men realized that there was no chance at victory, knowing that only death was in their future. Despite this, he watched as they pulled out their guns and advanced in formation against the Alliance. He watched as his brave men were torn apart in front of his very eyes. He kept his eyes open, for he dare not close them. He dare not look away from their bravery; for the very least he could do was acknowledge their courage within their final moments.

The scenes continued city after city, compound after compound. Then the screen flashed, showing a mass burial taking place as thousands of dead Dicade soldiers were being pushed into a giant hole within the ground. Damian swallowed hard, seeing some of the men still moving. Then watched as an Alliance soldier shot out a man's knee and, without hesitation, proceeded to push him into the hole. He watched as one of his men began to be slowly crushed by his dead companions. Kicking and struggling as his life slowly faded from his eyes, while thousands of dead men were piled on top of him.

"Screw this!" Kamon screamed while breaking into the Alliance broadcasting system. "I'll dig up their lies. We will show the world who the true scum is. We will show the world the truth. Pikon, grant me access to the station." Pikon walked up behind Coretheen as Damian remained motionless, staring at the screens as Kamon raged on. "Pikon, get over here. We have a job to do."

"Pikon…?"

"Damian…?"

"Damian, snap out of it!"

Coretheen grasped Damian tighter within her arms, releasing a soft whisper into his ear. "I know it hurts, Damian, but if I know one thing about you, it is that this will not stop you. You will persevere, for your sense of responsibility is too strong. Damian, without the Dicade, the worlds' hope will fade. Without hope, darkness will engulf the earth, leaving only the shadows of the Alliance. I know you will not go soundlessly into the night. I know you will unleash the truth. Not because of them, the evil within this world, but because no one else in this world can do what you can do. What you know, you must do." Coretheen paused, kissing his cheek. "Damian, for even the sun rises again after the darkest of nights. You will rise again. We will rise again, for their actions will not go unpunished."

"Damian," Kamon cried out, "I know this sucks, but we need you!"

He rose to his feet. Coretheen noticed his hands shaking as she gently let go of him. He turned, wiping a tear from her eye. "Pikon, it is time for us to stop these lies. We cannot, no; we will not let them tell one more tale, one more piece of fiction. We will not let them change the truth. We will not let them change our history! Let us be the ones who tell our own tale to the world. Let us be the ones to tell them the truth."

"Hey there, Damian, great speech and all, but I still need help getting the network feed. Pikon, I could really use your help... Anytime now." Kamon yelled while bent over the computer, typing furiously.

Damian walked forward, staring at the screen as Pikon turned the volume up even louder as the reporter declared. "This is truly a great day for the Alliance and the civilians they serve. Now that these terrorists are being eradicated from existence, it will open the Alliance up for a new age of prosperity."

Coretheen stood helpless; no longer able to bear the images on the screen, she turned her sight towards the floor. The television blared in the background as her eyes caught a glimpse of a thick black boot in the doorway. She raised her sight, following the boot to the one who wore it, to an Alliance soldier standing in the entrance. As her eyes met his, he raised his gun and began moving forward, and as more soldiers poured into the room, she unleashed a scream.

With that scream, Damian's attention broke from the panel before him. He turned towards the door as Alliance troops flooded the room, surrounding them. The sound of their boots masked by the television blaring in the background. Shots immediately fired as two members of the Dicade fell to the floor, dead. Crouching down, Damian pulled out four knives and threw them into the necks of the approaching troops. Picking up his cane, he lunged forward, screaming in rage against those before him.

Kamon's attention snapped back to his surroundings as the shots echoed within the small room. He stopped typing and attempted to roll towards the gun he had left on the desk, though it was already too late as the enemy tackled him to the ground.

Damian rushed forward towards the group of soldiers before him as more flooded into the room as if a tap was left on, releasing an endless supply of men. He moved forward as eight troops surrounded him. Holding his cane out in front of him, he clutched a knife in his other hand.

Hesitantly looking toward his four dead comrades on the ground, an Alliance soldier cautiously moved forward.

With that single glimpse, that single moment of inattention—Damian lunged forward—thrusting the blunt point of his cane into the soldier's trachea, collapsing it. The man fell to the ground, choking, clutching his neck within his hands. Without hesitation, without delay, Damian rolled over the soldier's back as another combatant shot towards his leg. The bullet missed as his knife slid down the attacker's gun, landing deep into his carotid artery. Blood poured profusely down the man's shirt as Damian grabbed his arm, flipping him into the approaching soldiers. He rushed forward, closing the distance as the troops attempted to push their dead comrade off of themselves. The only sound within the air was that of his vengeance, his anger, as he released a roar that exploded throughout the room.

"With the authority vested in me, by the power of the Alliance, I command all of you to seize and hold." A powerful and stern voice commanded, its familiarity settling upon his ears.

And as he attempted to take another step forward, the voice boomed again. "Damian, that means you too."

A high-pitched whimper rang into his ears, and with that whimper, Damian's stare rose to where she was standing, where Coretheen was standing.

Pushing himself off of the ground, one of the men stood up and grabbed Damian's arms. Spitting at him in anger as a hate-filled growl consumed his voice. "After the trouble you just gave us, we will make sure that little girl of yours will bring us some fun." A conniving smile slowly spread across the man's face. "And I mean a lot of fun."

Raising his line of sight towards the one holding Coretheen, towards the man who was talking, towards the one who had called his name. Damian growled, "Pikon!" Then glanced at Kamon, who was now pinned to the ground, being placed in handcuffs, as soldiers began fiercely kicking Jacob in the stomach.

"Damian," Pikon calmly placated, "I see that look of disgust on your face. I see the look of contempt."

"No, my friend, this is the look of sorrow." Damian roared, "For those you have betrayed. For those, you have misled. And for those that you have guided to the slaughterhouse, even after you shared a meal with them. This is not the look of contempt, my friend. This is the look of sorrow; this is the look I give to those poor, lost, and yearning souls, such as yourself." He peered towards Kamon, who was sitting up against the wall with tears running down his face. Damian returned his ferocious stare towards Pikon as he held Coretheen captive, and as he did, he saw Coretheen's face. Her face did not hold the look of fear, but what it held was even worse. It was consumed with the heartbreaking suffering of betrayal.

"What kind words, from a kind man, who will soon be lead to the same slaughterhouse that you just spoke of." Pikon paused for a second, looking down upon his captives as a tremendous glare shot through his eyes. "I will admit, though, at times, your motivation, your hope, and your laughter seemed to be contagious, spreading from one person to another. It was like a disease how it spread, even tugging at my heart, despite my best efforts. Damian, today was finally my time to leave, before that disease grasped at my soul forever. Even a child must leave their family when they grow up. Damian, I have indeed grown out of this family."

With those words, he lightened his grasp on Coretheen, and as he did, she lashed forward, breaking Pikon's grip. Damian hastily turned his knife in his hand, sliding it up the soldier's arm who was holding him—cutting into his subclavian artery while turning and positioning his leg behind the second soldier.

Pulling out her pistol, Coretheen began wildly shooting behind her while running forward as a bullet pummeled into Pikon's vest, knocking him back.

Quickly grabbing the second soldier's neck, Damian threw him over his leg, watching as the back of his head made contact with the floor below.

Pikon pulled out his sidearm and shot the two remaining Dicade soldiers against the wall. "One more step Miss Nerites and the next one goes in your head." She stopped running, allowing Pikon to grasp her arms within his once more.

Rushing forward, Damian attempted to close in on Pikon. And as Pikon pressed his gun against Coretheen's head, he released a sly, condescending, and arrogant tone that plagued their ears. "Now, now, Damian, let us not be too bold, or she will fall as your comrades just have. Do not forget. I know what I hold in my hands." A green flare erupted in the background over the city. "See, there is no hope now, for even the remaining Dicade are retreating. What's left of them anyway."

He looked upon the warrior whose artery he had cut a moment ago—the very soldier who voiced his interest in Coretheen. He looked at the man sway while grasping at his arm.

The man grabbed Damian again, this time driving his foot into the back of his knees.

Falling to the ground, Damian smiled at the man above him and began to explain. "You are now beginning to feel dizzy, aren't you? The blood is rushing from your body, and weakness is setting in. The comment that you had previously made summoned this precious gift to you. I cut a major artery in your body, located just inside the inner arm, where it rises close to the surface of the skin."

He was smirking even greater as the soldier braced himself upon his shoulder. "Shut up! Or I'll kill you now!"

"Quite the contrary, young man," he revealed, "for I have already killed you. Feel as the sweat pours from your body, and your heart begins to beat furiously. Feel as your breathing increases in an attempt to compensate for the blood loss. Nausea will soon set in, followed by your insentience." He paused as the man threw up next to him, "And lastly, death will take you."

The man let go of him, beginning to plead while frantically packing his wound, "Someone, please... Anyone? Please, stop it! Please, anybody. It won't stop. Ohh God, please help me! Ohh God, it won't stop." Damian watched as fear and panic spread across his face.

Not giving him the peace of silence, he continued. "You have already chosen your God, and he will not help you. Nonetheless, it doesn't matter. Unless you were at an Alliance hospital at this very second, your death is certain. Your body is helpless. You cannot stop the bleeding or even slow it to allow yourself a few more breaths, even if those breaths would have been used to cry out for help."

The soldier began to cry as tears strung down his face.

"I am glad you, too, share my sympathy for the Dicade brothers who have perished from the betrayal of one of their very own leaders." Damian shook his head, then returned his glare to Pikon.

"Damian, that is not necessary," Pikon interjected, "true, but not necessary."

He watched as the man ran to Pikon screaming, weeping for help, clutching onto his arm as he slowly fell to the ground.

Not even lifting a finger, Pikon let the man collapse to the floor and began to laugh without even acknowledging the man's agony.

"I am glad that I can provide my old friend with laughter once more." Damian said.

"You know Damian, through all of your skill, you have but one weakness. That one weakness has always weighed down upon your soul. One weakness that the second I asked Kamon to meet you, I instantly knew I could take advantage of. Your only weakness Damian is your trust. Your weakness is that you believe those before you are always good-hearted. That given the right vision and teachings, they will realize on their own the best course of action. Well, Damian, I will teach you one more thing, not all people, in essence, are good. You neglect the fact that some people just don't care if they kill thousands, just to climb a little higher on the totem pole. That if they cannot out-think someone, maybe they will just kill them, and claim what he had as their own."

"Damian, this is why you have failed. This is why you all have failed. You thought of every possibility, every outcome, except the betrayal by the one right in front of you. I know you will learn from this lesson Damian, but by the time you grasp it, it will already be your turn to die. It will be sad to lose such skill, such prowess from the dirt of this world. Yet, Damian, you are still but only dirt."

Kamon's eyes met with his old companions as he sighed. "Betrayed by my friend." Taking a deep breath, he attempted to mask his sadness. He attempted to mask his anguish, even as his heart was breaking in two. "Betrayed by my right hand. Betrayed by my friend. Betrayed, from the very beginning."

With those words, Damian felt a great pain erupt from the back of his head as the lights faded from his eyes.

CHAPTER THIRTY-FOUR

Raising his phone to his ear, Lorne's pitch rose as joy spread across his face. "Glad to hear it! I'll let him know immediately, and on behalf of everyone here, we welcome you back to the Alliance." He swallowed his food in his mouth while walking over to Eston and Ashling. "Hey Ash, I am glad to report that both the President and Damian have been apprehended at the broadcasting center. There were many casualties but a small price to pay to lure them out of their compounds, guaranteeing their capture."

Smiling towards Eston, Ashling declared. "Tonight, you delivered yet another great service to the Alliance and even more so to the Guardians Eston. This act will not be forgotten."

"My dear lad," Lorne slapped Eston on the back, "I knew you would do great things, beyond all expectations, great things, my boy."

Walking towards the exit of the room, stopping at the doorway, Ashlings' soft voice drifted across the room. "Eston, my child, come stand next to me as I gaze upon those that go against our wishes, that go against my wishes."

⊷⊶

Damian opened his eyes, seeing blurry figures within the dim light before him. As his eyes began to focus, the figures turned into the sad yet familiar faces of his companions. Looking above, he saw Coretheen's face peering down upon him, his head resting within her lap. Gazing to his right, Kamon sat against the wall by Jacob.

Forcing a hollow smile upon his face, Kamon attempted to mask his grief as he spoke. "Glad to have you back, Damian."

Squinting at him, he peered into the sadness within his family's eyes. "Kamon, I am sorry, I... there was nothing else I could have done. If only I would have seen it sooner. I should have seen it sooner. I am sorry that the one you placed your trust in the most has betrayed you. The one who helped you build the Dicade, from the beginning, under the guise of friendship."

"There is no reason to be sorry, Damian; you have always done your best, never delaying in any task given to you. Though you are wrong about one thing, he was not the one I trusted most." He paused as a glimmer in his eyes erupted. "That level of trust I only put in one person, and that person is you, Damian."

"I am proud to have a leader with as much passion, with as much wisdom, with as much ambition, and a sense of moral responsibility as you have, Kamon." Damian paused while peering at the thick steel bars surrounding them. "I am proud to have followed you, and I do not regret one day of my life next to your side. Not even now, as I am locked in this cell, looking towards my death, do I regret walking with you throughout my life."

"And I too, Damian, and I too." With those words, his hollow smile transformed into a genuine one.

Peering up at Coretheen, with his head still resting in her lap, he attempted to sit up. He clutched at the back of his head, grimacing as pain shot out from where he had been struck. He reached for his cane, then frantically scanned the room as his heart dropped.

"I'm sorry, Damian." She said, grimly confirming his worst fears, "They took it."

Glaring across the hall, he noticed his cane displayed in a clear bulletproof box attached to the wall. He sighed while hearing the door open as footsteps echoed down the hallway.

He raised his sight upon the man who now stood in front of him. The man who had etched his name upon their hearts, first in friendship, then in betrayal. "Pikon." Damian said, speaking slowly, letting his sarcasm drift with every word. "What do I owe you for this visit, that you have so gracefully decided to bless us with?"

"I have come for the President of the Dicade. For Kamon, for the public demands him."

"No, Pikon, you demand an execution." Damian growled.

"Not I Damian, the people of the Alliance demand it. They demand the leader be held accountable for his horrific deeds against the nations he was supposed to serve. Try to think on the bright side of things Damian, you'll get a martyr. Not that it will do you any good with your comrades, all dead or dying. Do not dismay, though. I am sure you'll soon be following in his footsteps."

"If you open this door," Damian roared as gold began to seep into his eyes, "I will tear your throat out of your intestines."

Gently placing his hand upon his shoulder, Kamon's calm voice began soothing his soul. "Damian, you once said this is a dream worth dying for; I will happily die for what I believe in. At least my torment will come to an end."

"But..."

"As long as one of us lives on Damian, our dreams will still exist. They will remain, always, through each other."

"But how can I live on without you here? Without you next to me and without you helping to guide me?"

Kamon jabbed Damian in the shoulder as his sad eyes faded, and a slight smile tugged at his worn cheeks. "If there is a dream worth dying for, then that dream is also worth living for. So, Damian, I want you to live. I want you to carry forward, not just for me, but for the world."

He lowered his gaze to the floor as drops started to rain down upon him from Coretheen. Then stood up, forcing a smile upon his face. "Ahh, you couldn't run this group of misfits anyway. I guess you're just taking the easy way out, huh?"

"Hey, the President does deserve the finer things in life, doesn't he?"

Coretheen attempted to wipe the tears from her eyes, though gave up as they continued to flood down her face to the frown beneath.

"My President does indeed deserve the finest of things. And the one who stands before me deserves much more than this world has to offer."

"And that is why I must move on to the next life," Kamon chuckled, "for only God, himself, can give me what is mine." He turned towards Coretheen, "Treat him well, for he is now yours to take care of. I am putting my faith and my trust in you."

"I will remain by his side until the end." Promising as her tears began to slow, she released a smile at the man before her.

"From the first moment we met Coretheen, I knew you two were created for each other, like the diamond for the ring. Sadly, I will have to break my promise to you, for I do not think I'll ever get to clean those dishes." With that, the door opened as soldiers grabbed Kamon, pushing him down the hall as his smile faded into the distance.

Watching his leader disappear from his sight, Damian looked upon him for the last time—as Coretheen embraced him, allowing her tears to stream down her face once again. Then he glanced over to Jacob, watching as a new stream of tears became plastered upon his face.

"Ohh, how touching, what a reunion." Pikon smirked, sardonically releasing his voice across the cell.

Another voice rung out, slowly plaguing Damian's ears as he walked down the hall. A voice he was all too familiar with, hearing it during almost every press conference and broadcasting. A voice that inspired hate, even within him. "So, this is the famous Damian Gardge I have heard about. He does indeed have an interesting look to him. Ohh, and I presume this is Coretheen Nerites. Pretty one, we will indeed have some interesting discussions."

"Ashling, the one behind the uprising of the Alliance. The one who convinced the world to give up their freedom for the betterment of the whole. When in truth, it is only for the betterment of yourself." Damian snarled, clenching his jaw shut between each word.

"You actually believe people are smart enough to live for themselves? Smart enough to hold their own will, their own wishes in their hands? Your ignorance is amusing." Pikon snickered, "I will teach you something, Damian. People are idiots, and in being so, they don't even know what's best for themselves."

"So, your answer is to have the Alliance guide them through the scope of their rifles?"

"That may be the case now, my unique Damian Gardge, but they gave it to me freely." Damian looked toward Ashling as he continued to reveal, "I will admit, it took some convincing, some manipulation of the economy. It was easy when you controlled the reserves. Many were paid off. Those that would not accept a payoff, well, in those cases, we took it by force. Ohh, and how the population loved it too; to watch those above them get torn down. They cheered and praised me for my efforts. It was so simple and so delightful. Looking back now, I realize it was a flawless piece of art. After that, everything moved so quickly. I am glad there weren't too many like you. Of course, you were only but a child then." Ashling started to laugh as Damian looked down at the ground in disgust. "Though, I will honestly say Damian, that this too is a high moment for me. I didn't think it would be so gratifying to entrap those who still had some fight left inside them. Who persevered against my wishes."

"And yet, it was so easy." Pikon mused, "From the very start, I helped Kamon build the Dicade. He thought I was breaking into the networks when, in reality, I possessed every single key. He thought I helped the Dicade evade the Alliance's prying eyes. When in truth, I was their prying eyes, waiting till every single person going against the Alliance were in our grasps. Yes, I killed some of my own men, but killing always makes me feel." Pausing, he closed his eyes as a sense of euphoria fell over him as he reminisced of the past. "Makes me feel, so... So alive!" His voice quivering with pleasure, "Damian, there is no better way to prove ones' existence than taking another's life. To hold it in your hands. . . Mhhmmm, it was always such a... such a delight. A delicacy of the highest degree."

Damian clenched his fists while staring at Pikon. Then he closed his eyes, forcing himself to remain calm, for he would not give him the gratification of his anger.

Pikon looked curiously upon him, upon the face that now showed no emotion. He shrugged while continuing, "It was easy. Even now, the civilians celebrate as the portrayed evil from the land has been eradicated, by their saviors, by us. Their morale is the highest it's been since the undying treaty between the nations. Their very ignorance was the key, Damian, our key to the world."

Taking a deep breath, Pikon felt their plans all finally coming together. He felt goosebumps rise across his spine, as the world was soon to be theirs, and theirs alone. "They embraced as America consumed Canada for their mutual financial and military protection, of course. They cheered as North America opened their borders to Mexico, for there is no reason to have borders when we're all on the same side. They celebrated as almost the entirety of Europe joined our ranks. And ohhh, how they applauded us when we told them there would be less of a burden on individual nations, as the military budget would be split between all; for the Alliance of Coordinated Governments tax was applied directly to military operations. Putting them under our very rule, without any means to resist as their nation's military force eroded, and ours only grew in power."

"Thank you for the history lesson, filled with your immense arrogance and pride." Damian slowed his speaking, attempting to hide his vast annoyance. "Pikon, can we be left alone till the time you choose for our death arrives? I do require some peace, my once honorable friend upon friends." He looked up at the four men who stood in front of him. One so large that the strain on his bones seemed far too massive to bear his weight, but to his shock, they did not break or even bend under the stress. The other standing behind him remained still. He looked upon that man, who seemed hesitant, who seemed cautious. He was unsure, but his eyes seemed different than the rest before him.

"In due time, Damian. The point is that we control the population. The very essence is that we control everything. Even now, they celebrate as their last hope fades. They celebrate while their last chance of survival dies with the Dicade, with Kamon, and with you. I will admit it was a pleasure to let both of you think you were making an impact against the Alliance. Watching you draw out all those who oppose us, highlighting the businesses, drawing out the population. Even as this very day approached, as you devised the plan to break into the broadcasting tower, knowing it was the only logical choice. Everything lined up so perfectly, everything went according to our plan, to Ashling's plan."

Damian watched as the fat one hit the young man on the back as he averted his gaze.

"It was perfect. When I assisted in opening the broadcasting tower's door, I sent a message to Ashling—letting him know that his moment—no, our moment was at hand." Pikon looked upon Damian one more time, watching his expressionless face, and then sighed in disappointment. "Anyway, though this is a thrilling experience, I have an execution to help with. The people will be so happy to see the death of the so-called President. I bid you adieu, my kind, and once old friend."

Eston watched Pikon turn, seeing his face for the first time. As he gazed upon his face, he noticed something familiar yet peculiar. The man before him not only had roots grasping at his heart, as he too did, but his pale white eyes pierced towards him. Walking forward, he turned, peering at Ashling, who bore those same white eyes. Pausing, he replayed the very moment he had received this gift within his head. The same moment that Ashling's eyes received their piercing white stare for the first time. Eston began grinning as he looked at Pikon, "Manus Furtim Proditione, it is a pleasure to meet you, or should I say, the hands of secret betrayal?"

Turning towards him, Pikon questioned. "But how?"

He continued, "It is an honor to meet one of the eight."

"My child, my Eston, I see your mind is as brilliant as ever." Ashling looked towards Damian. "I can't wait to converse with you, Damian Gardge. I can but only fathom the plethora of information and insight you must carry. Unfortunately, I must also bid you farewell, till another time. I promise it won't be long. I just have more important and pressing matters to attend to." Glancing towards the others, he began walking, "Eston, Lorne, let us depart."

Damian watched as they disappeared down the dim hallway. Then he sat down behind Coretheen and wrapped his arms around her.

She leaned back, resting her weight against him, still crying. In between sobs, he heard Coretheen's voice break, "I was useless. All I could do was watch my life fall apart in front of me. I was useless, just like the day you found me. I was useless then, and I am utterly useless now."

"Coretheen," he whispered, "you are anything but useless. You have a strength that you aren't even aware of, and that strength brings out the best in me. You, Coretheen, you were the only one to have the mind to manipulate the Alliances currency with our own supporters. No one else could have devised that plan. Not only that but having you by me made me the strongest I have ever been. Never in my life have I been able to do so much in such a short amount of time. Before you arrived, time seemed to stand still, never moving forward, never advancing. When you came into my life, the world no longer stood still. The world began turning as the Dicade moved forward, thrusting its might upon the Alliance."

She watched as tears fell upon her hand. "That might is no more Damian, and that dream is now dead, as we dwindle within this cage."

"We cannot let that dream die." He grabbed her hands in his, "We must continue to move. We must not die on our knees. We must rise, for we still draw breath, and as long as oxygen is in our lungs, we must continue to move forward. For Kamon's sake…"

She tightened her grip on his hands. Looking down as her tears now fell upon his hands too. "Damian. I want to learn. I want to be able to move like you do. I never again want to be held by a captor. I never again want to be but only prey for the predator to consume."

"Coretheen, with time, even prey can grow claws, as you will too." He said as he wiped a tear away from her eye.

She let a hint of a smile show on her face. "Yet, here we are in this cell, unable to do anything as those we love are struck from this earth. I will miss how he smiled. I will miss how you two joked, and I will miss him."

"We will all miss him," he whispered softly into her ear, "but I will not miss his smile. I will not long to see it, for soon he will be in a better place—getting the rest he deserves. And I refuse to plague his thoughts with sadness and yearning."

"Damian, a smile is a funny thing, isn't it? How it can bring so much joy, how it can change another's frown, and lighten one's mood."

"My Lady, it is a curious thing indeed, but in a world of a billion faces, I only wish to see one smile. Though I may be locked in this cell—I have the only smile I need to bring me joy, to bring me happiness, and that smile is yours, Coretheen. That smile is the only one I wish to see, and it is the same smile that I dream about when I close my eyes. That smile is the very smile that belongs to the face that I am lucky to gaze upon every day. Your face, my Lady, the face that I love."

With those words, Coretheen's tears stopped as a smile struck across her face.

"Yes, that is the smile I long to see. Thank you, my Lady." Damian glanced down upon her as she closed her eyes, resting her head upon his chest. Then he too closed his and let the silence take him.

CHAPTER THIRTY-FIVE

E ston gazed upon the concrete room. Upon the wall's bearing the flags of the Alliance and upon the concrete floor imprinted with the image of the congressional buildings. In the center of the room, there was a raised wooden platform with a finely polished finish. He raised his head towards the ceiling, noticing a giant skylight above him, with lights shining down on the shimmering platform. Upon the platform sat a stainless-steel structure. He remembered how in the past, it was said that a firing squad was vicious; that the electric chair was too gruesome; and that lethal injection was too inhumane because too many faced long and agonizing deaths. The Alliance claimed that the only logical solution was a quick severing of the spinal cord, but not by human hands, for human hands could deliver inconsistent blows. For these rare public showings, the Alliance built a large guillotine that was carved out of molybdenum, chromium, vanadium, and carbon. The vast blade fell from over twenty feet high, providing a high-energy impact on its target in a single blow.

He watched as soldiers strapped Kamon into the chair, resembling a witness stand from the judicial system of old. He turned as Ashling began giving commands. "I want a camera on top of the guillotine blade for the execution, and I want another one rotating around the guillotine for dramatic tension. During the viewing and deposition, I want a camera on both Kamon and myself.

"Mr. Ashling, the viewing will be ready in two minutes." The reporter notified.

Ashling smirked at Kamon, "Now is the time for the innocent to die."

"It is always great to have backstage passes," Lorne's entire body vibrated with every step he took while leading Eston to the side of the room, "to the most exclusive events, isn't it, my boy? This will be a spectacle to remember."

Eston gazed upon a screen set up in front of the camera crew, making sure the broadcasting angles were perfect for those viewing as the reporter began.

"We are here live, for a rare viewing, a viewing like none other. We are here to tell you that the Alliance has apprehended the leader of the Dicade, whom compares himself with the President of old. A man whose power was discontinued for a dire reason. This is quite a feat. Not only did the Alliance destroy and capture all those who go against them. But they also apprehended the most villainous of men, in the very same night, ridding our nations of the plague that kept our advancement at bay. The elite task force of the army, along with the planning, could have only been accomplished by one man—by one of our very own representatives. He will be doing the deposition tonight, hopefully leading to the removal of this evil man from our nations. The speaker and the greatest of our leaders. I present to you, your representative, Ashling!"

"Is this your flag?" Ashling began speaking, pulling out a torn piece of cloth and throwing it on the desk before Kamon. "Your symbol of rebellion against the Alliance?"

"That is the symbol the Dicade bear." Kamon sternly answered.

Ashling continued, "It has been reported that the Dicade partake in illegal substances, human trafficking, and organ harvesting, upon many other heinous acts of moral infidelity. To these, how do you plead?"

"The Dicade have never once trafficked drugs or humans. They have never once harvested organs, for it would interfere with our goal of personal freedom. That act alone would destroy another's freedom, and that is something we the Dicade hold very dear. We would never betray another individual."

"So, these images," Ashling smiled while proceeding to throw pictures on the table in front of Kamon. Then gestured to a large screen in the background, "and this video." The screen started playing the images that Eston had witnessed only a few weeks ago.

Kamon looked upon the screen before him, watching the horror and evil the human race could display.

"You admitted that this cloth, bearing an eagle with an olive branch clutched in its talons as a flame consumes each side, was the symbol of the Dicade." Ashling continued to pry, "Do you deny that these men bear the symbol of the Dicade? In which you claimed would never commit such heinous acts?"

He remained still, not allowing his anger to rise. For Kamon knew that his composure, his integrity, and his fortitude was the only tool he had that may inspire those watching. "I do agree that this is the symbol of the Dicade, but whose men they are, that is another question worth pondering."

"Does not the leader of the Dicade control his own men?" Ashling queried.

"What makes a person a member of the Dicade is not the symbol they bear, but their wishes and ideals. In the same manner, Ashling, I ask you, do you control your own civilians? For there is one thing I am sure about, you do not control me."

"A citizen serves the Coalition. They serve the Alliances' wishes for the betterment of the whole instead of the individual. The Dicade are not civilians. You are not a civilian, for you do not fit that description. So, let me recap. You admit that this symbol is that of the Dicade. You admit that in the images before you, men who proudly wore your symbol, did these acts?"

Kamon responded, "You say I do."

He shot Kamon a glare of contempt. "We had multiple reports that you claim to be the leader of the Dicade, a so-called President of the righteous. Will you confirm this statement?"

"Those who are moral. Those who value freedom. Those who are willing to put their life on the line for..."

"Mr. Kamon, that's called a terrorist."

"Those who are willing to put their life on the line for another's rights," Kamon raised his voice, not heeding to him, "not for personal gain, but because it is the right thing to do. Those who honor their contracts, their obligations, and those who thrive on freedom using the greatest gift that God from above has given them. To those, I am honored to claim to be their leader, elected by them, for them. I am their servant, and unlike the Alliance representatives, I will happily step aside so a new person with more insight, with better ideas, can use his mind to further the freedom in this land. Is it wrong for an individual to reclaim what was once his? Is it wrong for an individual to hold a thief who stole not only their possessions but their thoughts, responsible for their actions?"

"Self-sacrifice is the most honorable cause, for it is truly a sin to think of your own well-being over that of the masses. The Alliance thinks of the greatest good, in every single case Mr. Kamon. Let me recap; you do admit that you are the self-proclaimed President of the Dicade, their leader?"

Looking towards Ashling, Kamon once again calmly pronounced, "You say I do."

"The matter is settled. Mr. Kamon, with the power vested in me from the Alliance—in accordance with our laws—you have been sentenced to death for crimes against the Alliance of Coordinated Governments."

"I am happy to finally be free from the agony of the Alliance's grip and proudly die for the true members of the Dicade. Not those who bear our flag under the wishes of the Alliance, those who bear false witness." With those words, a soldier pulled Kamon out of his chair and begun dragging him to the guillotine.

Pikon entered the room with a smile on his face as Kamon looked towards him, with sadness filling his eyes, at his once close comrade. The soldier forced Kamon's head down upon the shimmering structure and proceeded to strap Kamon into the guillotine, positioning his neck where the blade would land. Eston heard the reporter start to speak again.

"You all heard it. The one called Kamon has acknowledged his acts as the Dicade's leader. You have already seen their horrific deeds. There is no denying their participation in these dreadful events that have unfolded before your eyes only moments ago. The Alliance has granted me permission to announce the weekly executions of the Dicade leaders from across our nations. Their names and their ruling will be released after more information is obtained from them. Also, next week we will list the businesses that participated, or funded, the Dicade movements."

His attention drifted from the broadcast as Lorne and Pikon began recalling their favorite parts of the hearing. "That was great, how Ashling trapped him," Pikon uttered, "first having him admit to the flag of the Dicade, then connecting it to the crimes."

Lorne rushed in, "Too bad for him that the population will never believe that the Alliance had something to do with those images."

Eston looked at Lorne curiously as Pikon continued. "I provided you with those flags and patches many years ago. I am glad the Alliance put them to good use. Without that evidence, it may not have gone according to our plans. We may never have had the support of the civilians. Heck, it could have even caused mass riots instead of overwhelming support. Ashling is indeed a genius in moving the masses."

Continuing to listen, Eston turned his head, contemplating what was being said as Lorne droned on. "Believe it or not, the final act leading up to their capture was planned by this young lad. Eston greatly helped in our cause."

Turning to look at him, Pikon inquired, "Is that so? No wonder why Ashling pushed for his admittance into the shadows, promoting him so quickly."

He stared deeply into the white eyes of Pikon, the same eyes Ashling had. The same eyes that the eight shadows of the darkness bore.

"Yes, it is. He is a prime example of one of the many minds the Alliance holds in its arsenal."

"Hmm," Pikon pondered, "he does show promise for great advancement."

"He sure does," smiling with pride, Lorne chuckled, "and just think I trained the boy. He is my greatest pupil." Lorne walked over to him, smacking him on the back, "Isn't that so, my boy?"

His mind raced as he replied naturally. "That it is Lorne, and I have enjoyed every step I took while assisting the Alliance."

Closing his eyes, Eston replayed the images of slavery and human trafficking. He accessed the quantum computer's mainframe and computed the light source, receiving a geographical position based in New York. He then continued pulling up another image, noticing it was in old Seattle, the now fenced off population. He sighed with relief as he matched the known locations of the Dicade against the pictures. It was indeed possible that the Dicade had done those acts, though Pikon's words still rang in his head. "I have to be sure." He whispered to himself.

Hesitating, he took a deep breath and then pulled up the most horrific scene he remembered. Once again, he gazed upon the small boy, whose body was lying upon a table with blood dripping from him. He tried to ignore the child's eyes, his piercing dead eyes; he tried to ignore the abdominal cavity split open. Focusing upon the small window in the background, he pulled up the night's sky, running the constellations, trying to pinpoint the location. He stared at the results, the height off the ground it would take to acquire that angle. It was only accessible in one place, from one height. Eston forced the computer to rerun the equations.

The longitude and latitude results were the same, positioned within the same building where he was now. Locating the window in the picture, he pulled up the floor plans of the octagon compound. The exact room was located on superior floor, G-49. He then accessed the security cameras, gazing inside the same room from the image before him. He clenched his fists together as the boy's corpse was still lying on that very same table, in the very same spot. His blood now dried on the floor as maggots feasted on his flesh. His death was recent. His fear was recent. The face of the girl from the decommission plagued him once again. The child's pale hand was reaching out, clutching desperately at her dead mother's hand. Growling as his sadness gave way to anger, "Ashling was recording me. He saw my weakness. He saw my tears, and he used my own grief against me. Knowing that I, that I would never want that to happen again."

"Hmmm, what's that, my boy? You say something?"

He opened his eyes and decisively affirmed. "Yes, Lorne. I was stating that Ashling knows everyone's weakness. He knows what causes grief in them, and he will always use it against them, if but only given a chance."

"That's right, my boy," Lorne started to laugh, "that's why we are glad to be on his side."

He forced a smile as the reporter broke in, "And now back to Ashling, as he leads us in our pledge to the Alliance."

He watched Ashling walk to the center of the polished platform, raising his hand to his heart as he began to speak. "Let us rise, to pledge our allegiance to the Alliance, as dedicated citizens. I ask you on these trying and crucial times to listen to your hearts, for we truly do feel with our hearts. Our hearts guide us; they allow us to forget our own wishes and live for the betterment of the world, for the betterment of these great nations. So, I ask you to raise your hands to your hearts and once again state the pledge as honorable and loyal citizens of the Alliance."

Lorne nudged him as he stood still, staring at his hand in front of his face, "Eston, my boy, raise your hand, and state your vows. Don't worry; the excitement will come soon."

Forcing another hollow smile upon his tired face, he raised his hand to his heart—as he stared at it, a realization from the past formed within his thoughts. "Our brains do indeed lead our bodies. Our hearts can be misled by lies, by falsified truths as we trust in those before us. Words easily deceive us, and our hearts are incapable of noticing this because we long to trust. We wish to trust. We wish to belong, and in that wish, with that yearning, we allow ourselves to be deceived."

The image of the girl once again flashed into his mind as she clung to the one she trusted, who too was led astray. Eston's eyes began to water, knowing that he was one of those individuals who led so many down the wrong path, just as Lorne and Ashling led him astray. He did not blame them. For he was the one ignorant enough to allow it to happen. He raised his gaze. Watching the others beginning to speak their pledge, as he too began stating the words that they had drilled into him since he was only a child.

I pledge allegiance, to the Alliance of
Coordinated Governments.
To promote the General party, to put
their needs above myself, an individual.
To give the Alliance my body, mind, and
heart, for as long as I stand.
To strive to further the Coalition under rule.
Our nations, indivisible, with health and
prosperity for all.

With those words, Eston removed his hand from his heart and looked at it with disgust. His mind raced as his life's work flashed before his eyes. His mind raced, seeing the women sent to his apartment as a prostitute, forced by the Alliance. His mind raced, seeing the poor struggling to breathe as he looked at his polished shoes and pressed suit. His mind raced as he sat in the most privileged city in the world, yet only the politicians could even take a step within it. His mind raced, knowing that the only true work he had ever done was ruin other's lives.

Lorne's voice came screaming from the past. He was taught not to cause too much of a ripple, for he might knock those above him off of the log. Eston now knew the truth before him; he now knew that those on the log cared about nothing other than themselves. They did not care about those below them as they acquired their power under a masquerade, preying on people's trust while spouting selfless acts so the world could see. They hid their true faces within their masks, away from the world in secret, just as he had done. He closed his eyes, pulling up the history of the Alliance. Then dug his nails into his wrist, attempting to conceal the tears forming within his eyes as he felt the moisture drip forward around his fingers.

Ashling was the one who decommissioned the President from the old rule. He was the one that permitted Congress to remain as he declared, "No one man should have that much power." Ashling was the one who became the speaker, granting himself emergency power while explaining, "Congress can repeal the decision with a two-thirds vote, whenever they wish, for they too know that action is necessary within these urgent times." Ashling was the one who destroyed the economy by building the national debt up, then collapsed the financial system underneath it—knowing that as he tore down the rich, the population would celebrate his very actions. Ashling was the one that knew that he could tear down the middle class, for they didn't have the time or the energy to resist him. He even tore down the poor in the end, taking the few scraps they had left. He was the one who took everything, leaving nothing. He was the one who cast the world into the darkness, into this decrepit state, into the shadows of Hell.

"Why?" Eston declared, "Well, that's simple, to rule the world."

"That's right, my boy, we will rule the entire world." Lorne said, beaming.

Opening his eyes, Eston looked toward Kamon, whose head was turned towards him. He looked into his eyes, seeing an honest man. A man who was happy to give up everything, knowing he had done something. Knowing he had made his choices freely, not playing to someone else's tune.

Kamon's eyes met Eston's as he looked curiously at the man who was staring at him. His eyes did not hold contempt. His eyes did not hold happiness nor even desire for his death. His eyes held remorse. He looked upon him, noticing blood dripping from his hand as he continued to dig his nails deeper into his own flesh. Kamon noticed that those eyes were not only holding remorse but within those eyes, he saw courage rising. He saw determination rising. He saw hope rising.

Time seemed to slow down as he watched Pikon's smile grow, while Lorne's laughter only escalated as Ashling released his command. "Now, let the civilians of the Alliance receive the justice they deserve." He watched as Ashling walked to the side of the room while rubbing his hands together furiously as if getting ready to devour a feast in front of him.

"I once made a promise to the Alliance," Eston thought, "proclaiming I would serve to their whim as long as they allowed me to live." He now separated his hands, wiping the blood on the inside of his jacket, hiding it from sight. "I guarantee that you will no longer wish for me to be alive after tonight, for now is the time that I finally become free." He peered towards Kamon once more, seeing him still looking curiously towards him. Moving his gaze towards the screen on the other side of the wall, he then returned his stare at Kamon.

Kamon remained still, his gaze fixed on Eston.

He repeated the motion as Kamon glanced towards the screen, seeing himself laying down with the guillotine towering above him. Quickly closing his eyes, he severed the screen in front of Kamon from the broadcasting connection. Then forced the reporter's microphone to re-amplify, creating a high pitch squeal across the room. Every person within the room quickly looked towards the broadcasting desk where the reporter stood.

Ashling began walking towards the reporter, and as the sound screeched around the great hall, Eston quickly inputted a message onto the screen.

Ignoring the blaring sound, Kamon looked upon the screen and read. "Freedom will reign, and the Dicade will rise again." The words quickly vanished as Kamon peered towards Eston, who opened his eyes and smiled. He nodded toward the screen one last time as he closed his eyes again. This time causing the Alliances screens to flicker as an even larger eruption of static blared forth.

A new message now flashed onto the screen. "Your allies will be delivered safely, for I now realize the horror of the Alliance. Go in peace knowing this, as I will go forth following my own will. I declare you, Kamon, as my true President. I am sorry, for I did not know what I had done. My word is my honor; they will live." With that, he returned the screen to the Alliance broadcasting feed, cutting his connection from the computers. The screens returned to normal as silence fell upon the room, all except for a single voice, Ashling's voice.

"Do not fail me again," Ashling roared, "for the world is watching."

The reporter nervously nodded, her voice squeaked in fear. "Sorry, there was some sort of interference."

"And if it happens again, there will be some sort of interference with your breathing in a more permanent manner." He snarled. "Do you understand?"

The reporter could but only nod as she took a long and slow breath, then returned to talking to the world once again.

Eston glanced towards Kamon, who was now staring at him, and as their eyes met, he watched tears begin to form and run down Kamon's face.

Kamon's eyes locked onto his as he mouthed the words, "Thank you, my friend. I wish I could have known you."

He smiled, acknowledging his new President as a calmness spread across the Dicade leader's face.

Taking a deep breath, Kamon closed his eyes as Eston watched the blade fall, releasing a harsh thud that echoed across the room. And as his head fell to the floor, the smile that he had once worn turned lifeless.

"Tonight, we celebrate, my boy!" Lorne slapped him on the back as clapping and cheering erupted from those lucky enough to attend.

Lorne's foul chuckle rung in his ears as Ashling walked up to him, "My child, I expect to see you tonight at the celebration, for you played a vast part in this."

Carefully picking his words, Eston responded. "To the true leader of the Alliance, it would be an honor to be at your side tonight and hopefully, with more to come." While he spoke, he thought to himself. For if I bore the skills and were at your side tonight, I would kill you.

"Till later tonight, then." Ashling exclaimed.

He slowly watched Ashling walk away as he restrained himself from running.

Another stinging slap landed across his back. "So, shall we go, my boy? I even arranged a certain someone for you again. Though first, let us eat and drink with our comrades on this glorious day."

He raised his hand out towards Lorne as Lorne took it in, "Lorne, I have known you for a long time, and you have taught me much tonight. I will indeed celebrate."

"That's the spirit, my boy."

"Although I do regret to inform you that I am hardly presentable after such a long night. Let me clean myself up, and I will catch up with you later."

"Ahhh, I see what you're doing, trying to make yourself ready for dessert later, ehhh? Well, have at it, boy, but don't take too long for the sooner you get there, the sooner you can get to her. If you know what I mean, ehh?" He said while jabbing Eston in the side with his elbow.

Forcing another smile upon his face, he hoped, would be his last. "You know me well, Lorne."

"Lad, you bet I do."

CHAPTER THIRTY-SIX

Eston briskly walked down the halls of the compound, knowing he had less than an hour before Lorne would come looking for him. Entering the elevator, he closed his eyes and bypassed the access codes, taking control over the elevator's security clearance. He opened his eyes as the numbers slowly changed on the screen, indicating his current floor. He looked down at his arm as the fresh wound on his wrist throbbed. Never again would he become a piece of clay for someone else's use. Never again would he be molded by anyone's wishes, except for his own.

As the elevator doors opened, he squared his shoulders. He dare not shake in fear, for if he did, he knew he would be discovered. He walked forward, showing pride, for pride was a sign of independence over his personal accomplishments. He walked forward, accepting what he was about to do. Knowing that it was the right course of action, the path a decent person would follow, and he now knew that those above him were anything but decent. Eston smirked as he thought to himself, "Blades may not be able to cut into the shadows, but I am sure those blades could slice deeply within their flesh."

Walking out of the elevator, he turned down the hall and looked upon three members of the Dicade, locked within their cell. He looked upon three members of a rare breed, who still deserved to be called human. He looked upon Jacob, upon Coretheen, and upon Damian sitting on the floor. "Your leader, your friend, and your President... no, not just yours, but my President too, is finally free from the pain of this world." With those words, Damian raised his head curiously towards Eston. "The time has come for you to rise once again, do not sit on your knees, for you still draw breath Damian Gargde; for you still have comrades at your side."

"Why should we rise? Does the Alliance enjoy watching us stand, only to be knocked down again?" Coretheen sorrowfully stated as she looked upon the man before her with disgust.

"I no longer speak for the Alliance, for I now know what they do. But Miss Nerites, there is one thing I can assure you, and that is they do receive pleasure from watching others get knocked down. They do receive pleasure watching others become consumed with misery, rising with every breath they take; it seems that this is their ecstasy, their ultimate pleasure within life."

"Why should we trust one who stood so close to Ashling, to the evil of the Alliance?" Jacob questioned.

"I will admit, my sins are grave. I will take full responsibility for them, and I know that absolute redemption for what I have done will never be possible."

Damian peered upon the man before him once again. Yes, his eyes were indeed different, and he spoke sincerely. "Does one blame a child if that child is misled by their father?" Damian queried, "The greater of sin rests not upon the one who has done the wrong but upon the one who taught it as an acceptable act, who commanded of it. You are but a child who has finally seen the truth of the world, no longer held captive by those who have forced evil into his mind. With that truth, you are finally free. Free to go against that very same evil."

"Then please, Damian," he pleaded, "let me help show this truth to the world."

Helping Coretheen to her feet, Damian nodded. With that nod, Jacob pushed himself up against the wall, grimacing in pain with his hand against his shoulder.

Taking control of the video feed, Eston closed his eyes. He rewound the feed until he saw the code that was used on the keypad of the cell when they were first brought in. He then pulled up the blueprints of the compound, forging the best escape route in his head. Accessing all the security cameras that were on his route, he cut the recording feed and disrupted the system's facial recognition software. Then placed all the feeds on a one-hour loop within their escape route, allowing only himself to observe the current images.

He quickly entered the access code as the cell door slid back, and as Eston opened his eyes, Damian stared within his.

Extending his hand out in front of him—towards his new comrade—towards Eston, and with that gesture, they embraced each other as friends.

"They will soon be looking for me at the celebration. That being the case, the sooner we get out of the city, the better chances we have at avoiding their vast reach." He rushed forward down the hallway as Damian remained still. "We must hurry." He turned around, pleading.

"May I ask a favor of you, my newly found ally?" Damian pointed towards his cane, "Could you please assist me in acquiring something that is very dear to me."

"Time is…"

"Time is indeed important, Eston, but we must not forget where we came from. Sometimes those around us are more important than a single task. Please, Eston; this is a favor I must insist upon you."

He quickly ran to the bulletproof box in front of him and pounded the access code on the keypad as Damian pulled out his cane. Then the three of them began moving to the end of the hallway. And as they opened the door, they peered upon two troops positioned on the other side.

They both turned, looking at him curiously, and then continued to peer past him towards the three once secured prisoners. The soldiers glanced at each other momentarily and quickly began raising their weapons as Damian rushed forward. He stared in disbelief at the speed of the man he had just released, faster and swifter than he thought possible for any human. He watched as Damian dashed between the two guards before they could even finish raising their guns.

In the middle of sprinting forward, Damian jumped, kicking at one of the guard's knees, breaking it in an instant while simultaneously swinging his cane down upon the other soldier's neck, collapsing his trachea within his throat. Then he grabbed the first guard's neck, as he began to reach down towards his broken leg, and threw him back into the wall. A crack echoed down the hall as the combatant's skull came in contact with the cement wall, then fell upon the floor below it. He now turned his attention to the second guard, who was bending over, gasping for air, desperately clutching at his own neck. With every step that he took closer to the guard, the fear in his eyes grew. Stopping in front of him, Damian pulled out the knife strapped to the soldier's leg and drove it deep within the man's chest.

Staring in disbelief, Eston watched the guard slowly fall to the floor. His hands falling away from the knife now lodged within his heart. He looked up at Damian, whose face showed no emotion. As if taking down two trained army personnel without a weapon was a normal occurrence. And as their eyes locked, Eston attempted to widen his stance.

Directing those around him, Damian kneeled down and grabbed the guard. "Eston, Coretheen, grab the other soldier and pull him into the cell. Jacob, clean up this blood." Remaining motionless, Eston stood still, attempting to take in everything that had just occurred as Damian's voice rose towards him again. "My kind Eston, I insist that you help Coretheen, for both stealth and speed are essential to our lively hood."

He quickly grabbed the dead soldier, and they began dragging him into the cell while Jacob finished cleaning up the blood. When he returned, Damian peered at him for direction.

Closing his eyes, the route lit up before him, highlighting the building's blueprints. He started to move forward as the others closely followed behind. Reaching the elevator, he quickly entered the access codes, and as the elevator rose, he began canvassing the security cameras along their route.

"Crap." Whispering under his breath as he noticed two politicians patiently waiting for the elevator to approach. Quickly connecting to the quantum computer, he stopped the elevator. Then proceeded to make the system believe that it was resting upon the top floor.

The politicians looked up at the floor indicator, with confusion spreading across their faces. Then shrugged and walked towards another elevator down the hall. Starting the elevator again, he allowed the doors to open as he led them south, away from the main lobby.

Quickly leading them through the maze of the defensive compound, he no longer walked with his eyes open. Keeping a constant observance on the blueprints, his current position, and the cameras within the computers reach, his reach.

Damian felt Eston's hands upon his chest, guiding him quickly into a room, as the others swiftly followed. He watched as Eston's eyes briefly opened, closing the door in front of him. Seconds later, he heard the sound of footsteps echoing from within the halls, growing louder with each step.

Resting his eyes upon Damian's cane, he peered at the symbol carved upon it. And as he gazed upon that symbol, upon the oddly curved lines, strange and ancient figures rushed into his vision. Hundreds and thousands of images flashed before his eyes as he fell to the ground, shaking. He grabbed at his head as the pressure grew stronger until it became unbearable. It felt like a fire was ignited inside of him, consuming every single one of his nerves.

Kneeling next to him, Damian watched the man before him.

"Never before," Eston's voice quivered as pain shot throughout his body, "have I seen with my eyes open."

"What? What do you mean you have never seen?" Coretheen trembled.

The look of confusion spread across Damian's face, only to fade moments later as he spoke with serene and commanding courage. "Eston, slow your breathing. Focus on the beat of your own heart, your own breath, no matter what the challenge, control is the key."

He squeezed his head, concentrating on his own heartbeat. He concentrated on the feeling of his blood rushing throughout his body, pulsing throughout his head, and even within his very toes. He slowed his breathing, concentrating on the great force inside of him until the images began to slow. Taking another deep breath, he relaxed as they trickled to a stop altogether. "That symbol you carry, do you know what it stands for? Do you know its history?"

"I know it is the symbol of hope. It was handed down to me from those I consider my ancestors." Damian's body relaxed as calming ease took over him. "It pulls me to it. It is the symbol of my ambition, the symbol of my endeavors, and the symbol of where I came from. Though it is so much more than just a symbol of hope to me, for it is the symbol of my spirit Eston."

"This symbol you bear is engraved into the Alliance. It was once and still may be the greatest force that ever went against them. Maybe even a greater threat than that of which the Dicade possessed. This symbol is not of an army but of a single man. It is the symbol of the one man who sat next to Ashling. The man who was once one of the eight. This symbol belonged to a man who secretly plotted against the Alliance, against Ashling himself, while bearing the mask of an ally. This man holds their greatest secrets and their greatest weaknesses. For he was the one who attempted to destroy them, hiding within their own ranks."

He looked upon Eston in astonishment, "And what happened to this single man?"

"That is the answer Ashling himself seeks, for even he does not know. He seeks it so he can extinguish his presence from the face of this earth. It seems that this was his sole reason for allowing the Dicade's presence in its entirety. For him. For this single man."

"Eston, my newly found friend, let us not allow our President to die in vain. It is time to unleash the truth; it is time for us to unleash the hidden filth of the Alliance upon this world."

"And I think I have the perfect way to showcase their despicable acts." Closing his eyes, he concentrated as he continued to speak. "Yes, this will do nicely. I have been made aware that you were told of the decommission of Seattle."

"That I was."

"Sadly, the truth is that this endeavor, carried out by the Coalition, was gruesome. It was a horrific tragedy for the Dicade, along with the civilians who lived there. They died in anguish as Ashling laughed at their torturous demise."

Damian looked upon the man who had freed them, a new member of the once strong Dicade. He looked upon the regret building within his eyes and the anguish behind every one of his words.

"I was there, Damian." He glanced at the floor, his face filling with grief. "I helped organize it. I helped cause that pain."

Coretheen put her hand on Eston's shoulder as Damian put his hand on his other. "Eston," her calm voice softly fell upon him, "you cannot change what has already occurred in the past. Live for the future and use that determination to never allow what happened that day to take place again. Use your pain against those who guided you into the actions you took. Not out of anger, but out of the wish to liberate those around you from the pain that you share, the pain that you now both bear."

Rubbing the symbol engraved upon his cane, Damian cast a quick smile. "Let us take this mark, this symbol of hope that the Alliance so hates, and unleash its light into the darkness."

The footsteps faded in the hallway as he pulled up the security feed, seeing that the way was now clear.

He opened the door, rushing down the hall, knowing that Lorne would attempt to summon him any minute now. "Damian, through that door lays the security relay system, and by using it, we can access anything within the archives."

Closing his eyes, he accessed the cameras inside the room and located the soldier's positions. "There are four men inside. Damian, do you think you will be able to handle them?"

"It would be my greatest pleasure, my newly found ally from the Alliance, and against the Alliance."

"Two will be at the entrance of the door; the other two are observing the cameras across this floor."

Allowing his cane to slide further into his hand, Damian grasped at it tightly, "Understood."

He entered the security code. Then quickly retreated behind Damian as he walked towards the door, causally knocking upon it. Tilting his head towards the entrance, he listened calmly as a few seconds passed. Then straightened his head as he slowly turned the handle and leaned back, kicking it open with all of his might.

The door collided with the two troops on the other side, sending them pummeling over a desk. Rushing through the door, he grabbed a computer monitor, hurling it at the man attempting to turn around in his chair. The monitor crashed into the soldier's head as blood streaked across the screens in front of him. Leaping across the desk, Damian raised his cane above his head and brought it down upon the man's temple, killing him with a single strike.

Eston began to yell as he saw one of the guards raising his sidearm towards Damian. Before a word could erupt out of his mouth, Damian launched forward. Grabbing the back of the troop's neck with his cane's curved handle, he pulled the man down while forcefully raising his leg.

A snap reverberated off the walls as the man's forehead collided with Damian's knee, then slumped down to the floor. He turned towards the last man, who was pushing the table off of himself.

The guard quickly looked for his gun, and as he located it upon the ground, terror struck his face. He rushed forward, throwing a punch at Damian with every ounce of force he could manage.

Damian shook his head as he sidestepped the man's futile attempt. Then grabbed the combatants' arm, wrapping it around the troops' back while seizing the man's neck within his other hand, and broke it with one swift movement.

Standing still, Eston observed Damian release his grip on the last soldier within the room. And as the man fell to the floor, he listened to the muffled thud that released him from his trance. He rushed forward, sticking a drive into the computer, and began downloading a file as images began to be displayed upon the screens around them.

Coretheen and Jacob entered the room, once again finding Damian standing still, mournfully taking in the images on the panels before them. He watched as thousands of citizens were torn apart by bullets and mines. He watched as men and women were entangled in steel as the wire fence was erected, only to be impaled by wire, after wire. He watched them take their last breath as horror took hold of them, and he watched as families—who once lived together—now died together.

Looking towards Damian, Eston's voice began to quiver. "I am sorry, Damian."

"The world will see this evil." Damian ensured as the scenes continued to show the true might and horror of the Alliance. "They will not only know and hear about what happened on that night, but they will also see it, and they will believe it."

"I'm sorry. I know they are but words, Damian, but I truly do mean them. It is my fault that the city met this fate. It is my fault that Kamon is dead. It is my fault that..."

"If not you, Eston," Damian pierced inside his sorrowful eyes, "someone would have only replaced you. You have been betrayed as I have. I by Pikon, and you by the lies of the Alliance. Let us move forward as new allies against a common foe."

A soft beep rang out, indicating the download was complete. He grabbed the drive as Damian nodded at him with approval. A weight lifted off his chest as his lies now crumbled behind the strength of veracity.

Eston left the room, leading the way through the halls of the compound, scanning the cameras, until coming upon a thick steel door. "We are almost to my vehicle, our way out of this city. The city of self-proclaimed kings." They broke forward, running through the door and into the parking structure. Quickly locating his car using the cameras, he yelled, "This way!" and ran towards the shimmering black vehicle.

Opening the front door, he sat down, bewildered by the controls in front of him.

"Let's get out of this wretched town." Releasing his grip upon the soft leather seat, Jacob called out. "The next time I want to see this city is when it is covered by ashes. Now, let's get moving."

Placing his hands on the wheel, Eston sat still. He had always been chauffeured from one place to another, never paying attention to the one behind the wheel. Turning towards Damian, a sense of unease began plaguing his face.

Pulling him aside, Damian grabbed the wheel.

He closed his eyes and disconnected the car's GPS signal.

Coretheen looked up upon the giant wall in front of her as the thick metal doors automatically began to slide back. Her mouth hung open as a row of tanks stretched down the entire road on both sides of them. She then gazed behind her as they pulled away, looking at the swirling lights of the great city.

"I was given the highest of security clearances when I was accepted into the Guardians of the Shadows." He explained, "If we are stopped, it will just be routine, stay calm and let me do the talking."

Slowing the car, Damian's voice rang with uncertainty. "Eston looks like we may have a problem."

Peering ahead, he watched as two tanks blocked the exit to New Chicago. As the car came to a stop, soldiers enclosed around the vehicle, their guns raised. The tanks slowly turned their turrets towards the car as Jacob swore under his breath, receiving a fierce glare from Damian.

Rolling down the window, Eston straightened his spine. His eyes pierced into the approaching troops, and with that stare, he allowed himself to once again apply the mask he once bore.

"State your purpose." The man demanded.

"I am Eston Tavernier." He spoke with a harsh and commanding voice that reverberated off the tank's thick armor. "A representative of the Alliance of Coordinated Governments, and I am leaving under political necessity."

"We have orders that no one is to leave the city unless directly approved." The man signaled his troops to move in closer. "And we have not received such an approval for anyone, except for the speaker himself."

Glancing up at the soldier, he observed the pin on his chest, the pin of the Guardians of the Shadows. He closed his eyes, exhaling, retrieving the files of the troops surrounding him. He quickly opened his eyes, squared his shoulders, and then reached into his pocket, grabbing the coin given to him by Ashling.

"I am Eston Tavernier, and you will grant me leave, second Lieutenant Phillips Barthow."

The Lieutenant peered upon Eston as both confusion and uncertainty spread across the soldier's face. He hesitated, taken aback at how the man in front of him knew both his name and his rank.

Eston continued, staring directly at the Lieutenant before him as he allowed the harshness of his voice to be released upon the men. "Sargent Johnathan Stevens and First Private Patrick Cunnings, all three of you will receive the full fury of the Alliance's might if this gate isn't opened within sixty seconds!"

They nervously exchanged glances as their Lieutenant spoke. "Representative Tavernier, I send you my sincere regards, but despite your merits, I have strict orders."

Flashing the Lieutenant a fierce glare, Eston reached out and handed the Lieutenant the coin bearing the iron tree. "Do not make me repeat myself, Lieutenant, for if I do, it will be the last thing you ever hear."

The soldier looked upon the coin and nodded as terror spread across his face. Handing the coin back to Eston, he attempted to prevent that terror from entering his voice. "My apologies, representative Tavernier, your credentials have been verified. You may proceed, true servant of the Alliance."

Damian, Coretheen, and Jacob watched in amazement as the troops withdrew from around the car, giving them their freedom from the Alliance's grasp.

With one last glance, Coretheen looked back upon the bright city. Upon the evil's magnificent wonders slowly shrinking in the background, and as they drove away from New Chicago, they drove away from the nightmare that moved past the realm of their dreams into reality.

EPILOGUE

Standing within the sanctuary of the shadows, the screens flickered around him as the eight silhouettes bore witness. Ashling calmly walked to the center of the room, towards the man kneeling on the floor. The speaker's voice bellowed across the chamber. "Lieutenant Phillips Barthow, you have been called here today to answer for the crimes you have committed. Against not only the Alliance of Coordinated Governments but against the Guardians of the Shadows themselves. How do you answer for the transgressions you have rendered against us? For you, Lieutenant Barthow, have committed the most abhorrent of sins."

He grasped his hair tightly within his hands and pulled back the Lieutenant's head, revealing the sockets where his eyes once were. "I swear," the Lieutenant begged, "I did not mean any harm to the Alliance, to the shadows, to you Ashling, to you!"

Ashling let go of his hair, then began pacing around him, "And yet my child, nonetheless this act was still carried out by your hands, by your words. You gave the order to free them, to let them escape."

"My leader. My king," Barthow began to sob, "have mercy, for he bore the coin of the honored. I only did..."

"You bore the ignorance of a commoner who lacks the insight to think!" He growled, then once again re-sumed to slowly walk around the Lieutenant; until he released a hissing whisper that pierced into the inner depths of Barthow's soul. "Your sins bore blood against the Alliance, and for this, you shall repay with your blood." He walked towards one of the screens as the Lieutenant fell forward onto the ground, sobbing.

"This is indeed a sad day. Not only have we lost a prom-ising member of our own, but we have also lost those we held captive for the world—those important and neces-sary members of the Dicade. Even though this act has passed, the Dicade are still broken, their ranks destroyed, their leader killed, little hope remains for them. We will hunt them. We will find them, and we will extinguish their breaths from this world, grinding their bones into dust, only to be returned to the dirt in which they are."

"The world is ours, Ashling; our destiny is set in stone." Pikon assured, "There is no longer hope for those who stand against us. We will find him, and we will destroy him together."

"That is as certain as the sun rising in the morning, never faltering from its schedule set out before it." He turned his gaze back to Lieutenant Phillips, "Now, my child, it is time. We breathed life into you, lifting you from the scum of this world, and now it is time to return what was given to you."

The eight shadows spoke in unison, "According to our laws, we find you guilty. Let you return to the shadows and no longer show significance upon this earth that we had once deemed you appropriate for. In accordance with our laws, we release you from our service."

The tree's iron roots began scraping against the ground, slowly wrapping itself around Lieutenant Phillips Barthow. A shriek let loose as the thick and cold iron roots entangled themselves around the Lieutenant. Ashling started walking towards the exit of the room as he began to hear bones breaking, one by one, and as each one broke, it was followed by a weaker whimper.

He turned at the door, looking upon the Lieutenant as his final scream rang within his ears, watching as the roots slowly pierced through Barthow's lungs. Digging themselves deeper inside of him, slowly weaving their way up his throat, until climbing out of his mouth, twisting with every movement they made.

Ashling smiled as he heard the Lieutenant gargle, asphyxiating on his own fluids. "Such beauty." He whispered serenely as the roots lifted Barthow off of the ground, showering the marble floor with blood.

"This will be your fate Eston; the world will not watch you fade from this earth. You will be forgotten. Your name will have no meaning, and your pain will be but for my amusement, as you cease to exist in this world, drawing your last breath."

– Three Weeks Later –

Coretheen looked down upon the decaying city as the warm breezed licked her chapped and bleeding lips. She smiled while grasping Damian's hand within hers, knowing that God himself had realized that this world was worth saving, for they were no longer alone within this frigid place she called home. She looked towards him, the man that she loved, with Jacob and Eston standing at his sides. Damian tightened his grip upon her hand, peering upon the city lined with fog in front of him. The sun slowly set in the background, piercing through the deep red clouds behind the city. She looked upon the decaying buildings. The sun's light reflected off the scattered specks of glass that were still hanging onto the window frames as a towering needle broke above the fog in the distance.

"My Lady, you will become strong, for you will become a true fighter of freedom. One who thinks before they move. One who anticipates the enemy's movements, almost knowing what they will do before they themselves do. Your movements will be based on strategy, on insight, for those overpower even the greatest of forces." Damian's cool blue eyes looked down upon Coretheen as he kissed her forehead. The forehead of the one he held closest to his heart. "For my dear Lady, we now start your training."

The swirling fog briefly broke as Eston peered upon the city in front of him, once again. Upon the decaying buildings, once again. And he gazed upon the steel fence encasing the city once again. Though this time, he did not look upon the city with sadness, he did not look upon the city with plans of destruction in his eyes. Eston looked upon the city with resolve and with hope for the future.

Damian started to walk forward, towards the town before them, determination rising within his voice. "The Alliance deemed this city and the people inside of it useless. Yet, this city lashed out against those who held it hostage. This was the city that fought back. This was the city that refused to let the Alliance starve them to death. This was the city that rose from their knees, against their masters, against the Alliance."

They began following Damian into the fog as he continued to speak with valor and strength. "We will rise again. Against those who oppress us, against those who hold us down, for we are no longer on our knees." The thick haze slowly turned over the city once again, hiding it from view. "Because my friends, the Dicade, will rise again."

Eston, Jacob, and Coretheen spoke as hope radiated from within their eyes. "For together, we will stand taller than the Alliance itself."

ACKNOWLEDGMENTS

First off, I would like to thank any and all who purchased, read, and reviewed my book.

I especially would like to thank those who have written a review, followed by those who have left some stars. It may not seem like much to you, but for me, it means the world and helps my material spread.

If you have not yet done so, don't worry, there is still time. So please go and leave a review, of any kind I might add. And in return, I send you my multitude of thanks.

Although this is my first piece of work, I do have some other projects in the works. Some of which are very intriguing, and though I might be biased, are also wonderfully crafted. If I may say so, it is even more brilliantly crafted than this one. So if you enjoyed this book, you will enjoy my next one even more!

www.ingramcontent.com/pod-product-compliance
Lightning Source LLC
Chambersburg PA
CBHW030549180626
46816CB00005B/1465